I0638989

LABYRINTH
QUEST

YVONNE HERTZBERGER

ISBN:9780987826091

I would like to express my profound gratitude to all those who supported me in the creation of this book. Special mentions go to my beta readers: Janet, Lyrra, Carolyn, Ian, Laurel and Pam. You all made this a better book by far.

To Ed, thank you for all the insights, suggestions and encouragement as I struggled.

To the members of my critique group. I may not accept all you say but it made me think and that's priceless.

To my spouse, Mark, who understands that writing is "real work" even though it adds little to our budget.

And not least, to all my readers who have read my Earth's Pendulum trilogy, taking a chance on a new author and letting me know that, yes, I AM a writer. Your faith and support are invaluable.

Finally to all those who took the time to write honest reviews on my previous books. Every author depends on that kind of support. You keep me writing.

I

M'RAIN SHOOK HER waterskin, knowing even before she did that it was almost empty. With a sigh she wiped her face with one forearm, leaving a dirty smudge on her forehead. She lifted her heavy, waist length hair, tied out of the way with a woven grass lace, off her back in the futile hope the non-existent breeze would cool the back of her neck. The sun beat down on her head and the arid desert air dried her sweat as soon as it formed. Her mouth felt like sand.

She had wandered farther from her home village than was wise in her quest for food for the communal cook-pot. The meagre contents of her woven grass gathering basket mocked her in mute rebuke; three fibrous cactus roots, one cactus fruit, and one skinny desert mole. Her small, bone knife lay on top, hardly used, her digging stick lax in her other hand. The elders would not be happy with the results of the day's foraging.

The long trek back would be harder knowing that others likely had no more success than she. The contents of the cook-pot would not fill their bellies tonight. Adults would go hungry so children could eat.

This season had been drier and hotter than usual. The burrowing animals had retreated deeper underground to avoid the scorching heat and so were harder to scare out of their dens with the result that meat was scarce. The cacti that usually provided fruit had produced less than usual because the rains had not come. Even their roots had become tough and dry. The hunters had also been less successful than in other seasons. Perhaps their prey also hungered and fewer survived. Her stomach rumbled at the thought of food, reminding her of her current task.

Shielding her eyes with her hand she judged the position of the sun in the sky. She would have to head back soon to reach home before dark. Darkness brought out the predators; scorpions, poisonous snakes, and a few of the nastier burrowers like the needle toothed rat. They all remained hidden until the sun sank low and the desert cooled for the night. The scorpions were the worst. In the darkness she would not see them. Their sting was sudden and sometimes deadly if not tended quickly. She must not delay long if she hoped to avoid them.

Scanning the sand for any more possible sources of food she spotted a dark shadow on the far horizon. Caves were scarce but she knew what they were. Her people, living at the edge of the desert where the sand gave way to more rocky terrain, used several small ones near where they lived to store dried provisions and protect them from the rains and animal thieves. They were too small to use as shelter. They reserved the largest one for some rites.

Against her better judgement she decided to explore the dark shadow. It was indeed a cave opening, a big one, inviting and scary at the same time. She decided to check it out. Caves were cool and she might be able to rest a few moments out of the sun. Then, perhaps, she would not miss having more water quite as much on her way home. She hesitated outside the entrance, knowing she ought not to linger.

Midday had passed some time ago but the sun still baked the desert, leaving it shimmering and sere. M'rain shook her waterskin again, knowing she would find no watering hole to refill it between here and home. She let it fall back on its thong around her waist, her decision made. She needed that rest before heading back, though she would have to keep it short.

The coolness inside, along with a profound silence, welcomed her as she stepped in. Awed by its strangeness she chose to sit facing the entrance, comforted by the sight of the world she was familiar with: the sand with waves of heat shimmering off it, the dunes, the occasional cactus standing sentinel, the dunes on the horizon beckoning her home.

This cave felt different from the shallow ones near her home. It had no friendly village within sight and it kept the light out deeper back so she could not see into it much past where she sat. It was as well she could not stay long. The coolness that had seemed so inviting became chill, even foreboding. Goose bumps rose on her arms and she wondered if they came from the chill of the cave or from a sensation that this place did not approve of her presence. She could not shake an uneasiness. It made the tale the storyteller recited about the legendary Great Caves and how her people came to live in this desert much more ominous, more real. The story had been repeated around the evening fire so many times she could recite it word for word.

In the time before time, the time before we were here, we lived very far away. Water was plentiful. Each day the hunters brought back fat game. The sun did not parch the earth and we lived in abundance. We were provided all these things by the One Who Gives.

Only one thing was forbidden us. The Great Caves. A dark and jealous spirit ruled the Great Caves, one that stole the lives of all who ventured inside. It is said that no one who dared enter the caves ever returned home. The darkness swallowed them up, to wander, lost, until death took them.

But there lived some who did not believe in the danger of the caves. "Together," they said, "we will best the spirit. We will find a way to discover what he hides from us. The caves will give up their treasures to us. They will give us more power".

These few lured others away, into the forbidden labyrinth, to seek the power and riches of the caves. Many went on that journey. The darkness caught them. Food ran out. They wandered, lost. Many died.

But the One Who Gives took pity on the people and showed those who remained a way out. But that way did not take them back home. It led them into the desert, this desert. The One Who Gives told them they must make a new home here.

Life was hard but the people learned how to live in this new world. We grew and had children. Now we are two villages. But the Great Caves remain forbidden to us. We can never return.

So it is told, of the time before time. And now we live here. It is a good life. It is our home.

M'rain shivered again in spite of the oppressive heat outside and reached for her basket. Her single grass wrap, which covered her torso down to mid-thigh, offered no warmth against this chill.

She had not yet stood upright, ready to leave, when a hand covered her mouth and strong arms pinned her down. The hand left her mouth but before she could utter a sound she felt something coarse and prickly stuffed into it. It tasted greasy and had hair on it that threatened to go down her throat. She felt she was choking and could hardly breathe.

No amount of bucking or kicking helped loosen the grip of the one who hauled her to her feet, and with the help of a second pair of hands, dragged her deeper into the cave. When they turned around a bend the last of the light from the entrance faded. Total blackness enveloped her, increasing her terror.

Before pushing M'rain to sit on the cold stone her captors tied her ankles and wrists. The coarseness of the cords bit into her skin and she could feel her hands and feet begin to go numb from the tightness of the bindings. She struggled without success to push the wad out of her mouth with her tongue. It just seemed to go deeper. Panic threatened to rob her of her last efforts to breathe. Just when she thought she must surely faint she felt a soft breath at her ear.

"Sssst, stay quiet." The disembodied voice had a strange, clipped accent but M'rain understood the hissed whisper. That calmed her enough so she could listen.

"Ssssst, we must not be discovered. The monster might find and kill us...you, too." A hand reached out and touched her face. "Do you promise to keep quiet if we take out this gag."

M'rain nodded vigorously so her captor would know. The hand reached up and pulled the gag out of her mouth. She spat the dirt and remaining hair out and took two deep breaths. Her training on how to deal with danger began to come back to her. She did her best not to cough while she tried to order her wild thoughts. With each breath she felt calmer. The attack and threat of murder warned her she must choose her words carefully. She was the prey now.

She heard her captors retreat a few paces back the way they had come in. They whispered between themselves. She did not understand how she could hear their furtive whispers when they stood so far away and wondered if it might be due to something about the way the caves were formed. It surprised her she could make out most of what they said and it puzzled her that they did not seem aware of that. If they were, they showed no concern. *No, they must not know, else why would they have moved off?* She kept still and strained to hear. Perhaps she would learn something that would help her escape.

"Light...are we lost?"

"How...get here?"

"Cannot be...are no others."

"Chosen one...

"...must we do?"

"...K'kor do to her?"

"...should have let her go."

"But if...can help us...."

"No...must take ...K'kor."

"but...find way back?"

"If chosen...will get back."

"But...K'kor do?"

"...no choice....the black rocks..."

"...not enough food...will kill her..."

"...no choice...must not let her go..."

They must have come to an agreement because M'rain heard an almost inaudible scuffle back in her direction. Hands untied the bindings around her ankles and she was lifted to standing. She stumbled as the blood rushed back into her feet. The two must have understood because they held her still for a moment, just long enough for her to regain control and remain upright on her own. They still kept a tight grip on her arms, one on each side.

She felt another breath near her ear before one of them whispered again. "Sssst. Stay silent." One let go of an arm. A tiny glow appeared revealing the blurry image of dirty, bony hands holding what must be a lamp. Its light reached no further that the holder's wrists making them appear disembodied. M'rain could see no flame and wondered how this could be. It looked as though the hands carried only embers. The person turned and began to move away

The one who held her gave her a small shove indicating that she was to follow. The only sound, as she tried to walk, was the scuffling of her own feet. Her captors moved in utter silence. It made the hair on M'rain's neck rise. Even in sunlight, walking the desert sand, she knew she would be able to hear the whisper of her footsteps. *But these two make no sound as they walk. How can this be? And why is silence so important?* She recalled what the one had said. *"The monster would kill them"*. What was *"the monster"*? She shuddered in fear.

When, after a long time during which it became impossible to remember all the twists and turns, a strange, pale light appeared in the distance, her captor blew out the lamp. *That light must be our destination. With it in view they no longer need to create their own.* M'rain's eyes had adjusted to the darkness just enough that she could make out shadowy figures moving across the circle of light they approached. It wasn't until they were mere steps from the entrance to a new, inner cave that she heard any sound. It appeared that even here, deep within the earth, silence was important.

One of her captors tugged her to the side, out of sight of the entrance as the other entered the cave. The woman, or M'rain thought it was a woman, reappeared almost instantly and jerked her head to indicate they were to enter the lit cave. Once inside M'rain was led to its central fire and pushed to the ground to sit. There one removed the bindings from her wrists and relieved her of her waterskin. Her hands burned and prickled as blood returned to them.

She looked around and saw roughly twenty pairs of eyes staring at her from the perimeter. In the dim light she could not make out facial expressions, only the reflections of the whites of their eyes.

When no one moved or spoke, M'rain made herself take a longer, more careful look around. She knew she must control her fear and learn as much as she could if she hoped to escape. She expected to see more of the little lamps bringing light to the cave. Instead, to her awe, she noticed that the very walls seemed to glow of their own accord, an eerie pale green. Was this some kind of magic? Could rock create light? She shuddered again, a cold chill running down her back, and hugged her knees to keep herself from shaking. *Breathe, breathe and think.*

Still no one moved or spoke. The air held a pregnant expectancy, as if the people could not act until what they waited for occurred. M'rain discovered she was holding her breath again and forced herself to resume breathing. Another look around showed her that every one of the others in the cave had begun to gather in a half circle along, but not touching, one wall of the cave and sat cross-legged facing her and the fire. An opening was left between those closest to the entrance. All sat in complete silence. The only sound was her own breathing and the drumming of her heart in her chest, seeming inexplicably loud. These people expected something, and M'rain suspected she did not want to know what that might be.

She kept her head turned to face the cave opening and hugged her knees tighter to contain the next shudder that passed over her. *Remember what you have been taught. Fear is your enemy. It must be controlled.* She tried to remember the lessons her elders had taught her. *If you must stay still, and cannot run, think about something pleasant. Breathe slowly and deeply as you remember.* While she still kept an eye on the cave entrance she forced her breathing to slow and lengthen. She pictured her home: the communal fire in the centre, the pot cooking over it, the huts forming two circles around it, children chasing each other laughing, people talking and going about their tasks as the sun began to go down. An image of her pregnant sister came to her. Her first child would come before the next full moon. That she, M'rain, had been named her birthing sister was an unusual honor for a young woman of barely seventeen. But she had

13

learned the lessons taught by the eldest birthing sister well and had been deemed ready. Hers would also be the honour of naming the child, a special honour, one not bestowed on one as young as she within living memory. She pictured herself sitting beside her sister, N'iri, as she placed the amulet around the babe's neck before the celebratory feasting and dancing.

The realization that she might not get back for that event brought M'rain crashing back to the present.

A shadow darkened the entrance to the cave.

II

K'KOR HALTED IN the dim light of the cave mouth, arms akimbo, legs planted apart, waiting for all eyes to turn his way before he made his entrance. The luminous, blue rock powder he rubbed onto his skin made him glow. It helped him impress upon 'his' people that he had been chosen by the spirit of the caves. K'kor believed there was no cave spirit. At least he had never encountered one, but it served his purpose to have the men and women under his control believe it. The spirit didn't give his name because, as K'kor explained, using the name would rob the spirit of some of its power. *Oh, I am a clever one.* The real reason he had not named the spirit was to prevent anyone else from trying to use that knowledge against him. With a name they could claim to have contact with the spirit. He wanted no competition. K'kor's grip on his small band was total and unassailable. He intended to keep it that way.

When he could see he had everyone's full attention he strode to the centre and stopped in front of M'rain, his toes almost grazing her knees. He jabbed a menacing finger at her face and glared slowly around the cave, making certain he met the eyes of everyone there, and growled, "What is this?"

No one responded. The silence seemed to grow deeper. Satisfied that no one had the courage to challenge him, or even speak, he plopped down cross-legged in front of M'rain in a single, swift motion. He knew his speed of movement and his physical closeness to her had achieved

15

its desired effect when the girl gasped and shrank away with a jerk. He thrust his face so close to hers their noses almost touched, his eyes a narrowed glare, his mouth a scowl, his knees brushing hers. It pleased him to see it had its desired effect. Her visible tremor satisfied him that he had another captive who would be easy to control. K'kor made sure she saw his gloating leer, the widening of her eyes feeding his satisfaction.

He reached out with one bony finger and poked her ribs. Then he twisted her hair with his other gnarled hand and yanked her face toward the light of the fire where he pulled her lower lip down with his free hand to examine her teeth. When the girl didn't yelp he felt a glimmer of admiration for her before realizing the importance of it. This one was stronger than the others. He would have to go even harder on her to break her to his will. To this end, he made a great show of examining her, She uttered no sound. Only her eyes and the rigidity of her body gave away her fear.

When there was nothing more of her to examine he let her go and sneered as she fell over onto her side, then scrambled to sit back up and hug her knees. He rocked back on his haunches, his eyes never leaving her face, and glared at her for a long time. When that tactic seemed to have no effect he changed his strategy. His face split with a maniacal grin. "I have a new miner," he crowed, then sprang to his feet and pulled M'rain up to standing by her hair, twisting it so she was forced to turn slowly, so everyone could see her from every angle. He grabbed her arms one by one with his free hand and waggled them in front of his people. "See. This one is strong." Then he shoved her back down to the floor so hard that she lost her balance again and almost fell into the fire.

He bent down and thrust his face close to hers. "See that you keep up or you will be food for the beast. I do not keep those that will not work." He sat back, looked around the cave and demanded, "Where is my food?"

Two scrawny women scurried forward. One filled a bowl, the only one M'rain could see, with the ladle in the clay pot hanging over the fire. The other picked a wooden spoon off the ground and placed it in the bowl.

The first woman held the bowl out to him with trembling hands. He flashed her one of his gloating grins before taking it from her. He had eaten half of the contents by the time the two women resumed their places in the perimeter.

When he had emptied his bowl he paused to seek another woman in the circle, and held out the bowl to her. "Feed the others." There was never enough food to satisfy everyone and it served him to watch the person he chose to dole it. How they divided what was left in the pot over the fire told him a lot about the characters of his 'subjects'. If the person made sure all got an equal share it told him that they valued fairness and justice. That made them more malleable but also told him they had a limit and might fight back if he pushed too far. If they began with generous portions and ran out before the end they were careless, perhaps even stupid, and thus easier to control. And it meant that, as the server always ate last, that one would go without that night. If the server saved more for the end, to eat themselves, it meant they were greedy and could challenge him at some point. There was only one bowl and one wooden spoon, so portions could not be adjusted. Once served, each portion had to be eaten before the next person got any. K'kor's keen observations served him well in keeping his little band where he wanted it.

Tonight, however, he had one who would not be given any food. He needed the newcomer to be hungry. He needed to break her.

III

WHILE K'KOR'S ATTENTION focused on the feeding ritual, M'rain had an opportunity to observe. Once K'kor had shoved her back down she felt a measure of relief, believing he would not kill her, not yet, at any rate.

The light from the small fire only dimly reached the perimeter of the cave but she could see enough with the glow from the walls to count the number of occupants and thought she could detect their sex, though they looked so emaciated she could not be certain. There appeared to be sixteen women and only two men. All were naked except for something wrapped around their loins, which might be leather, but could also be woven grass. She could see no children at all. The more she thought about this the more uneasy it made her. Nothing made sense. *Why are there only two men? Why no children? And why are they so afraid of noise and light? Where did they come from? Why are they here?*

The bowl had gone around the circle and was placed back beside the fire. When M'rain realized she would not be given any of the food she watched K'kor with great care, looking for clues to explain how the group lived. Where did the food in the pot come from? What had K'kor meant when he said he had another miner? What was a miner? She could see nothing in the cave that gave her any clues.

K'kor reached into a pouch dangling from his waist and took out a nondescript grey mass. In the dim light M'rain could not tell what it was. She watched him go around the circle and, one by one, give a small bit

19

of it to each person. Each one took it with what appeared to be reverence and held it on an outstretched hand until everyone had some. At the very last he stopped in front of M'rain and handed her a piece. It felt a bit spongy, like a fungus. She held it to her nose and the aroma supported that idea, but if this was a fungus it was different from any she had eaten back at her village, stronger smelling, with the scent of the cave about it.

K'kor returned to the fire. Still standing he faced the circle and said, "Eat and dream".

M'rain noted that he, himself, did not eat any, but all the others obediently chewed and swallowed their portion. Curious, M'rain lifted her hand toward her mouth to taste it and felt the bit knocked out of her hand. Since K'kor stood two paces away from her he could not have done it. She looked around for the piece but could not find it, its colour being so similar to everything else in the cave.

Something tapped her hand. She jerked it away. When she looked where her hand had been she saw a small creature, unlike anything she had known. It was about the length of her hand, shaped like a lizard, covered in small, grey scales that blended into the cave floor. It had huge eyes that bulged from the top of its head. Those eyes had an eerie intelligence in them and could move in opposite directions. As M'rain looked at it she felt a strange tug at her mind. The creature spoke. Yet she knew it made no sound and could not be seen by the others. *This is forbidden to you. Watch and be ready. Act like the others."*

Just as she found the courage to ask a question the creature disappeared. A quick look around the cave showed her that no one else had seen it. Then she noticed the people in various poses, in apparent stupor, some already lying where they had been sitting, seeming asleep.

All but K'kor, who turned and leered at her.

The warning had startled M'rain so that she had not fully taken it in.

K'kor's eyes narrowed. "You did not eat my dream-fungus. Here, eat this piece. It gives most wonderful dreams and takes away the hunger." He thrust another morsel of the strange fungus at her and, when she hesitated to take it, growled, "Eat it." The threat in his tone was unmistakable.

At the point of almost putting it into her mouth, she felt it knocked aside again. This brought back the warning. So she pretended to chew and swallow, knowing it would gain her a few moments to think. She looked at the others, saw how they slumped and appeared to sleep, or be near sleep, and remembered the admonition, "Act like the others".

She glanced back at K'kor, who still stood over her. Knowing that the fungus was supposed to put her to sleep she let her body grow lax and her eyes unfocussed.

K'kor made a show of licking his lips suggestively as he waited, feet planted apart, facing her, toes almost touching.

Though she let herself sink to the floor it seemed he knew she was still aware of him. He grabbed his crotch and shook his rising phallus at her. "It will be your turn tonight. New blood. Perhaps you will be the one to bear me an heir." A cruel chuckle emerged from deep in his throat. "I know you can hear me. They all can. Sleep does not come so quickly."

M'rain could not have moved if she tried. Terror immobilized her as completely as the drug would have.

With a final hoarse laugh he reached for her...and crumpled on top of her, snoring.

M'rain held her breath. Her mind roiled in confusion and terror. The fetid odor of the man lying on top of her and the foul breath that he blew into her face made her retch. Though her stomach heaved in protest nothing came out.

When K'kor did not move M'rain resumed breathing and did her best to apply the calming techniques she had been taught. *Breath in, longer breath out. Make each breath longer than the last.* Her breathing slowed and became more regular. Soon she found she could think more clearly. The body on top of hers lay lax with apparent sleep. The man snored. He showed no signs of waking. This made no sense. He had been wide awake and full of lust moments ago. He had not eaten of the fungus. What had happened?

Knowing she would not find the answer doing nothing she turned her attention to her situation. She placed the palms of her hands against K'kor's shoulders and gave a tentative push. No response. She tried a harder shove. Still nothing. Gathering all her courage and strength she gave one great shove. K'kor rolled off and lolled in a limp heap beside her. She froze, waiting for him to wake. He continued to snore, a satisfied smile on his face.

She noticed her hands. A little of the glowing powder had rubbed off onto her palms. The sight made her whole body spasm with revulsion. She rubbed her hands wildly in the dirt to get the loathsome stuff off.

Still seated, she turned her attention back to her plight and tried to plan. *I need water.* Surely these people drank water, too. Had she seen them drink? *Think. Breathe. Look around.* She rose to standing and strained her vision as far as she could to the edges of the cave. *There. What is that darker spot?* She tiptoed over to it, taking care to make no sound. *Yes.* A glimmer of orange light moved on the surface. That meant movement; the ripple reflecting the glow from the fire. Was it the flow of water into the pool or something alive?

She squatted by the edge, alert. The glimmer had disappeared so the pool must be still. *Something alive, then. Be careful.* She moved to one side so that she did not block the meagre light from the fire and bumped into something that fell over with a clatter. The noise sounded to M'rain like the crack of lightening during a wild storm. She froze, certain that it would wake everyone. When no one stirred she reached a tentative hand to the object. It was smooth and round with a hole at one end. *A water vessel. This really must be where they get water.* She worried about whatever might be alive in the pool so she lowered the vessel only a fraction into it, ready to spring back. A tiny splash, followed by a flicker of reflection confirmed her suspicions. Something living dwelt there. She held very still but did not remove the vessel from the water. When nothing happened, driven by her thirst, she lowered it further to let it fill, taking care to cause as little disturbance to the surface as she could.

The liquid had an acrid, mineral taste but she drank greedily, emptying the small jug completely. With her thirst slaked she revived somewhat and calmed so that she could think more clearly. *Where is my waterskin? I need to fill it.* She rose to her feet and made her way to the entrance of the cave where she spotted a small dark lump. *There!* She reached for it and heaved a sigh of relief when it proved to be what she sought. She took it back to the pool and hesitated. Should she fill it directly or use the vessel? Which would disturb the water less? Someone moaned and rolled over. That decided her. She quickly dipped her waterskin under the water and held it there until it was full.

With it tied securely back around her waist she turned her attention to escaping. She would need light. She saw no sign of the tiny lamp her captors had used. She knew that, even if she did find it she would not know how to use it. The fire still had some glowing embers. She thrust one end of a knotted stick she found beside the fire into the embers. If the knot lit it might glow enough without burning out before she found her way. Could she find her way? M'rain struggled to remember the feel of each twist and turn her two captors had taken in bringing her here. She knew this cave must be one of many. She could easily get lost.

They had taken several turns after she had been captured. Trying to remember proved futile. Fear had made her forget the survival lessons she had been so carefully taught. She slumped in defeat. What good was light if it only led her deeper into the maze of caves? She would die of starvation or thirst. But the alternative? To be controlled by this monster, raped by him, perhaps bear him a child? *Can I bear that? No! I would rather die of thirst or starvation.* The thought of food made her stomach growl loudly. She sent a wild glance at K'kor. Had he heard?

Seeing that K'kor did not move M'rain pulled the branch, now glowing at the knotted end, out of the fire and sidled to the entrance of the cave. The orange glow helped her see obstacles in her way but nothing beyond the range of it. Upon reaching the entrance she turned to look back. The dark lump that was K'kor still lay unmoving by the dying fire. What had caused him to fall asleep so abruptly, she wondered again? He had not eaten of the fungus.

One of the women stirred in her sleep, rousing M'rain from her musing. She must go...now. Something caught her eye just inside the mouth of the cave. When she brought her torch closer she recognized it as her gathering basket. Empty. Thinking she might have a use for it later she put it over one arm and eased out into the emptiness she knew must be the first tunnel. Without the glow from the fire the darkness was even blacker. Her branch gave almost no light as it had only the smallest gleam at one end. She tapped it on the ground and waved it from side to side to waken the embers. It helped, but only a little.

How was she to remember the way? She forced her breathing to slow and closed her eyes in concentration. Away from the cave it was easier to think. *Was it left or right? Right. Yes, that was it.* She turned and edged along the wall, feeling with one hand.

But when the women brought me here there was no wall close enough to touch. Panic assailed her at that realization. She waved the branch about wildly again, desperate for more light. It glowed stronger for only a moment and died back down to the slightest orange glimmer. The knot in her stomach tightened and she found it hard to breathe. The sorry light from her makeshift torch illuminated less than a step ahead. Trying to walk across an open space was out of the question. *Think.* She slowed her breathing once more. *Walls lead to openings. If I follow the wall I will come to the opening through which they brought me.* She resumed her slow progress, once more keeping one hand along the wall. Not long after, she came to a break in solid rock. Fresh air flowed in, raising the hairs on her arms. Her spirits rose. *That must lead out.* She quickened her pace as much as she dared lest she fall. Even as she turned into the direction of the air flow the last glowing ember on her torch sparked and died, leaving her in total darkness. But the air gave her hope and offered her a direction. She dropped the useless branch and continued along the wall of the new passage.

After a time she felt, more than saw, that the darkness was not quite as black. Light! She must be approaching the exit. She quickened her pace as much as she dared. As she moved forward the darkness receded by small increments. Hope rose with the increasing light.

Later still, she could actually see enough to walk upright and let go of the wall. The pale light drew her forward. The fresh flow of air grew stronger. Each gulp of it raised her spirits more - until she entered the new cave and discovered the source of the light.

Above her, very high above her, gaped a great hole. Moonlight poured through it, bathing the new cave in an eerie light. What made the light blue?

M'rain looked around. The walls shone with blue, luminous patches of all sizes. The floor appeared strewn with bits of glowing, blue rock and dust, some of it in small piles, as if made deliberately.

Craving the light M'rain ran to stand below the opening and lifted her face to it. Far above, directly over her, shone a full moon, the same moon she had known all her life, the one that had comforted her dreams. She reached her arms to it in silent supplication, knowing, even as she did so, that the moon could not help her. Desolate, she sank to her knees and let her chin drop to her chest. Without realizing it, she lay down in the strange blue dust and wept.

She must have fallen asleep for a short time. When she opened her eyes again the moon had passed over the opening and the light inside had dimmed, though she could still see enough to make out the edge of the cave and its mouth. She raised herself to sitting. The only opening in this cave was the one by which she had entered. She had taken the wrong path.

Her eyes' gaze dropped to her bare arms. They were covered in the dust from the floor and where it clung to her skin she glowed blue – *like K'kor. So this was the source of his blue glow. It was not magic after all.*

She shuddered remembering K'kor's hands on her and his leering lust before he fell asleep. She tried vigorously to rub the dust off but only succeeded in spreading it more. Ragged sobs escaped her. After a time she fell back asleep, overcome with exhaustion, grief, and despair.

IV

WHEN M'RAIN WOKE, and by the rose tint through the hole over her head, she knew dawn had come. If this really was the cave where K'kor got his glowing dust she had to be gone from there before he came back. Another look at her skin revealed, to her relief, that the blue glow disappeared when the light hit it. *Perhaps it only lasts as long as the darkness.* She moved to the entrance to the cave and peered into the blackness beyond.

I have to keep moving or I will surely be found. Which way? I came in from the left. I cannot go back that way. But where will the other way lead? How can I go there if I cannot see? Dread of leaving what little light she had kept her rooted to the spot. Her stomach growled. When she took a small drink from her waterskin it only growled more loudly.

To her left an almost imperceptible shuffling noise broke her dilemma. Someone, or something, was coming. She slipped out of the entrance into the darkness to the right, and as she had before, crept along the tunnel, feeling her way along with fingers and toes. A few steps out, when the tunnel took a bend, even the suggestion of light abandoned her *"Keep moving. They will see you. The dust will give you away."*

That voice in her mind felt familiar.

"Keep moving."

The little lizard. That was the source of the voice? It had a lot of clicks in it, giving it not only a strange accent but also an air of brusque authority. Knowing the lizard had saved her once convinced her to push back the next wave of fear that threatened. Then she looked down at her skin and panicked. She glowed again, just as K'kor had, in spite of there being no light here. That must be what the voice in her head meant.

"The dust needs no light to be seen," the voice came again, answering her unspoken question as though the creature had read her mind. Had it read her mind?

"Look down."

M'rain looked toward where she knew her feet must be and gasped. There it was. She could see it now. It had the same blue glow.

"Follow me." It scuttled silently away in front of her. When M'rain did not immediately follow, it turned back. *"Would you prefer to be caught again?"* M'rain sensed a definite impatience in the tone.

She looked back in the direction she had come. No, she certainly did not want to be in K'kor's clutches again.

When the lizard turned and headed away into the darkness once more its tiny blue glow was the only thing M'rain could see. She took a few hurried steps toward it, stubbing her toes on a stone and nearly falling.

The lizard turned back. *"My apologies. I will go more slowly. Come."* Now the tone sounded somewhat contrite, which helped quell M'rain's panic. She decided she had no choice but to trust this creature. With that decision made she calmed more and concentrated on placing her feet one in front of the other in the direction the lizard led her.

With no more stumbles to interrupt her she had some time to think. She wanted to speak with the lizard but did not know how. What was its name? Why was it here? Why was it helping her? What did it know about K'kor and his little band? She dared not break the silence by asking aloud. Somehow she knew that even whispering would meet with censure from her rescuer.

When her stomach growled so loudly the lizard could not help but notice, M'rain heard, *"There will be food soon. Come."*

Of course, the message came into her mind without sound. That made M'rain wonder if she, too, could send a message with only her mind. Perhaps if she concentrated very hard. *"Who are you?"* She stubbed her toe on a stone and stumbled again, causing the lizard to turn back to look at her.

"Not now. You will learn. Later."

It worked! The thrill of discovery vanished as soon as she saw the lizard scurry forward again and realized she would lose sight of it if she did not pay attention. She watched it turn left and disappear. Then it stuck its head back out just enough so she could see it. *"Hurry. There will be food soon."*

It gave her no time for even a sigh of relief but twitched around again so that only the tip of its tail remained visible. M'rain hurried after it and found herself in another small cave with an irregular hole in the ceiling that let in some light. The walls of this cave had no blue patches. It was all grey stone.

The glow on her skin faded as did the lizard's. But she could still see it, waiting beside a small mound, twitching its tail back and forth as if losing patience. *So does the glow only show when there is no other light?*

"Come, eat."

At the mention of food M'rain's stomach emitted another loud growl. She moved to the mound indicated. There was nothing there she recognized. It resembled a small pile of dried fungus, no different in appearance from the stuff K'kor had given to his band. Certainly not appetizing. She wasn't sure it was even edible. Nor did she want to be drugged into sleep.

The lizard seemed to understand her hesitation. *"Eat. It will sustain you."*

With nothing to lose, and recalling her decision to trust the lizard, she reached into the grey mass and pulled out a small lump. She held it to her nose but could discern no odour other than that of the rest of the cave. It felt squishy. She put a small piece into her mouth. When she began to chew she almost spat it out again in surprise. It tasted like the stew her people made in the communal pot at home. How could that be?

She sensed an amused satisfaction from the lizard. Then she heard it in her mind again. *"It is the food you were thinking of when you put it into your mouth. It will taste of whatever you wish it to. I can do that."*

With the familiar flavour making her saliva run freely now, M'rain dropped all caution and gobbled the entire mound in a matter of moments, followed by a long draught from her waterskin.

Finally, replete, she remembered the lizard, and looked around wildly to make sure it had not left her. She spotted it, apparently asleep, under a slanted shaft of sunlight that made it onto the cave floor. Indecision followed relief. Should she speak to it? And if so, should she whisper aloud or try to use her mind again?

The lizard stretched and seemed to yawn. It looked so comical M'rain almost laughed, clapping a hand over her mouth just in time, fearing the lizard might be angry.

"Time for your lesson in mind-speak."

When M'rain jerked in surprise it said, *"No, I was not asleep, only resting. The sun felt good. Now, ask me a question, but do not speak aloud."*

M'rain concentrated and thought, *"Who are you?"*

"Do not shout. That hurt." Its tail twitched in agitation.

Chagrined, M'rain hung her head.

The lizard did not answer her question. Instead it said, *"Try again, more softly."*

"I am sorry. Who are you?"

"Better. Still loud, but better. Next time send it even more softly."

M'rain tried again. *"Please, may I know who you are?"*

"Ah, much better. You are beginning to understand this." M'rain warmed with relief when he added, *"You learn quickly."*

When M'rain made to try again it stopped her. *"You may call me Glick, although that is not my true name. I am known by many names. No one may know my true name. I am your guide, and yes, I have magic."* It gave her a studied look, curled into what M'rain assumed to be a comfortable position, its tail settled over its front feet, and said, *"Sit and listen. Do not interrupt."*

M'rain settled herself cross-legged and waited. She needed answers and this seemed the best way to get them.

"The signs suggest you have been summoned here, that you have been chosen. There are tasks you must perform. I have chosen to help you." Glick stopped and turned one keen bulging eye on her. He, as M'rain had decided it must be a he, said nothing more.

M'rain needed more, much more. Her attempt at patience vanished with a frisson of anger. *"What do you mean, summoned? What must I do? I still understand nothing. I only want to return home."*

Glick twitched as though he had been struck. *"If you cannot stop shouting I shall leave you. Shouting is rude, to say nothing of painful. Have you been taught no manners?"*

With what felt to M'rain like a huff Glick turned his back on her and began to scuttle in the direction of the mouth of the cave.

"No, Glick, please. I will be more careful. Do not leave me alone here. Please." M'rain hoped that in her fear she had not raised her voice too much. This mind-speak was more difficult than she thought. How was she to keep her emotions out of her tone so that she did not hurt the little lizard?

Glick turned around and came back to his spot. He regarded her with a studied look. *"Very well. You need not fear. I would not have abandoned you in any case. The work is too important."*

"What work is that?"

"You must rescue all the people under K'kor's control. They are not meant to be there. It is contrary to nature."

M'rain almost blurted that she was only a stranger here, so how was she supposed to do that, but stopped herself. If she was ever going to be able to return home she needed the goodwill of this lizard. Instead she composed herself as best she could and thought about which questions might tell her what she needed to know.

Though he said nothing, M'rain thought she sensed approval from Glick. That encouraged her to think even more carefully before she spoke. Yes, she decided "speak" was the correct word, even if the speaking was in their minds. What was most crucial to know?

"Will I ever see my people again?"

V

GLICK DID NOT even acknowledge the question. Instead he turned and headed for the exit to the cave. *"You need to remove that glow-powder. It will make you ill. Come."*

"Make me ill?"

But Glick did not seem to notice and she had to hurry to catch up with him. He led her through several more tunnels, all winding and narrow, until he entered a very small cave where M'rain could barely stand upright. She could hear the trickle of water. Glick disappeared with a splash.

"What are you waiting for? Follow me into the water."

M'rain sidled forward until her toes entered the water. She stooped down to take a handful and rub it on her arms.

"Come. Did I not tell you to follow me? You need to immerse yourself. Bah, what is wrong with you?"

"I am afraid."

"Why? Because of the darkness?"

"No. The water. My people never immerse themselves. It is dangerous. I might die like little D'nel."

This clearly puzzled Glick. M'rain could sense his confusion, mixed with disbelief. After a long pause he said, *"Do your people not bathe?"*

"What is bathe?"

At home water was hard to find and M'rain knew of only one shallow stream that sometimes dried up at the peak of the dry season.

Anything deeper than her ankles was alien to her. The memory of the one small child who had drowned after falling face down in that stream had taught her that water was dangerous. During the dry season their only source of water had to be dug or gleaned from the sap of the fruit cactus.

After a short silence Glick answered, *"Bathing is immersing your whole self in water to get clean."* After a short pause he added, *"How do your people get clean? Or do they remain dirty?"*

Insulted, M'rain could not hide the scorn in her voice. *"We are not dirty. We take bowls of water from the stream, or dig it up, and scrub our bodies with wet grasses. Then the sun dries us."* That memory triggered another wave of homesickness. Would she ever laugh with her family under the desert sun again? She gulped back tears, refusing to let them escape.

"Oh." While Glick did not apologize, his tone had lost its biting edge. Then he reverted abruptly to his former air of authority. *"That will not suffice here. Come. Immerse yourself. You will not die. Do not make me wait any longer."*

When she still hesitated he shouted, *"Do it now!"* The sharp pain in her head made her realize how painful her early attempts at mind-speak must have been for Glick. It jolted her out of her inertia. She stepped forward into the pool – and gasped, breathing in water as she lost her footing and the frigid liquid enveloped her head. She flailed around desperately, not knowing which direction was up, certain she would drown. When she finally found the bottom with her feet and got her head above water she coughed, fighting for breath. Her head went under again as she once more lost her footing on the slippery surface.

Before she could react she found herself on her back on the dry floor of the cave, still coughing, her chest heaving with the effort to take in air.

"It is no deeper than your neck. Silly girl. What is wrong with you?"

While the words were a rebuke M'rain detected some concern and even remorse in Glick's tone. That calmed her enough so that when she could breathe again she was able to ask, *"How did I get out?"*

"That was me. Magic. Remember how K'kor fell asleep? I did that, too." He

34

paused, then added, *"Look at your skin."*

"I cannot see it." Then she understood. *"Oh, the glow is washed off. It is gone."*

"Hmph."

"But now I cannot see you either."

"I can remedy that."

M'rain felt Glick climb onto her leg.

"Touch my eyes and then touch yours. Make sure they are open so you touch the eye, not the lid – your eyes, too."

"But I still cannot see you. Where are your eyes?"

Though he did not answer her M'rain soon saw two orange orbs glowing in the darkness. They gave her an eerie feeling that sent gooseflesh over her entire body and made her shiver.

"Well." The volume told her Glick was losing patience.

M'rain reached out with both her forefingers and gingerly touched one finger to each of Glick's eyes. As soon as she withdrew she could no longer see them.

"Now touch your eyes, both at the same time, mind. And not the lids."

While M'rain wondered why it was so important to touch both at the same time she thought better of asking and did as she was told.

Fire seared her eyes. The pain was greater than she had words for, blocking all other thought from her mind. She fell over backward and writhed on the floor of the cave, screaming aloud. Then she lost consciousness.

When she came to she heard, *"It is a good thing this cave is not near any of the others. That scream would have brought them running."*

M'rain kept her eyes squeezed shut, afraid to open them lest the pain return. Her eyes felt strange, but she sensed no more pain and wanted to keep it that way.

"What have you done to me? Have you blinded me?"

"Hmph. Certainly not. How will you complete your task if you cannot see? Silly girl. Open your eyes, now. There will be no more pain." When she still hesitated he added, *"That is why I told you to touch both eyes at once. If you had touched only one you would have refused to touch the other. It only works if both eyes*

are magicked. Now open them and look around."

M'rain ventured one eye open just a crack. When she saw that Glick had spoken the truth she opened both eyes and looked about herself in amazement. She could see. Not the way she was accustomed to seeing but she could make out everything around her. It all looked like red shadows and shapes on black. The outlines were hazy and unclear, but that did not hamper her from being able to see everything. A glance toward her feet revealed the pool she had fallen in. She crawled to its edge and looked in.

"See," Glick said, *"it is not deep. You can stand up in it and still keep your head out."* His voice took on a tone that seemed a mix of gleeful satisfaction and remorse, a very odd combination. *"You see, I had to make you get all that powder off, even out of your hair. I had no choice."*

That made M'rain angry. *"You mean you almost drowned me on purpose? How could you? I trusted you!"*

"Not enough to get your head under water."

"You do not know that! I did everything you told me to. You did not give me a chance."

"Hmph. It was quicker that way." Before she could reply he twitched around and scuttled to a small pile of something on a stone at the other end of the cave. *"Here. More food. Then sleep."*

"First I need to know something. The others in the cave, K'kor's group, do they have the same magic to see? Can they see me as easily as I will see them?" A frightening thought came to her. *"Will I ever see the way I used to? When I return to the sun, will my sight be the same as it used to be? Will it?"*

"Stop shouting!"

"Answer me. Please, I need to know."

M'rain had not known lizards could sigh but she was sure that was what she sensed from Glick before he answered her. *"No, the others do not see as you do. They see far less. But the fungus that induces their dreams also affects the eyes so that they need less light to see. But they see less than you."*

That calmed M'rain a little. *"But my sight. What about that?"*

"The change will not affect you in the open. It only works in the caves."

"Thank you."

"Now eat, and then sleep."

M'rain thought about the food she missed most and took a bite. It worked. The grey mass tasted and felt just like the roasted Running Bird her people hunted. As she swallowed the last bite a strange lethargy overtook her. The food must also contain something that induced sleep. That thought was her last as she felt herself slide onto her side.

VI

HIDDEN AMONG THE strange, pale trees growing in front of the last of the stalagmites in the gigantic cave behind her, M'rain saw stranger things than she had ever imagined.

She shrank back even more as a young man with golden skin, slightly paler than her own copper colour, and carrying a small animal that squealed and struggled, strode in her direction. He tucked the animal under one arm and opened a strange door into what must be a hut of some kind. But it was unlike any hut she had ever seen. Her people made round huts of dried mud, with conical grass roofs. This one had flat straight walls that met at four corners, and a peaked roof made of some kind of grass. At least that looked familiar, dried and dark gold in color like the grass used in her village. She watched the young man enter the hut and come out empty handed. He closed the hard door behind him, barred it with a long piece of wood and walked away again. Her people never barred doors. He must need to keep the strange animal inside.

Good. He had not seen her.

Though the squealing had stopped she heard other noises unfamiliar to her, the calls of what must be many birds, other animal noises. One sound was familiar – the sound of human voices calling to each other and answering. So, though she had seen only one young man she knew there were others in this strange place.

She crept forward to peer through the trees and saw more of the strange huts of varying sizes, some with smoke rising from the top of a special pot on their roofs. The things that belched smoke looked almost like the hollowed out gourds her people used, but these tapered at the top, as though the stem was hollow. Her people made the *foamy drink in them that was shared around the fires when they danced together. They did not catch smoke in them on top of huts.*

Around those huts she saw patches of green with plants of many shapes and sizes. These, too seemed to have been laid out with straight sides. And there was light – a lot of light, though she could not see its source from her hiding place.

All around, behind the huts and patches of green, grew tall trees, unlike any she had ever seen. They looked lush and green suggesting an abundance of water.

Nothing looked familiar. Yet, it had an order about it that told her it must have been made that way by the people who lived there, different from her home, but with a similar sense of planning to it. In spite of its strangeness she felt drawn to it, as if this was where she needed to be.

M'rain woke feeling rested, if a little stiff from sleeping on the cold stone floor. It took her a few moments to realize she was still in the cave and that what she had seen was only a dream. But, unlike most of her dreams, every detail of this one remained vivid in her mind. Her people believed that when the shaman dreamed it always meant something. *Does my dream mean something?*

She sat up and stretched, looking behind her for the rock where the food had been, hoping to see another small pile of the wonderful grey stuff that tasted like whatever she wanted it to. Disappointed to see the spot empty she reached, instead, for the waterskin at her waist and swallowed a few mouthfuls.

That erased the last vestiges of sleep from her mind and she became, once more, acutely aware of her predicament. She examined her surroundings. To her relief the shadow vision Glick had given her was still present. She could see, after a fashion.

Spotting the edge of the pool reminded her that she ought to keep her waterskin full so she crept to the edge and dipped the mouth under the water. When she noticed that the water in the pool was cooler than what remained in the waterskin she poured out the old and filled it with fresh, cool water. She took another long drink and filled it to the top again. There. Now she would not go thirsty for a day or two.

Since Glick was nowhere to be seen M'rain used the time to explore the cave more closely. When she approached the entrance she spied a gossamer thread of light running along the floor of the next tunnel. This thread was green in colour, quite different from the red and black of her shadow vision. She followed it for several steps and then turned back to see if it remained behind her. To her relief it did. She could still see it. That gave her the courage to explore further, checking every now and then to make sure she could still see the thread behind her.

She had gone far enough that she could no longer see the entrance to the cave she had left when she heard a noise that made her freeze in her tracks - footsteps, careful and shuffling, but definitely footsteps – human ones. She could not see who made them but could tell the direction they were coming from – toward her. She had nowhere to hide in this tunnel and the entrance to the nearest cave was too far away to run to. Hoping that whoever was coming would not spot her when they entered she shrank against the darkest far edge and crouched under the slanted roof, making herself as small as possible.

No sooner had she done so than the silhouette of a person appeared at the mouth of the tunnel. The figure swayed and stumbled, as if too weak to walk, or possibly drugged. M'rain thought it looked like one of the women from K'kor's cave.

The woman moaned, and when she almost fell she put out a hand to steady herself against the wall. It looked like it took all her strength to place one foot ahead of the other as she made her way toward where M'rain huddled. About halfway there she gasped, bent double and clutched her abdomen with her free arm, another moan of pain escaping her lips. She tried to straighten, but after two more faltering steps, slid slowly down to sitting. She bent forward with both hands around her abdomen as if cradling it and rocked back and forth, accompanied by a low sing-song moaning.

M'rain watched for a few moments, undecided about whether to reveal herself. The woman was obviously in pain. It occurred to M'rain that she had seen something similar at home in her village - a young woman writhing in pain holding her abdomen. Was this the same? Was the poor woman having a miscarriage? As M'rain watched she spotted a gleam on the woman's hands that told her there was something wet there. Was it blood?

Her desire to help overrode her fear. She uncoiled and stood up to approach the woman. That was when she recalled what Glick had told her – that she must rescue all the women under K'kor's control.

Her movement must have caught the woman's eye because she jerked her head in M'rain's direction and let out a low cry of fear.

M'rain approached slowly. Keeping her voice low and soothing she said, "I will not hurt you." When she was close enough to touch the wretch she asked, "What is your name?"

The woman gave her a puzzled look and then seemed to think, her eyes wandering away in the distance. "I do not know." Her voice cracked as though long unused. "I think I had a name once. Now we are all nameless." A spasm overtook her and she doubled over again with a long moan.

"Do you know what is happening to you?" M'rain knelt beside her and placed what she hoped was a comforting hand on the woman's shoulder. "Are you losing a baby?"

Frightened eyes looked into M'rain's. "He will kill me...his heir..."

"No one is going to kill you. I can help you." When the woman sent her a look of disbelief and began to shake her head M'rain added, "I have been sent." She pressed the woman down gently until she lay on the floor. "May I look? I have assisted with childbirth before."

The woman turned her head away with a resigned nod. "Too late...the one who gave him an heir...would be his queen. He promised...Now..."

Just as M'rain spread the woman's knees and began to probe between her thighs a sticky lump the size of a cactus fruit slipped into her hands. "Yes, it is too late for this one. I am sorry." She massaged the woman's belly with one hand and waited a few moments. Soon a second slippery mass slid into her free hand. "The afterbirth has come. It is finished now." She continued to massage for several more minutes, hoping it would slow the bleeding. She had not enough light to see well and nothing to offer the woman to soak up the blood that continued to seep out. But the woman gradually calmed and M'rain thought that the flow of blood had slowed almost to nothing. "Can you walk?" Though the woman was small and painfully thin, M'rain did not think she could carry her far. "We cannot stay here."

When the woman made no move to answer or rise M'rain slipped an arm under her shoulder and attempted to lift her to sitting. "Come. You must try. I can save you but I need you to help, too." M'rain did not know where the thought that she could save this poor woman came from but she sensed it to be true.

"...cannot go back..."

"No, I will not make you go back. There is another place, a safe place. We will find it together."

The woman began to shake her head but when she looked into M'rain's face it was as if she saw something there, something that gave her a sliver of hope.

M'rain saw the change in the woman's eyes so she tried again. "Come. Put your arm around my shoulder and I will help you up." The woman obeyed and M'rain struggled to get her to her feet. With that accomplished she looked in both directions. Where could she take her? She had no more idea now of where to go than she had had when she woke that morning. The only place she knew was the cave she had left earlier. But that cave had fresh water, at least. She decided to head back there and give the woman something to drink and possibly wash her off. The light showing the way was still visible. After that...well...maybe Glick would re-appear and give some ideas. If not she had lost nothing.

The woman leaned heavily against her, dragging her feet along the ground as she moved one foot ahead of the other, the sound seeming to echo in contrast to the silent steps of M'rain's captors. M'rain staggered under the weight but managed to keep both of them upright until they arrived at the cave and she could lay her burden down. She reached for her waterskin, wondering why she had not thought of it before, and offered the woman a drink. When the woman had drunk enough M'rain lowered her head back down and watched until she fell into a restless sleep, muttering and twitching.

VII

WHILE SHE WATCHED her charge sleep M'rain had time to reflect. She had made a promise, a rash one. She had told the woman she would take her to a safe place. What had made her make such an impulsive statement, one she had no guarantee she could fulfil? M'rain was lost herself. How could she have felt so confident? Yes, Glick had told her she must help all the people under K'kor's control. But he had given her no hints as to how she would accomplish that task. The more she thought about it the more impossible it seemed.

On the other hand, had Glick not provided her with food and water? Had he not given her some sight in the darkness? Had the thread of light not led her to this woman exactly when she needed help? The more she tried to understand the more frustrated she felt. Her previous life had been predictable, which had given her a sense of control. Now, that sense had been stripped from her.

And what of the dream, with its strange huts, plants, animals, and light? *Does it mean anything? Am I supposed to find it, or take the woman there? Does it even exist?* Dreams did play an important role in helping her people understand things. But in her home village only a few elders and the shaman had dreams that anyone considered important. And she, M'rain, was no shaman or elder. Her dreams would not have been considered valuable. *I am an ordinary girl, almost a woman.* She recalled the women who had captured her. One of them had told her companion

45

that she, M'rain, was "the one". *What does that mean? Why am I different? I do not feel different. Am I different?* No matter how hard she tried she could not come up with anything that set her apart from the other women of her village. Yes, she had been a headstrong child and had often wandered too far from home but she did not consider that significant. She decided, with a mental shrug, that the woman must have come to that mistaken conclusion because M'rain happened to wander into the cave and had managed to escape from K'kor. *But then, why do I see Glick? And how is that he is able to speak with me? And why has he told me I must rescue the people under K'kor? I do not want this. I want to go home, to forget about this dreadful place.* The thought struck her that this might all merely be a dream. She had had dreams before where, at some point in it, she knew it for what it was and was able to wake herself. She tried that now. But this felt different from those times. None of her tricks worked. Dream or not, she knew she would never go home until she had completed the task Glick had set for her. And she would have to rely on herself. Glick could not be relied upon to be present whenever she wanted him. That had already become plain to her. His help seemed unreliable.

During her musings she glanced down at the floor and noticed, to her alarm, that the thread of light was gone. She still had the ability to see but all trace of the thread leading into the tunnel had disappeared. Had she imagined it? *No. Otherwise how did I find the woman and bring her back here. It was there for me to follow.* She rubbed her eyes. When she opened them the line was still gone.

Anger replaced the panic that threatened to rise in her. So...Glick meant to keep her here. *"Glick."* She shouted the mind speak as loud as she could, thinking that either the blast would hurt him and make him answer her, or if he was far away, he might hear it and come to her.

When she got no response her anger ebbed again in a deep sigh. She sat, dejected, shoulders hunched, feeling sorry for herself. When her gaze fell upon the stone that had previously held the food she noticed it had been replenished. When had that happened? Had Glick returned? But Glick was nowhere to be seen and the food looked the same as the last time so she wondered if it would put her to sleep again. She wanted to stay alert in case the woman woke. Not only would her companion need her but M'rain had questions for her - and she had to make sure the woman didn't run away from her.

M'rain studied her guest again and noted that her breathing had become slow and steady. She looked about as comfortable as anyone could be on the cold, stone floor of the cave. M'rain concluded she would not wake for some time and decided to do some exploring. Even though she had no thread of light to guide her, with the magic vision Glick had given her, she could scrutinize the cave more closely and even see part of the tunnel.

Having something to do helped settle her mind somewhat. This cave was small. Within only a few moments she felt she knew every part of it and stepped out into the tunnel. She again recalled Glick's assertion that she must help all the women. And now one of them had already come into her care. Perhaps she was meant to remain in this cave until all of them had been gathered here. *No, that does not make sense. This cave is too small.* So, though she had no answers to her many questions, she came to accept that, against all reason, she would rescue the women. Somehow the means would present themselves when she needed them, just as the food and water had. And, since Glick kept disappearing, she would have to find some of the answers herself.

Food. The grey pile on the stone reminded her how hungry she was. *If I am destined to bring the women to safety it is unlikely I will oversleep and lose the first one.* Reassured by the rhythmic breathing of her sleeping charge and the logic of her conclusion she closed her eyes, imagined the boiled p'ona her people ate in the morning and chewed. As soon as she finished the last morsel she curled up on the floor, head pillowed on her hands, and fell into a dreamless sleep.

A shrill scream shattered the silence and brought her bolt upright. The woman cringed behind her, her look of terror directed at the entrance of the cave.

What M'rain saw there made her recoil. A creature the length of her body, massive in width, grey like everything else in this maze, stood limned in the entrance to the cave. It had a long snout filled with wicked looking teeth and huge yellow eyes that bulged out from each side of its head. It blocked the entrance and swung its head from side to side as if trying to see them but could only use one eye at a time.

"It is the monster! K'kor has sent it. It will eat us!" The sheer terror in her charge's voice mirrored that in M'rain's mind, though she remained silent. When the creature stopped swinging its head and began to lumber in their direction, M'rain could think of only one thing to do. Making the volume of her mind-speak match the terror she felt she shouted, *"Glick!"*

"Stop that! I am right beside you."

"Where?" I do not see you." M'rain spoke this aloud, forgetting, in her fear, to use mind-speak. She glanced down to see Glick uncurl the tail he had wrapped around himself and stretch as though waking from a comfortable sleep. When she spotted him all M'rain could do was point, mute, toward the cave entrance. The creature had, by now, lumbered half-way across to where she and her companion cowered.

"Oh, that. That is the flesh-eater lizard." His tone sounded almost bored.

When the monster took another two steps in their direction, no longer swinging his head from side to side but keeping one eye firmly fixed on his next meal, Glick moved to position himself between it and the women. He raised himself up on his hind legs...and grew. Before M'rain could register what was happening, Glick swelled to three times the size of the creature, his head touching the top of the cave. He looked terrifying. One forearm, bearing claws now a long as M'rain's arm, reached out and gave the monster's snout a solid swat. This caused its head to swing to one side so that it saw Glick towering over it. A guttural rumble escaped the creature's throat. It turned tail, and with astonishing speed, disappeared out of the cave and down the tunnel.

"There. He will not bother you again." Glick returned to his normal size and settled himself beside M'rain.

M'rain glanced behind herself to find that the other woman still cowered against the wall staring wide-eyed at the entrance to the cave.

"She does not see me. Nor did she see what just happened. You are forbidden

to tell her."

"*How can I explain why that creature left us alone?*"

"*Simple. Tell her you have magic. With the evidence of her own eyes she has no choice but to believe you. And she will do whatever you ask as well as tell everyone she meets.*"

"*But that is not true. I have no magic.*"

"*It serves the purpose.*"

"*You want me to lie?*"

"*It is no lie. You see me. She does not. Is that not magic? You have the vision I gave you. Is that not magic? She need not know the limits of your gifts. Nor does she need to know about me.*"

M'rain sensed the warning tone that made her decide not to press Glick further on the point but it did not sit well with her.

"*Now, look at the ground.*"

"*Oh, a green line. That was not there before.*"

"*You did not need it before. More magic.*"

"*Am I supposed to follow it?*"

"*What do you think?*" Glick's sarcastic tone took M'rain aback. "*Of course you must follow it. And take the woman with you. When you reach the cave with the stalactites stay hidden, but tell the woman to go into the village.*"

"*The village?*"

"*You will know it.*" With that Glick seemed to wink out. M'rain could no longer see him even though she searched the entire cave. *He is the one with the magic. Not me. And I will not lie.*

"Has it gone?" The woman had found her tongue.

"Yes, it will not bother us again."

"What made it leave?"

M'rain thought quickly. "Magic. I am protected by magic." There she had managed to keep to the truth. She did not need to lie.

With that realization something changed in M'rain. A new confidence grew in her she had not felt before. She had a task to complete, and however impossible that task looked, she would succeed, with or without Glick. However little it might be, she believed she once more had some control. She would remain true to herself. It felt good.

VIII

K'KOR LASHED OUT in fury, spittle spewing from his lips. "Where is she?" When he received only blank stares from the women and two men in the cave he took the only spoon from the pot, thrust it into the dying cook-fire and withdrew it filled with fiery embers. With one wide swing of his arm those embers went flying toward his captives, hitting several, making them yelp in pain.

The victims cried out and rubbed wildly where they had been hit. A few had only minor burns but three of the women moaned in pain, holding their hands over blisters that came up on naked arms and one belly. The others mewled in fear and hugged themselves, eyes on K'kor to see if he would do it again. Yet, despite the pain, terror kept them in their places, none dared reach for water to ease their hurts.

K'kor took a grim satisfaction from that. His power remained intact. He swung the spoon around to emphasize that he could do it all again. "Where is she? She stole my heir." He took two steps toward the nearest woman and leaned into her, face thrust out, almost touching hers. "Tell me."

The woman began to shake so hard she almost fell. "I...I do not know. Sh...she was bleeding." With that statement she flung her arms protectively around her head and stumbled backwards. When K'kor raised the spoon as though to hit her she took another step back and fell into the cave wall and down to the ground where she curled into a ball, arms wrapped around her head.

51

Instead of stretching out to hit her K'kor swung the spoon sideways and clipped the woman to his right. She yelped in surprise and grabbed her arm where the blow had landed.

The news that the missing woman had been bleeding caught K'kor by surprise. He had brought the women to this cave so certain that he would sire a new people who would look up to him as a god. These women were all supposed to produce sons and daughters to work the mines and make him rich. They would dig out the black rocks he had discovered, rocks that burned longer than wood, and produced heat. The men in his home village, reluctant to burn the trees that took so long to grow back, would trade for his rocks. And they would worship him as the one to discover the black rocks. He was the favoured one, the one they would remember long after all the rest were dead and forgotten.

Before leaving the village, before his little band followed him into darkness, K'kor had come upon the dream-fungi. By experimenting with it himself and having a few followers try them he had learned that the dream-fungi made people sleepy and suggestible – even to the point of forgetting who they were for a short time. K'kor had taken this discovery as a sign that he was meant for greatness. He had also made certain that no-one learned what he had found out or where this special rock could be found.

The dream-fungi would give him the power to make his ambitions come true. A short time later, using its hypnotic influence, he had enticed his mate, a few young men, and several very young, and he hoped, fertile women away from their homes in the village to this great cave. Finding the glowing dust in another small cave a short time later had reinforced his drugged delusions, and convinced him that he was a god. Nothing, not the loss of two of the men and three women to starvation and overwork in the mines, nor the darkness, nor his own failing health, could sway him from his quest for power or his faith that he had been chosen.

So. She ran away. And she was bleeding. That means she no longer carries my heir. Traitor!

He made a dismissive gesture with one arm. "Bah, she was not worthy. She was weak." In his delusional state he now dismissed the missing woman as easily as though she had never been of any consequence. "Now one of you must give me a strong son. She did not deserve that honour." He gave each one a suggestive leer, eyes glittering. "Who, eh? Who is strong enough?"

With an abrupt motion he sat down next to the fire and jabbed the spoon at one of the two remaining men. "Show me how much you have mined."

The two brought forward two shabby reed baskets, placed them in front of K'kor, and backed away.

"What?" K'kor shrieked, causing all the others to jerk back and shrink toward the wall. "That will burn in one night. I must have the black rocks to trade." His voice rose even higher. "Fools! Lazy fools! Do you think you deceive me? Do you think I do not see how lazy you are? I am a god! You swore yourselves to me. I see what you are doing. Traitors! All of you!"

Then, just as quickly as his voice had risen, it fell to almost a whisper, even more menacing than his rage. "Those who do not work do not eat." He kicked out one foot which toppled a basket. Several pieces of black rock rolled out onto the floor. He gestured to one of the men. "Empty them."

As soon as the baskets were emptied, leaving a small pile of rocks beside the fire, K'kor stood up, the spoon still in his hand. He tapped one young woman on the head with it, almost gently. "You will remain with me," He pointed to the ragged grass pallet beside the fire. "Lie down."

Not waiting to see if she obeyed he turned to the rest. "Back to the mines. Do not return until the baskets can hold no more. No one eats until I have my fire rocks."

K'kor turned back to the woman half sitting on the mat, like an animal ready to run. He plopped himself down, cross-legged, in front of her, tossed the spoon at her, crossed his arms and said, "Feed me."

IX

"HERE." M'RAIN HANDED the woman her waterskin. "Drink your fill. And eat as much of that food on the stone as you can. Then we must leave."

"Leave?"

"Yes, I will take you to safety...but I do not know how long we must walk." When the woman gave her a doubtful look, she added, "You do have the strength to walk, do you not?"

The woman handed her back the waterskin with a slow nod. "I think so. And I remember my name."

"Good. I was about to ask you to make one up. It feels wrong to speak to someone without a name. What is it?"

"L'lowen."

L'lowen had an awed expression on her face. It made M'rain wonder whether it was due to remembering her name or because she knew M'rain had magic. Not sure L'lowen would remember M'rain's name she repeated it for her. "I am M'rain." While she refilled her waterskin, and chewed down the fungi L'lowen had not eaten, she told her, "I know the path to safety. When we get there I must leave you and I must return."

"Leave me? I am afraid to be left alone."

"There are others there, ones who will look after you." *How do I know that? Is it true? Will there be others?*

"...oh..."

M'rain hoped what she had told L'lowen was true, that she would be looked after when they reached wherever the thread was leading them. *Otherwise what is the point of rescuing the women as Glick says I must?*

The soft whisper and the way L'lowen lowered her gaze and shrank into herself told M'rain the woman's awe had grown, though it still held a note of fear.

Both of those responses made M'rain angry. She had to bite her lip to prevent herself from chastising the poor woman. M'rain wanted neither fear nor worship. *I am not special. I do not have magic. I only have a task to perform before I go home.* She took a deep, steadying breath before answering. "L'lowen, I am an ordinary woman like you. I have been sent to help you." Not knowing what else to say she spun on her heel toward the entrance of the cave, waterskin securely tied at her waist, and strode away. "Come."

L'lowen scrambled to catch up.

As her annoyance faded, M'rain slowed her pace. She needed to concentrate on keeping the new green line of light in sight.

They walked in silence for a time, M'rain in the lead, through tunnels of various lengths and depths, and past several side caves. It startled M'rain when she heard L'lowen begin to speak, voice low, almost dream-like.

"He was so beautiful."

M'rain kept silent, hoping L'lowen would go on.

"He was strong. A good hunter. Well-liked by the other young men. Ambitious. He could have chosen any woman. He chose me. I felt so lucky."

Though L'lowen stopped speaking again M'rain sensed that prodding her would only serve to send her deeper into silence. She did not respond and kept walking...and waiting for whatever might come. She did not have to wait long.

"But I was not enough." Her tone held such sadness. "He chose a second mate. No other man had two wives." After another silence L'lowen said, "I think it made him feel powerful...He was...powerful." A long, heavy sigh escaped her before she repeated, "I was not enough...I hoped...the baby..."

M'rain heard a short sob, like a single hiccup, then nothing more. The anguish in that one sob told her not to pry further, lest L'lowen break down and become too despondent to keep walking.

With no sunlight to help gauge the passage of time, M'rain thought they must have travelled for about half a day when she saw light that had a different quality from the shafts that had come through the roofs of the occasional cave. The green line led directly toward it. The closer they got the more inviting it looked. M'rain sensed something familiar about it. Then it struck her. This was sunlight – real sunlight – like at home. A wave of longing almost made her forget L'lowen and run toward it. But what she saw next stopped her in her tracks.

This was nothing like her own home. The stalactites that stood in her way also kept her hidden. Ahead, just as it had appeared in her dream, was the gold and green village. Beyond the stalagmites, between her and the village, stood a thin forest of trees, very pale where they rose under the lip of the opening of the giant cave she stood in and deeper green where they received more sun. Even this far back M'rain could see the top of one of the strange peaked roofs from her dream and the smoke that lifted in a lazy spiral from its funnel on top.

"It is real."

L'lowen's guttural moan covered M'rain's awed whisper. She turned to see L'lowen on the ground hugging her knees, rocking back and forth. M'rain could not interpret the look on her face. It seemed to have both longing and fear, but those emotions did not usually appear together.

"L'lowen, what is it? What's wrong?"

"I cannot...."

"Cannot what?"

L'lowen kept her gaze on the scene ahead of them as if transfixed. M'rain had to strain to hear the low whisper.

"I cannot go back."

"What do you mean?"

L'lowen stretched out one arm as if to pull the scene toward herself. "Home."

"Home? This was your home?" Some of the pieces fell into place in M'rain's mind. This must be where K'kor had taken his following from. But that knowledge only brought more questions. How had he been able to lure them from such a beautiful place? What hold did he have over them?

L'lowen slowly let her arm fall by her side, her hand coming to rest, lax, on the ground. "They will not want me back. I cannot..."

M'rain thought quickly. She had to get L'lowen into the village without being seen herself. She had to convince the woman to step forward past the stalactites, through the trees, and to attract the attention of a villager.

"L'lowen, remember when I told you I would bring you to safety?"

L'lowen finally shifted her gaze to meet M'rain's. "I cannot..."

"Yes, you can. Because of the magic. Remember? I said I was protected by magic. Well, you are, too. You will return home and your people will welcome you and take care of you. It is fate. It is meant to be." *Glick, this better be correct.*

A faint glimmer of hope came over L'lowen's face. Her gaze swivelled back and forth between the village and M'rain. When it rested on her again, M'rain gestured with her head in the direction of the village. "They wait for you. Go." She took L'lowen by an elbow and helped her to her feet. "Go. It will be well."

When L'lowen still hesitated, staring unmoving at her home, M'rain slipped unheard back behind another stalactite where L'lowen would not see her. She watched L'lowen look around for her, her face full of fear once more. When she did not see M'rain the woman turned to watch the village again. She stood there for so long M'rain thought she might have to prod her some more. Just as M'rain decided to show herself L'lowen took her first hesitant steps away from the stalactites into the trees.

That was all M'rain needed to see. Confident that L'lowen would continue into the village she turned back the way she had come hoping the green thread would still be there to guide her back. It was.

Leaving that sunny glow and re-entering the labyrinth of darkness was one of the hardest things M'rain had ever had to do. *Why must I stay hidden? What will happen if they see me? Why may I not go with L'lowen into the village?* She received no answers to those thoughts.

X

THE GREEN LINE still led M'rain but after some distance she got the feeling it was not taking her back the way she had come. She could not know for sure, since these caves and tunnels all looked so much alike, but she knew if she strayed from that guiding thread she would be hopelessly lost. And she suspected that, while Glick might come to rescue her, he would likely make her wait until he had punished her for disobeying him. As much as she wanted to make her own decisions she realized her life depended on Glick and knew she would die if he abandoned her.

Her stomach grumbled and it occurred to her that she might have been walking for most of the day without eating or drinking. Time passed differently here in the darkness. She was tired, hungry, and thirsty. The weight of her waterskin reminded her that she could, at least, have a drink. The cool water refreshed her enough that she could push her other discomforts to the back of her mind.

Before she had walked much further she heard what appeared to be soft voices from the direction in which she was heading. The green thread led toward the sound. When she had come close enough she could discern two distinct voices, both female. One was weeping. The tone of the other had urgency about it, as if the speaker was desperate to get her companion to do something.

M'rain crept closer, staying hidden in the shadows, until she could both see and hear. She spied two women, looking like the ones from

K'kor's cave, one, with dark hair, standing, the other with hair that might have been lighter but was so dirty it looked as grey as the caves, sitting against the wall.

"I cannot. I am so hungry."

"If you stay here you know he will find you."

"I do not care. I just want to rest...to die. K'kor lied to us. Where are the riches he promised?"

"What about me, then? I dare not go back without you...or with an empty basket." The dark-haired one grabbed the arm of the one sitting on the ground and gave it a tug. "Come on. Please. I do not want to die yet."

"I cannot. I have no strength left." She tugged her arm free and curled into herself. "Let me alone...let me die here."

The dark-haired one looked around, eyes darting down the tunnel and back. "You must come. He will kill me, too. You can rest while I mine the rocks and fill the basket."

The other gave her head a disconsolate shake. "We have not even come as far as the rocks, yet." She raised her gaze to her partner. "I have not even the strength to walk to the mine." She paused, looking at her friend, "...and you have not the strength to fill the basket alone."

"Yes, I can..." The words seem to catch and die in her throat. The dark-haired woman let herself slide down beside her friend. "You are correct. We are already dead. There is no hope."

"Yes, no hope..." It reached M'rain's ears as a despairing echo.

The two women sat together in silence. Then one said. "I am so thirsty. I do not want to die thirsty."

That made M'rain decide to step into view. "I have water."

The two women gasped and yelped, clutching at each other.

M'rain held up her waterskin and repeated, "I have water." She approached the women, untying the neck of the waterskin as she did so. "Here. Not too much. We need to make it last." She held the neck of the skin to the mouth of the nearest woman. "Here. Drink."

As soon as the woman felt the water on her parched lips she overcame her fear and took several greedy gulps. When M'rain made to take the skin from her she tried to hold on to it with both hands but she had not the strength and sank back against the wall.

M'rain repeated the offer of the waterskin with the second woman. "Not too much at once or it will not stay down."

Before M'rain tied the neck closed again she took a few sips herself.

The dark-haired woman whispered, "Who are you?"

"I am called M'rain."

Recognition dawned on the face of the second woman. Her declaration came out in a croak. "You are the one...the one from the outside..."

"Yes."

"How...?"

Before she could answer M'rain spotted another thread of light, blue this time, leading from the cave into the tunnels. "There is no time for that. You must come with me."

The two women looked at each other but made no effort to get up. When M'rain turned back to them one reached out to the waterskin. "More water..."

M'rain hefted the skin to see how much was left – less than half. How long would it be before she would be able to refill it? A look at the women showed her that both of them had recovered a little but she had no way of knowing how far they could walk. She had never seen women so thin and with skin that looked so dry. And if they drank too much too quickly they could become ill. But the first drink seemed to have had no ill effects. She relented. "Just a small drink. I do not know when there will be more – and too much will make you retch." She held on to the bottom of the skin so that she could pull it away if the women tried to drink too much. There was not much left when they finished.

"Now will you come with me?"

"Where?"

"Home."

"No! We cannot go back."

"It will be safe."

The women clung to each other again. "K'kor will kill us."

With some chagrin M'rain realized her error. "No, not to K'kor, but back to the village."

M'rain watched first confusion, then hope, then doubt cross the faces of the two.

"How?"

"We will be lost."

"They will not want us back."

But even as they spoke the words M'rain could hear that glimmer of hope in their voices.

"They will. And I have magic that shows me the way."

While one woman moved to get up the other grabbed her arm and pulled her back down. "Magic. K'kor has magic. It is bad."

This was not the response M'rain had expected. The sense of urgency she felt, coupled with the distrust the women showed, made her impatient. She expected gratitude, not resistance. Could they not see that she was nothing like K'kor? Did they not understand what danger they were in if they did not follow her?

The thread of light had grown brighter and pulsed, now. Something about it made her sense they must hurry.

"Would you rather be found by K'kor?" M'rain's anger rose as she spoke, and her voice grew stronger. "Do you want to die, or be killed?"

When the women jerked in fear and looked at each other, still not rising, she took another tack. "Fine, I will leave you here, then. There are others I must rescue." She spun on her heel and began to stride away, taking care not to look back. *Glick is wrong. I am not meant to do this. It is too difficult. How can I rescue women who will not follow me? Glick chose the wrong person.*

M'rain had gone several steps when she heard, "Wait."

She stopped and waited but did not turn around, still angry.

"We will come."

M'rain heard shuffling as the two got to their feet.

When they reached her one touched her arm. "You can keep us safe?"

"Yes, but we must hurry." She began to follow the thread again, this time at a slower pace to allow for the weakness of the women. When she heard one stumble she turned and saw that the light-haired one could hardly walk. Her anger ebbed. She stepped back and took the woman's arm to support her. The lack of flesh under the skin told her just how close to starvation the poor creature was.

They had just reached the tunnel and chosen a new direction when M'rain heard voices – male voices, and the sounds of something heavy being dragged along the ground. She stopped and pressed the two women against the wall, hoping they were far enough into the tunnel that the men would not spot them.

One of the women whimpered in fear. The other quickly put a hand over her mouth. M'rain gestured to them to remain against the wall and crept back to see what was happening in the tunnel they had just vacated.

The two men she had seen in K'kor's cave dragged a basket between them. It emitted an occasional gleam as the dim light fell on the contents. These men looked no better off than the women with her, weary, bone thin, and weak.

"It is still not full. He will not feed us."

"He must. We can do no more."

"He is mad. You know that."

The other agreed with a tired nod. "We are all dead."

For a moment M'rain forgot caution and almost jumped out to invite the men to follow her as well. A sharp pain behind her eyes made her pause and press her head between her hands. As soon as she stepped back into the shadows the pain stopped.

"Not yet. Later."

"Glick?"

But Glick, if indeed, it had been Glick, did not answer.

M'rain slipped silently back, close to the two cowering women, and put a finger to her lips. The wait felt endless. When the men finally shuffled past their tunnel without noticing them M'rain beckoned to the women to resume their trek, offering the weaker one her arm for support.

To M'rain's surprise the thread led them into a small side cave she had not seen before, and then ended abruptly.

Her confusion must have shown because the woman who had her arm clenched it tighter. "What is it? What is wrong?"

Not at all sure that what she told them was true, M'rain said, "I think we must rest here. She freed her arm from the woman's grasp and began to explore the cave. A single reflected gleam led her to a pool. "There is water here." As the women came forward to confirm this she spotted a rock with the, by now familiar, grey mass on it. "And food. Look."

"Dream-fungi" The women reached out eagerly and took a piece. "We will sleep. No hunger in sleep."

M'rain knew this was not K'kor's dream-fungi. This kind would sustain them and give them back some strength. "No, not dream-fungi. This is food. As you chew imagine the food you like best. That is what it will taste like. Eat more. It will restore your strength. Then you may sleep. When you wake we will walk again."

The women hesitated until they watched M'rain eat with apparent gusto. With nervous glances in her direction they followed her example and ate several bites. M'rain noticed that the pile dwindled more quickly than the amount they appeared to eat. She guessed that Glick controlled how much they ate so the women would not overindulge and become ill.

After another longer drink from her refilled waterskin both women lay down and soon slept.

"*You have done well.*"

"*Glick?*"

"*Right beside you.*"

The tone of condescending amusement irritated M'rain. "*Why do you keep leaving me? And why do you not tell me what I am supposed to do? This guessing is dangerous. I need to understand.*"

"*You know all you need to. Have you not seen success?*"

"*I want to know more. I do not like not knowing what will happen and what I must do next."*

M'rain thought she heard a chuckle from Glick, the kind a parent uses when humouring a recalcitrant child.

"You will know what you need when you need it. Is that not true of many things? You must show some trust."

That prickled M'rain even more. *"Trust? When every step is full of danger? Do not treat me like a child."*

"Then do not act like one. Have I not provided all you need every time?"

"But I need to know."

"No, you do not." His tone softened a little. *"Even I do not always know. I, too, must trust."*

M'rain had not expected this. She thought Glick knew everything and had deliberately withheld information from her. The revelation brought more and different questions to mind. It changed things – a lot –and not for the better.

"But, if you do not know then how can I trust that I am shown the things I need?"

She sensed a mental shrug. *"What choice do you have?"*

An emptiness in the air told her Glick had gone.

Indeed, what choice did she have? The thought was not at all reassuring.

XI

TRUST. NOW THAT the seed had taken root in her mind M'rain could not brush it away. At home, in her village, she had known that she could trust everyone who lived there. Some were more likeable than others but her people understood that they needed to trust each other and work together to survive. She knew what was expected of her as did everyone in the village. And a young man had shown interest in her. She had reached the age of maturity and would undergo the rite of womanhood. Soon it would be time to decide who would be her mate. Would he be the one? Would she agree? *Is that what I really want? To go back and forget all this? Am I still that woman, the one who would be content with the way things were?* Thoughts of her village and the young man brought on a wave of home-sickness. She wrapped her hands around her knees and rocked back and forth, near tears. Would she ever see her family again, or her home, her people? What of her sister's new infant? Did they miss her?

A wail of grief and longing threatened to spill from her throat. It took effort to push it back down so she would not wake the two women. She could not allow herself the luxury of self-pity. Those would not lead her home. She hugged her knees harder, squeezing tight, and refused to give in to the tears that threatened spill onto her cheeks.

Trust. The more she thought about that, or rather how little of it she felt in her current situation, the more frightened she became. She had believed, blindly she now realized, that Glick would be there if she truly needed him and would intervene if she were in real danger. That belief now evaporated like dew in the morning sun. Until now she had given no more thought to the monster that prowled the caves. What if Glick was mistaken when he said it would not bother her again? Or had he meant the promise only for while she was with L'lowen?

One thing she still believed with certainty. She would never be permitted to go home until she had completed the quest she had been assigned – that was if she would ever be allowed to leave these caves at all.

M'rain wrapped her arms around her body and lay down on her side on the cold stone floor, silent tears of despair and loneliness finally leaking over her lower lids, rolling across her nose and cheeks and dripping onto the floor. A tentative touch on her leg pulled her back from her desolate reverie.

The dark haired woman had wakened and now regarded her with an expression M'rain could not understand. She saw wonder, fear, doubt, hope, and even a desire for life there. The emotions all seemed at odds with each other and played in rapid succession across the woman's face.

"Oh, you are awake."

The woman nodded. "More water? Food?"

M'rain handed her the waterskin. As the woman drank, M'rain looked for more of the grey stuff that had sustained them. "No food, I fear. But when you have had enough I can refill the waterskin."

Their conversation woke the other woman. When the first had drunk her fill M'rain indicated the first one could hand the skin it to her companion. "Drink up. Once I have filled the skin again we must go." A new green line leading from the cave pulsed in a way that looked impatient to M'rain. It was time to go. "I must take you home."

The two looked at each other in consternation. One turned back to her asking, "Home?" echoed by the other, "No. We cannot." They clutched each other, eyes wide.

M'rain quickly amended her statement. "To your village, not back to the cave." Perhaps they had forgotten her earlier promise. "L'lowen is already there. She waits for you."

When the two stared at her in wide-eyed disbelief M'rain added, "I took her there."

"...L'lowen." The word came out as though foreign, as if they had heard it before but were not really familiar with it. Then a wild eagerness replaced the puzzled expression. "L'lowen lives?"

The light-haired one echoed the phrase. "L'lowen lives?"

Recognition dawned on her companion's face. "I remember...I remember..." She grabbed the arm of the other. "We have names, too. Remember? You are N'nuni." A smile broke over her face. She turned and knelt to face her companion. "You are N'nuni and I am P'pani."

Upon hearing her name N'nuni seemed to wake up as though from a spell. "I am N'nuni...yes...I remember."

The memories of who they were seemed to fill the women with renewed energy. N'nuni sprang up and tugged P'pani's hands until she too stood on her feet. They hugged each other in delight.

"And I am M'rain. I am here to lead you home to your village."

The two turned as though surprised to see her there, as if they had forgotten her, or were seeing her for the first time.

"L'lowen waits there for you. Come. We must hurry." M'rain knelt by the pool to refill the waterskin. Without waiting to see if the women followed she headed for the mouth of the cave, where the new thread of light beckoned. Then she stopped mid-stride at the memory of the monster. *A weapon. I need a weapon.* The cave was bare, not even a small branch in sight. A look at the expectant women made her ask, "Have you seen a creature, about this big, with sharp teeth?" She raised her hand above her head as high as she could to indicate size.

The two looked at each other, fear returning to their faces. P'pani nodded. "The monster. K'kor says it obeys him. He says it will eat us if we do not do his bidding."

M'rain thought for a moment. "You say it obeys K'kor? Have you seen it? What does he do to control it?"

"K'kor says it is afraid of fire so it will not come into the big cave."

The pulsing of the green line told M'rain that they had to leave immediately even if they had nothing to counter the monster with. "But does he not have a weapon? What does he use outside the cave where there is no fire?"

"He carries a stick with a point on one end. I have not seen him use it but perhaps that is what it is for."

M'rain let out a frustrated sigh. "Well, I do not have a pointed stick." Seeing the fearful reaction of the women, who had by now lost all of their previous exuberance, she softened. "We need to leave, weapon or not. Let's keep our eyes open along the way for a stick. If you see one, please tell me right away. And let us hope we do not see the monster." She went to the entrance once more and when she saw the women hesitate, added, "Come. We cannot stay here...and they wait for you at home". She exited into the tunnel without looking back, knowing that the women had no choice but to follow her.

The thread led them without incident to the same spot where M'rain had left L'lowen. She still had no stick to fight off the monster. The trek felt shorter this time. The women had not asked for more water so her skin was still full. A glance at the ground confirmed that the green thread that had led them here was gone. Nor did she see another. Now what was she supposed to do?

P'pani touched her arm and broke into her train of thought. "M'rain, will you come with us?" She looked nervous, as did N'nuni. "We are afraid to go alone. What if they do not want us?"

M'rain shook her head. "L'lowen is already there. They will take you back. I cannot come. No one must see me."

"Why?"

Why, indeed? What difference would it make if the villagers saw me or met me? Why did Glick instruct me to remain hidden? But something told her that this was not the right time. She tucked the question away in the back of her mind for the next time she spoke with Glick.

She shook her head. "No, I must go back. I must help the others." She turned around, looking for a thread to lead her away. There was none. Weariness and hunger made her impatient and angry. She turned to the women still waiting for an answer. "Go. I need to think. Just leave me. Go." She waved her hands in front of her waist in a dismissive motion as she spoke and gestured in the direction of the village. "I must not be seen. Go." She turned her back on the two and strode out from between the stalactites back in the direction she had come. As soon as she knew they could no longer see her she turned back to see what the women had done. She spotted the back of one as they disappeared between the trees in the direction of the village.

With still no thread of light to follow weariness got the better of her and she sank to the ground. There she lay down and, with her head pillowed on one arm, fell fast asleep.

XII

K'KOR DID NOT notice the sores on his skin, oozing, with blisters formed randomly everywhere. He had stopped noticing long ago that it burned when he applied the blue dust. Pain no longer registered. He had discovered the glowing stuff in the tiny cave only he knew the location of. *More.* He needed more. Not satisfied with the amount that stuck to his skin from rubbing it on with his hands he jumped into the heap and rolled wildly in it. *They see a god. They worship me and obey me.*

Next to the dust lay a smaller pile of the dream-fungi.

These two things were the source of his power over the group in his cave. Before they came here he had used the power of persuasion. He no longer needed that. The dust made them see him as magical, as a god, even. The dream-fungi kept them docile, made them sleep, and made them forget. As long as they were under the influence of the dream-fungi they believed anything he told them, would do anything he wanted them to.

He rarely ate dream fungi himself, knowing that they made him see strange things and that they put him to sleep. He could not afford to sleep, at least not in the presence of the others. He believed he did not sleep at all. Gods did not need sleep. The short periods in his secret cave when time seemed to disappear did not count.

So when he fell, exhausted, on top of the blue dust, he had no awareness that he slept. This happened more and more, recently. He dismissed those episodes as of no consequence and convinced himself that they did not exist. No, K'kor did not need sleep.

Nor was he aware that he seemed to feel weaker than he used to, or that the periods that disappeared were growing longer. Nor that his limbs no longer obeyed him as they used to; they had not the same strength.

When K'kor came to on the pile of dust he didn't notice that he staggered after he got up, or that he no longer strode with purpose or in a straight line. It didn't bother him that he had difficulty remembering the way back to the main cave. When he reached it he grinned with satisfaction on seeing piles of black rocks next to the fire. Watching his people backing up to the wall when he entered increased his sense of contentment. *I am all-powerful. Let them fear me.* The reactions reinforced his delusions of power.

He usually counted the number of people in the cave. This time he forgot. He sensed vaguely that something wasn't right but didn't have the energy to find out what it was so he dismissed the thought.

He waved one arm loosely in the direction of the nearest woman, "Feed me," and lowered himself onto the ragged grass mat in front of the fire.

K'kor fell asleep without going through the feeding ritual, or giving the others their daily dose of dream-fungus. The women and two men in the cave eyed each other, and shuffled their feet, not moving from their places. This had not happened before. It confused them.

It soon became clear that K'kor would not wake up. One of the women closest to where K'kor lay leaned over to a man next to her and whispered in his ear. When he nodded, still looking worried, she stepped out, took the kettle from the fire, spooned what was left in it into the communal bowl, and began the feeding ritual. When she had finished she put the kettle, bowl, and spoon back in their places and returned to her customary spot.

They all watched K'kor sleep, afraid that he would wake at any moment. When it looked like the fire might die the woman who had distributed the food crept close and added a few coals, prodding it back to life with the charred stick kept beside it for that purpose. Still K'kor did not move.

This time, when the woman returned to her customary spot along the wall, she noticed that two more spots were empty, two more women had not returned to the cave. That meant that there were now three missing. She thought about that for a while then sidled over to the one next to her.

She pointed to the empty spots and murmured, "Where are they? Do you know?"

The second woman, who had until now been sitting inert with only an occasional fearful glance at K'kor, took a more interested look around. When she saw the two empty spots indicated her eyes widened. "No."

As others noticed the two whispering and looking around, they too began to realize more women were missing. A faint buzz went around the cave as the rest of them began to speculate about what had happened and whether K'kor would wake up. A few gathered their courage and crept close to examine K'kor. One man took the spoon and staying as far back as he could and still reach him, gave K'kor the tiniest of pokes with it.

When K'kor showed no sign of waking the man reached, with great care, for the small pouch at his waist in which he kept the dream-fungi. K'kor jerked and gave a grunt that made the man jump back. But K'kor settled back again so the man made another attempt. This time he managed to lift the flap, reach in and extract a handful of the dream-fungi. He hurried back to the circle holding his prize high, a triumphant grin on his face.

Soon all of the others crowded around, hands held out for a share of the pilfered bounty.

The man did not show the others how much he had, but handed them each only one piece, just as K'kor always did. When each person had received their piece and returned to their spot to sleep he cradled his hand close to his chest and examined its contents, making sure no one else could see. He had several pieces left. Before anyone could challenge him he shoved all of them into his mouth at once, chewed and swallowed.

Not long after everyone in the cave slept.

XIII

P'PUCK LISTENED INTENTLY to the stories the women told, how K'kor had lured them with promises of riches, and kept them drugged and enslaved with magic. And how a strange young woman escaped the cave and returned to lead them back here, back to their home.

One of the first things children of the village always learned was that the caves were forbidden to them. There were monsters there that would eat them. And even if they eluded the monsters, the caves formed a labyrinth that could not be learned. Anyone venturing into them would be lost and never return. No one ever ventured past the first stalactites behind the trees at the edge of the great cave. At least, no one who had done so had ever returned.

Yet these three women had returned. They looked near death, it was true, but here they were, the first ever to make it back.

From his seat at the edge of the circle around the central fire he heard one of them say, "But she would not come with us." He watched them as they ate and it occurred to him that the woman who had led them home must also be hungry.

Some discussed whether any ought to go to the edge of the trees to look for M'rain, as she called herself, and invite her into the village. But the elders remained adamant. To go beyond the trees spelled disaster. It was forbidden – and for good reason.

P'puck stood up to get the attention of the elders. "I am not afraid.

I will take food for her. I will look for her." He was afraid, but this was too exciting to let it stop him.

"No, we have spoken. It is forbidden."

P'puck sat down again knowing that to argue with the elders showed disrespect and would cost him status within the village. He had only recently undergone the rite of manhood after bringing home a small boar from the hunt. They had held a feast in his honour and danced around the fire, he wearing the head-dress of a man who had made the big kill in the hunt for the first time. He had been on many hunting parties before. They had tried to teach him all he needed to know, but his aim was seldom true. Now, as he reached his seventeenth summer, his turn had come to undergo the rite. He had to make his first individual kill before he would be accepted. So, when the party had trapped the boar between two tree trunks and their spears P'puck had been given the honour of spearing the beast. P'puck knew his hunting mates had made it easy for him. But that would never be spoken of.

Even after all the training killing a trapped boar was dangerous. They were unpredictable beasts at best and when trapped could rush out without warning and gore a hunter with their sharp tusks. But, when his mates held the boar at bay he had thrust his spear true and the boar had sunk, bleeding, to the ground. Before it had ceased struggling P'puck had taken a second spear and driven it into the beast's eye, finishing it off. His companions had held back while P'puck had gone in and cut the throat so it could bleed out, feeding back to the earth some of the sacred spirit of the animal, in thanks for the bounty and the safe hunt. He was now considered an eligible man and could take a mate. But inside, P'puck knew that he had received more help than was usually given. For that he was grateful.

If he argued with the elders now they would say he had not earned his rite and had behaved like a child. He would lose respect and the young women would no longer cast interested glances his way or send sideways smiles at him. He could not risk that.

Yet, P'puck disagreed with the declaration of the elders. *They are wrong. The woman brought ours back. She travels the caves and is not killed or eaten. And this is the second time she has come. So she does not get lost.*

As the light of early evening bloomed into a brilliant sunset of orange and red streaked with deep blue, and began to fade into indigo, he made up his mind. He crept to the platform where the women had not yet cleared away the meat, p'pone cakes, and greens of their evening meal. He wrapped some up in two serving leaves, lit a small torch from the central fire, slipped out of sight and stole unseen into the trees that ended inside the cave. The light had already faded so he hurried in the direction the women had come from. As darkness enveloped him he began to have second thoughts. *What if she has gone? I will be lost in the caves. What if she sees me? What will she do? Will she speak to me? Will she cast a spell on me for finding her when she made it clear to the women that she must remain hidden?*

P'puck looked behind him, taking courage when the waning light still showed him the mouth of the cave and the way to the village. He could still find his way back. He was not lost – not yet. By now he had reached the first stalagmites. Beyond this point all was blackness. He waved his torch about, and, seeing nothing within the small circle it illuminated, had just decided to return home when he spotted something at the base of the next stalagmite, something round, a shape that he would not expect in that barren rocky place.

He crept toward it, the bundle of food still warm in his hands. *It is her. It is the woman. And she is asleep.* P'puck kept still for several moments, watching the soft rise and fall of the woman's chest as she breathed. It surprised him that she looked much like the women who had returned to the village – dirty, small, and vulnerable, although not quite as thin – certainly not to be feared. And yet, she had done the impossible.

P'puck made up his mind. He would not wake her. She looked too peaceful, sleeping there. He backed away a few steps and placed his offering of food down where he hoped she would find it when she woke, then made his way back to the village. The light had almost disappeared but he saw just enough of a glow ahead that he could make out the direction of the opening from the cave.

Next time I will go while there is still full light. And I will take two torches.

Elation filled him with a sense of triumph. He had gone beyond the trees and made his way back.

That night his sleep was restless, filled with dreams of caves, monsters, and a young woman filled with mystery.

◇◇◇

The woman led as they trod a thread of pale light. She was surprised that he could see it, too. "Do you have the magic, too, then? Have you also seen Glick?"

"Who is Glick?"

She gave him a puzzled look. "So you see the thread of light, but have not seen the small lizard that speaks to minds?"

"…no,…but the totem of our people is a lizard. No one alive has seen him. Have you?"

"Yes, and he is very haughty and has magic."

"He must be real, then. I have wondered if he was only myth. If I ever see him I must apologize. I hope he is not angry with me."

They had followed the thread into the caves. Now, in a blink, it disappeared. The woman cried out, "It is gone," and groped for his hand in the dark. "We are lost."

"I am sorry! Please, do not abandon us. I believe in you. Forgive me."

◇◇◇

P'puck woke in a cold sweat, the nightmare vivid in his mind. The first glow of dawn already lit the morning sky. When he stood up, his legs wobbled as though they would not hold him. He looked around, relieved to be in his own hut. *Just a dream, it was just a dream.* He made his breathing slow back to normal. *Just a dream - or is it a portent?*

XIV

M'RAIN WOKE TO silence. It took her a moment to realize she was still near the back of the cave that led to the village. She sat bolt upright, swiveling her head from side to side to make sure she was still alone. Had anyone spotted her? No. If they had they were not with her now. She allowed herself a small sigh of relief and took a more thorough look about her. Something was different. At first she could not determine what it was. She stilled her mind and concentrated on what her eyes and ears could tell her. But it was another sense that gave her the clue she sought.

There. A tantalizing aroma. An image of roasted meat dripping with hot fat made her mouth water. The growling of her stomach reminded her how long it had been since she had eaten. Where did this smell come from? The village was too far away for the scent of food cooking to reach her here. That could only mean one thing, or rather two things. She had been discovered and there was food nearby – real food.

She sniffed the air trying to detect the direction the aroma was coming from. Her nose led her to a small mound, barely discernable in the dim light, at the base of the nearest stalagmite. Taking care not to make a sound she crept to it. There, wrapped in strange, glossy leaves she found large chunks of a meat she did not recognize. Next to the meat lay something green and another small pile of something like p'ona.

She reached in and picked up a chunk of the meat. It still held the barest hint of warmth, telling her it had not been there long. She studied her surroundings again for signs of life but saw none. Nor did she get the sense she was being watched. Yet, someone had found her. That meant the villagers, or at the very least someone from the village, knew she was here and had left this offering for her.

They know I am here. But they did not stay to meet me. I am not captured. She looked again at the food in her hand and on the ground. *The women must have explained that I have not eaten. So they left food for me. Or the women snuck back with food for me.*

Deciding it must mean that the villagers intended her no harm she took a bite of the meat. It was so tender it almost melted in her mouth, and just as she had imagined, dripped with delicious fat. But it tasted different from any meat she had eaten at home. The big birds her people caught and roasted were stringier than this and did not have as much of the delicious grease. This tasted sweeter. The green stuff had a slight bitterness to it that helped to cut the greasiness of the meat. The cakey stuff tasted bland, similar to the p'ona her people cooked. Soon there was not a morsel left on the leaves. Replete, she licked the last of the fat from her fingers. The weight at her waist told her the waterskin was still almost full. A long drink completed her first meal of real food since her capture.

The kindness of the villagers made her want to go into the village to see if they would accept her as they had the women she had rescued. *But those women are already from the village. They belong here. These are their people. And if I go there they may not allow me to leave.* She crept much closer until she could see the village through the trees at the entrance to the cave. Hidden behind a large trunk she watched until the last hint of dusk faded into deep indigo. She could smell more cooking aromas and watched several spirals of smoke curling up from the strange funnel shapes on the roofs of the square buildings. Now and then, the sounds of human voices and the occasional animal noise reached her, the noises of a people settling down to sleep. *I must ask Glick if I really need to stay hidden.*

The familiar cadences of human voices, even muffled, made her think of home. The longing to be home, to see her own family, her own people again, was so strong she sank down at the foot of the tree and let silent tears track down her cheeks and drip off her chin unheeded.

The increasing darkness soon hid the village from her view. The air grew colder. A shiver shook her out of her reverie.

M'rain rose with great reluctance, almost losing her balance. She had sat motionless in the cool air so long her legs had become stiff. One had gone to sleep and tingled as it woke up. She stretched in silence, shaking first one leg, then the other, to get rid of the prickling and turned to re-enter the world of the caves. On the ground, leading back the way she had come, a new green line showed the way. M'rain followed it with feet as heavy as stone. Her newfound confidence had abandoned her.

M'rain hardly noticed where the thread led. Her head hung so low her chin rested on her chest. She forced one foot ahead of the other, barely lifting it, scuffling the ground. She followed the light more out of habit than awareness. When she found herself back at the small cave with the pool of water it almost surprised her. Dark thoughts had occupied her for the entire journey and she had lost track of time and distance.

She gave no heed to the mound of fungus on the stone. Nor did she take a drink from her waterskin before lying down on the cold floor and wishing her mind into the oblivion of sleep.

"Silly girl. What is the matter with you?"

M'rain woke with a start. It took a moment to remember where she was. She had been dreaming of home. The reality of her current situation hit hard. She pushed herself to sitting. A look around showed her Glick, stretched out beside the food stone.

"Eat...and drink. You have work to do. It will not be done if you grow too weak to finish it."

"I do not want to do this. I only want to go home. Why must I do as you say? Why? And why am I the one? Perhaps you have chosen the wrong person."

"I am beginning to wonder about that myself. I expected someone who would

cooperate more. I wonder if I have made a mistake. A weak, silly girl. Bah!"

That stung but M'rain could not help but wonder if Glick was right. *"So why did you think I was the one chosen for this work? I have never been special. I am only an ordinary girl, like all the others in my village."*

"Hmph." Glick remained silent for a bit. His tone lost its angry edge when he answered. *"Because you were there. You came to the cave. I thought it was a sign."*

"But that was an accident. I had wandered too far while gathering and needed to rest."

"Yes, yes. Just as it was shown to me."

M'rain did not know what to make of that. And, since Glick showed no signs of saying more about it she decided to wait. *Perhaps he will see that I am the wrong one. If he does, perhaps he will show me the way out of the caves.* Even as she had these thoughts M'rain knew they were futile. She was here. K'kor's prisoners were here. Who else could rescue them?

Glick confirmed it when he finally spoke. *"No, there has been no other. It must be you."* He grew silent again.

After a long pause Glick shook himself, as if out of deep thoughts. *"Eat, drink, and then sleep. There is much more work to do. The others await. You must be strong."*

Knowing she had no other choice, M'rain obeyed, all the while still wondering if this was not a big mistake. There was nothing special about her. But even as the thoughts lingered in her mind she knew they were untrue. She had always been an adventurous child, prone to wandering beyond where she ought to. She had always been restless and felt constrained by the rules for the girls of her village.

She recalled the sense of purpose she had felt earlier and drew it back into herself. She would do what she had to.

Tired from her long trek she chewed on a few pieces of the fungus on the stone, thinking about the meal the villager had left for her, tasting once more its succulence, and took a drink from her waterskin before she lay down to sleep.

◇◇◇

Her sister emerged from the hut she shared with her mate, her infant in her arms, and came to sit around the communal cook-fire. There she put the infant to her breast, looking content and proud.

Why didn't M'rain know if the babe was a boy or girl? Surely she ought to. Why wasn't she sitting in her accustomed place beside her sister? Why did she feel so alone, so disturbed?

There, just walking into the light from the fire, came T'entri, the young man who had eyed her with such admiration. He sat beside another girl and said something in her ear. The girl rewarded him with a huge smile and eyes that clearly said she enjoyed his attentions.

Would he choose this one for his mate? Did it matter? After all, M'rain was not there. Did she even want him to think of her? He looked so young. Younger than she remembered. Too young? Why? She was no older. Or was she?

Her dream twisted and roiled with confusion. She tried to reach out, to show herself, but no one seemed to be aware that she watched them. She tried to cry out but could make no sound.

Why did everyone look so normal, so content? Why were they not seeking her? How could they go on as if she had never existed? Why did they not see her, hear her?

M'rain watched her mother join her sister, a bowl of food in her hand, which she set on the ground beside her, a sad smile on her face. Did Mama miss her? Is that why she looked sad.

"Mama."

But her mother heard nothing. She rose and, with a few words to her sister, turned her back on the fire and walked in the direction of the hut she had shared with M'rain.

M'rain tried to follow her but found she could not. Something rooted her to where she stood watching, unable to disengage her feet from the earth no matter how much she fought for some control.

◇◇◇

"Mama." The sound of her own voice woke M'rain. She sat bolt upright, the sweat of terror covering her whole body. She shivered with the damp chill of the cave on her clammy skin and hugged herself. One more anguished, "Mama" died on her lips as she became aware of where she was and realized that she had been dreaming. This time, she let the tears flow freely, the desperation from the dream overwhelming her self-control. For a long time she sat, head on her knees, arms wrapped around them, her whole body rigid, rocking back and forth in grief and desolation.

The dream replayed over and over, vivid in her mind. *Have they forgotten me? Have they searched for me? Have they given me up for dead? Did the dream show me truth?* Knowing she had no answers to those questions brought on a fresh flood of tears as she rocked.

Where do I belong? I do not belong here, not in this world. I am barred from the village of the women. I belong nowhere.

Over and over again, the questions and grief assailed her afresh, until she had no more tears left and she sank to the ground, spent. After a time sleep claimed her again.

The young man with the golden skin and green eyes placed a garland of bright yellow and orange flowers around her neck, a fond, shy smile playing about his lips. The people gathered around the ceremonial fire in the centre of the village and watched.

"Now you are one of us." He gave her a formal bow. "Will you feast with us?"

M'rain looked around her, saw the women she had rescued among those in the circle, saw the old, the children, mothers holding infants, children restless to be allowed to run. Every face looked solemn, as though waiting for her to speak. But something was still not right. She was supposed to do something first. She was not finished yet. It was too soon. What was it? Why could she not remember? And who was this young man?

When she woke Glick sat beside her, his tail curled around his front toes, eyes alert and bright, fixed on her face. M'rain couldn't say exactly how she knew but something told her he had sent her that last dream and expected her to have questions about it. She rubbed the sleep out of her eyes, which still felt swollen from her previous tears, and tried to clear her mind before composing her questions. The ones she most wanted answers to, she knew, would not be the ones he would be willing to answer.

"Very good. You are learning self-control."

The tone of Glick's comment made M'rain feel as though he deserved the credit for her changes. It prickled her. And how was it he knew what she was thinking? Her thoughts ought to be hers, alone. So, to guard against more tears she relied on her anger to give her strength. *"I am not stupid. I know you will not answer me if I do not ask the way you want."*

Glick's only response sounded like an amused chuckle. This made M'rain even angrier.

"You think I will ask about going home again, do you not? Well, I will not. I know you will not tell me." When Glick showed no signs of responding she asked herself what she most wanted to know that she had not already been told in Glick's cryptic way.

"What are you? How is it I never saw you before I was captured in the caves?"

"That is two questions." Glick's tone was still amused but M'rain decided not to take the bait. She waited, knowing he would tell her as much as he chose no matter what she said.

"I serve the nameless one who controls this world. That is the answer to your first question. You did not know of me before because you did not need me before. That is the answer to your second question. And I do not know if what you saw in your second dream will come to be. That is the answer to your third question." The tone of the last turned smug, though it still held a note of amusement.

"But I didn't..." M'rain caught herself. He had read her mind again. She bit off the retort she wanted to spit out and made herself stop and think about what Glick had revealed. *"So is there magic in my home village as well? Do all places have magic?"*

"Of course. The nameless one cares for the entire world. How could it be otherwise?"

"Then why have I not learned of this?"

"Your people live in harmony. We show ourselves only when needed. Your people have had no need of such as I to reveal himself — or in the case of your village, herself. A different guardian serves your people. I cannot look after everyone .The magic lives with your people, as well, even if you do not see it."

M'rain was both astonished and puzzled. Her people had their own guardian from the nameless one? And their guardian was female? *"What is our lizard's name, then?"*

"Oh, not all guardians are lizards. Your people's guardian is a snake. Her name is Senett. But I have not spoken with her in a long time."

All this gave M'rain so much to think about she forgot, for the moment, how angry she was that Glick had read her thoughts. When she finally looked back down at him he had curled up with his tail over his snout and appeared to be sleeping. The sight of him, so comfortable, brought her back to the present and re-awakened her anger. She had learned only one thing that would get a reaction from him. *"GLICK!"*

When Glick jumped a thumb's width off the ground M'rain allowed herself a moment of satisfaction. Then she got to what was really on her mind. Before Glick had a chance to berate her she said, *"You are a rude lizard. I do not care if you are a guardian for a nameless god. I want you to stay out of my mind, to stop reading my thoughts. You have taken everything else away from me. Surely you can leave me my thoughts."*

"Very well."

If M'rain sensed anything from Glick it was, perhaps, a small note of approval. He did not get angry at her. Instead, with a hint of his old amusement, he added, *"I have no need to read your thoughts. Most of the ones I need show quite clearly on your face. As for the rest, I have no real need of them."* He cocked his head to one side, and fixing one bright eye on her, blinked, and vanished, leaving M'rain somewhat astonished and a trifle triumphant.

XV

K'KOR CAME BACK *from the hunt bearing the front half of a fat boar over one shoulder. Behind him, hefting the heavier rear half, strode his hunting partner. As they entered the clearing a young woman looked up and beamed at him. He knew she adored him, desired him, hoped he would choose her for his mate.*

L'lowen rose from the stone where she ground the grain for his favourite flat p'pone cakes and sashayed over to where he waited. The way her hips swayed roused desire in him. She was the most beautiful woman in the village. Her coal black braid swung from side to side, brushing her long back suggestively as she approached.

He knew others wanted her, but she had eyes only for him. Yes, it was time to make her his. It would show the rest that he was best, that he always got what he went after. He would be leader one day. Soon. The chief elder was old and frail. He would not live much longer. The people would choose him, K'kor, to replace the chief. He knew it. He was the natural, no, the only, choice. He deserved it.

He stopped and waited for L'lowen to reach his side, ignoring his partner who still shared his burden. Just before L'lowen reached him he caught the eye of another man and beckoned him with a jerk of his head. The man hurried up and took over the burden of meat that K'kor handed him.

His hands now free, K'kor reached for L'lowen, wove fingers into her silky braid and another around her waist and drew her into a deep embrace, knowing she would feel his desire pressing against her. Without releasing her he drew his head back to look into her face. "I have decided. You will be my mate. You will sit beside me when I am chief elder." He knew he did not need to ask if she would agree, as

91

was the custom. It was a given. And her expression confirmed it.

Her eyes dilated with joy. She gasped one breath, did her best to compose herself and, in a husky whisper, answered, "I am the most honoured of women."

He grinned and let her go then strode purposefully to the central fire where many of the villagers had gathered in preparation for the evening's meal. K'kor noted that some of the other hunters had not yet returned but decided his news was too important to bother waiting for them. He raised his arms high to get everyone's attention. L'lowen had followed him a few paces behind. He reached a hand out to her and drew her by the wrist to his side.

"I have an announcement."

All eyes had fixed on him, as he knew they would after his grand entrance.

"I have chosen L'lowen as my mate." When he noticed a few questioning glances he added, "She has agreed. The boar I killed will be my contribution to tonight's ceremony. The hunt was good today. We will add the mating rite to the celebration of the hunt."

K'kor woke feeling dizzy and it took him a few moments to remember where he was. A look around showed him all his people sleeping and the fire down to mere embers. He was cold and hungry. The feeding bowl was empty, as was the kettle over the dying fire. He tried to remember the feeding ritual but could not. A quick search inside his dream-fungus pouch revealed it to be almost empty. He never let it get this empty.

A black rage washed over him. He tottered over to the nearest sleeping body and gave it a hefty kick, eliciting a pained yelp from the recipient.

As the woman struggled to come out of her drugged stupor and get to her feet K'kor repeated his kicks on the rest, roaring incoherently as he did so. He missed one attempted kick and fell over, which fuelled his rage even more.

The last woman struggled to raise herself up and join the others cowering against the wall as K'kor arrived at the first of the two men. When a nasty kick produced no results he repeated it. Still the man did not stir.

By now the commotion had roused the other man. K'kor noticed he was still only half upright and turned his fury on him, showering him with blows from hands and feet. The man rolled into a ball and did his best to protect his head until K'kor ran out of strength and stood over him, chest heaving with exertion.

K'kor lost interest in him when he noticed that the first man still lay inert on the floor. This aroused his curiosity. He looked at the man more closely, and nudged his leg with a foot. The leg moved under the pressure and then fell back into its original position. A second nudge produced the same result.

K'kor tilted his head to one side, waited a moment and tried again. Again the leg moved and settled back. He sensed that something was seriously wrong. He bent down and poked the man's chest with a bony finger. No response. He stood up for a moment and backed away a step.

The complete silence in the cave amplified K'kor's feeling that something had gone dreadfully awry. He looked around to where the others huddled together, watching. The fear he saw among them mollified him somewhat. He approached the prone man again and, when another nudge with a foot produced no new result, decided there was no danger to himself and squatted down a pace away to study the man. There was something strange about him. His chest did not rise and fall like it was supposed to. Very carefully, very slowly he reached out a hand and placed it on the man's chest. The skin felt cold and clammy. When one of K'kor's knees disturbed the man's arm it rolled to the side and a single piece of dream-fungus fell out of the semi-curled hand onto the floor.

K'kor erupted in rage again, screaming, "You stole it." He grabbed the man's hand and pried the stiff fingers open wider to retrieve more but found it empty. With a jerky, furtive motion he placed the single bit back into the pouch at his waist.

It struck him that the man still had not moved. That was when he knew. "Dead."

He began to giggle. His laughter grew until he was doubled over, screeching and hooting, pointing at the body. "Dead. Hahahahaha!

Dead." Just as abruptly as the laughter had started, it ended. K'kor sat back on his haunches and observed the body. Soon the whole performance repeated itself. This time the word that K'kor repeated was, "Meat, hahahaha, we have meat." He rolled on the ground in glee until he ran out of breath. When he had regained it he sat up and looked at his people. They stared back at him, shock and fear on their faces.

K'kor knew he needed to remember something – something to do with meat. What was it? Ah, yes. Preparing meat required a blade to cut it up with. He knew he had one somewhere – somewhere safe, out of reach of the others. Where? He felt around his waist and under his loincloth. No, no blade there. But he had one, he knew. *Where did I hide it?* An image came to his mind, of a rock behind another bigger rock. *Where? Yes.* He remembered. He rose, grinned at the group watching him, and staggered out of the cave, into a tunnel to the left and through an entrance into a tiny cave several steps away. *There. The rock.* He got down on hands and knees and scrabbled in the dirt behind the big rock. *There – the smaller stone.* He shoved it aside and pried with his fingers until they hit something solid and hard. *The blade.* K'kor pulled it out and sat on the floor cradling it in his two hands, rocking slightly back and forth, a blissful smile on his face. He pressed the bone blade, not noticing the how chipped its edge was, reverently to his chest.

A few moments later he remembered why he had come for it. *Meat!* He hoisted himself back up and returned to the big cave where he found his people still sitting, huddled close together. The murmur of conversation, and all movement, stopped the instant he entered.

K'kor jabbed the point of the blade in the direction of the nearest woman. "You." The blade moved in the direction of the next woman and then settled on the only remaining man. "And you – and you. Prepare the meat and cook as much as will fit into the pot." He stood erect and stuck out his chest, grinning. "The hunt was good. We celebrate tonight."

The three chosen eyed each other for only a moment before they moved in unison toward the body at the other end of the cave. When they had dragged it close to the fire and the cook pot K'kor knelt to make the ceremonial first cut at the throat, the traditional privilege of the hunter who brought down the prey.

What ought to have been a clean swift cut turned into a sawing motion as K'kor struggled to force the dull, damaged blade through the now cold skin and flesh. When thick blood finally pooled under the corpse's neck K'kor rose to his full height once more and, with a flourish, handed the blade to the man beside him.

He turned to the rest of the women in the cave and waved his arm in a wide arc, not quite managing a majestic flourish. "Go, my people. Bring back the black rocks for me. We dine well tonight." With that he strode with a slight stagger, out of the cave and out of sight, secure in the belief that his will would be done.

XVI

T HE THREAD OF light, yellow this time, making M'rain wonder why the colours kept changing, pulsed with urgency. M'rain stuffed some of the fungus into her mouth, chewing without thinking. This time it tasted just like it looked, acrid and dusty – earthy perhaps. This surprised M'rain. She thought about it while she filled her waterskin and came to the conclusion that she had better think of a food before putting any more into her mouth.

It did occur to her that Glick might have removed the magic from the fungus, though she did not imagine he was angry enough with her for that, at least not yet. If she was still the one chosen for this quest surely it would not do to make her so upset that she would refuse to do his bidding.

She had a few pieces of the fungus in her hand as she followed the yellow thread. Still hungry, she decided to experiment. She thought of the red fruit that grew on the cacti in the desert around her home and popped a small piece into her mouth. As she chewed her mouth filled with the sweet-tart juice of the fruit. *Good. The magic still works.* She vowed, going forward, not to put anything else into her mouth without wishing for a food she liked. As she had enjoyed the fruit piece she continued with that wish while she ate the last bits, and followed with a long drink.

M'rain had no sooner hung the waterskin back at her waist when a scraping sound and a low murmur of voices told her she had reached the next members of K'kor's band. The tunnel looked familiar. She recognized it as the same one in which she had discovered the last two women.

She found no one there so she followed the sounds a few steps further to the entrance of another large cave. This time, when she looked in, she saw three women bent toward a black patch in the wall of the cave, low down near the floor. They hacked at the patch with rocks or scrabbled at it with bare hands, their movements labored and awkward, as if they had neither the inclination nor the energy for the work. Behind them M'rain spotted one of the baskets she had seen before. It looked about half full of the black rocks that fueled the fire in the cave.

As she watched from behind she saw one of the women hack at the wall with another rock, pry a black piece loose and drop it into the basket. All the while, the women spoke very little and when they did their voices remained so low M'rain could not make out what they were saying. A look around the cave told M'rain that there was neither food nor water to be found there – no pool, no vessels and no mounds of fungus. *How can they work like this all day with no food or water?*

She had not thought that through before, that K'kor expected his band to slave over this impossible task without even water. She realized that likely the only food they got each day was what she had seen in the pot during the feeding ritual when she had been captured, or what they drank from the pool in their cave. With no vessels to carry water they would have no other access to it.

This new knowledge changed something in her, though she was not aware of it, as though she was beginning to accept something she had been resisting. Nor would she have been able to put her new feelings into words if she had been aware. Some of the resentment, the fear, and the desperate longing for home receded, or seeped out of her and she felt lighter, freer. The sense that she could help these people began to overshadow the old fear and resentment – and the longing for home.

M'rain stepped forward into view and cleared her throat to get the attention of the women who toiled with their backs to her.

As one, the women jerked as though struck, whirled to face her, and froze, backs to the wall of black rock.

Realizing that they expected her to be K'kor, M'rain hurried to break the silence. "I am M'rain and I have come to take you home." When the women's expressions of fear only increased she recognized her mistake and hurried to correct it, mentally chastising herself for the repeated error, " – er, that is – back to your village. Your friends wait for you there, the ones who have gone missing." She watched the expressions change from terror, to suspicion mixed with curiosity, and then to recognition.

The smallest woman, on the left with a matted braid in her hair, slowly raised one arm to point a bony finger. "You. You were there."

The voice came out not much above a hoarse whisper, reminding M'rain that the women needed a drink and she had water for them. She reached for the waterskin at her waist and untied the neck. "Look, I have water." She reached out to hand the skin to the woman who had spoken.

The woman began to reach for it then jerked her hand back again. "Poison?"

"No, not poison. See?" M'rain tipped the skin to her own lips and swallowed some of the cool water, then held it out again for the woman to take.

When that woman still hesitated, the one in the middle stepped forward, jerked the skin out of M'rain's hand, lifted it to her lips and took a drink. She stopped after a few swallows, needing a breath, and with her elbow still in the air ready to drink more, seemed to stop and think. She lowered her arm reluctantly and handed the skin to the third woman. "If it is poison we lose nothing. We die soon in any case."

M'rain was moved by the woman's generosity toward her companions. She had taken a half step forward ready to retrieve the skin from her before she drank too much, but the woman herself had stopped to share with her friends. The third one, whose deep brown eyes stared out from skin blackened with coal dust, drank. Then, before

M'rain needed to stop her, she, too, handed the skin back to the first woman. That one emptied it in four swallows. When M'rain reached out to take it back the woman regarded her with suspicion again for a moment, then held it out, pulling her hand back quickly when M'rain took it from her.

"Do not be afraid of me. I am here to take to back to your village." The confused looks on the faces of the women reminded M'rain that they, like the others, likely had no memory of their origins.

Something about the woman with the braid triggered a memory. When M'rain tried to recall what made her so familiar she recognized her as one of the two who had captured her that afternoon. It seemed so long ago, now. "You are one of the women who took me into the cave to K'kor are you not?"

When she got no response she decided to tell them what she remembered. Perhaps a new approach would make then trust her. "I heard some of what you said to each other that day. You mentioned that K'kor might kill me. You wondered if I should be allowed to go. But you were afraid to. Am I correct?"

The woman with the braid shrank back. "You heard?"

"Yes, some of it." M'rain decided to forge boldly ahead. "I have been sent to rescue you from K'kor. I must take you away from here." M'rain let that sink in before continuing. "Will you follow me? I will take you to your friends. They are well and wait for you." The simple act of stating it aloud made her quest more real to her, gave her a stronger sense of purpose and destiny. These women would follow her and she would take them back to where they belonged.

The three looked at each other as if asking what they ought to do. The middle one, the one who had taken the waterskin from her, nodded and took a step forward. "I will come. I have nothing to lose."

M'rain turned and began to lead the way out of the cave. She did not wait for agreement from the other two, judging that if one came the others would follow. The yellow thread still pulsed with urgency so she knew it was imperative they leave quickly. "Come, we must hurry." M'rain did not turn back as she spoke. The throbbing of the line told her they had no time to waste. She heard the women scrabbling to keep up with her. Then a new sound made her heart beat faster.

"Meat. I am a great hunter. See the meat. We feast tonight. See? Did I not promise?" A short silence followed, during which M'rain detected the shuffling of an uneven gait, then raucous laughter which ended in a fit of coughing.

The thread of light took an abrupt left turn into another tunnel. M'rain looked over her shoulder to see how closely the three women followed her. They stood frozen in fear several paces back. Behind them M'rain thought she could see a pale blue glow advancing in their direction, wavering back and forth.

M'rain sprang back to the women and gave the first one a shove in the direction of the new tunnel. In a harsh whisper she ordered, "In there, now, or you will be seen." Then she grabbed an arm of each of the other two and propelled them bodily after the first into the tunnel. She pushed them further in, behind her, and pressed them against the wall. She crept out to see, then shrank back into the darkness. "Shhhh."

The warning was unnecessary, as the three women stood rigid against the wall, holding their breath.

The shuffling came nearer. When it reached close to the opening of the tunnel in which the four hid, a hand reached into the opening of the tunnel as if searching for the wall. With the loss of support K'kor stumbled and fell to the floor almost at M'rain's feet.

M'rain held her breath, not daring to move. The other women also made no sound.

After what felt like an eternity a soft snoring escaped K'kor's lips.

M'rain looked for the thread, uncertain what to do, and saw that it had changed direction, now leading back out of the tunnel and to the left, continuing in the direction it had shown her before the unexpected aside to where they now stood.

M'rain took a steadying breath and, without saying anything, touched each of the women lightly on an arm. She bent close to them, put her finger to her lips and beckoned them to follow her. Making sure she made no sound she tiptoed past the sleeping K'kor and resumed following the thread. She dared not look back, lest it cause one of the women to try to say something that might wake K'kor. Not until she thought they were well away did she turn back. To her relief all three women followed not far behind. They had moved so silently she had wondered, for a moment, if she had lost them.

XVII

ONCE THEY WERE well out of earshot of K'kor, M'rain slowed down. She could hear the women behind her breathing heavily and remembered that, in their weakened state, they had to struggle to keep up with her.

The slower pace gave her the opportunity to take notice of the path the thread took. It ought to look familiar since the previous trek had begun at the same tunnel. Yet, when she looked for a familiar landmark she could not find one. The thread led in a different direction. *Why are we not going the way we did last time?* A prickle of anger at Glick teased the edge of her mind. *Is this another trick? What am I to do with these three? I cannot take them to the village this way. Why does it need to keep getting more difficult?*

Not long after, she found herself leading the women into an unfamiliar cave, larger than any before except the big one controlled by K'kor. In the centre hung a single stalactite, almost united with a corresponding stalagmite, both gleaming wet from the trickle that seeped onto them from the roof of the cave. Around the stalagmite lay a shallow pool of water. The reek of the cave reminded M'rain of the time she had broken a running bird egg that had gone bad. It made her wonder if the water was safe to drink. She turned to the women to caution them. Too late. All three had rushed over and knelt by the pool, cupped water in their hands and were drinking greedily.

M'rain looked around for the thread of light. It had disappeared.

Instead she spied Glick curled up on a large flat stone, half of which held a tall mound of fungus. *"They must eat. Then they must sleep."*

"The water — is -?"

"Yes, it is safe, though it tastes foul. Do you think I would allow them to drink if it were not safe? Fill your skin. You may need it later."

M'rain's nose curled in disgust.

"Do it. If you are too particular to drink it, then perhaps they will. Now tell them to eat. Then they will sleep. I have something you must do before they waken."

"They cannot see you?"

"No."

M'rain looked over to see all three women watching her with puzzled expressions. *"If they do not see you they must think I am mad just standing here doing nothing but stare at a stone."*

But while she had looked away Glick had disappeared — again. Pushing back her annoyance, M'rain gestured toward the mound on the stone. "Please, eat. This food will refresh you and give you strength." Even as she spoke it occurred to her that the taste magic would work for these women as well.

"Imagine your favourite food before you put it in your mouth. When I do that it tastes like what I am thinking about. Try it. The magic may work for you, too."

Three heads swiveled to look at her, eyes wide. The one with the darkest eyes examined the lump of fungus in her hand then addressed her two companions. "Wild boar." She popped the piece into her mouth and chewed, a delighted grin spreading across her face. She swallowed and, eyes dancing, announced, "Wild boar! It is!" Soon all three were eating, delight and amazement on their faces as they called out their choices.

M'rain had also eaten quite a bit before she remembered that Glick had told her the women would sleep but he still had something for her to do. *Will it put me to sleep? Was I supposed to wait until I had finished whatever I am supposed to do?* Even as she watched them the three women became drowsy and curled up on the floor, asleep. Yet she did not feel the least bit sleepy. *So Glick can control that, too. Fine. I need Glick's aid to help these women and they need me. Next time I see him I will demand he promise to see me back home. If he has other plans for me he can think again. He'll have to wait for another "chosen one".* With that decision firm M'rain lost much of her fear, not only of Glick, but of the caves and the beasts they might hold. *Glick wants these people rescued. Nothing will happen to me or to them as long as they are not all back at the village. He needs me.*

As soon as all three women slept, a new thread of light caught M'rain's attention, green again. She rose with renewed purpose and followed it out of the cave and to the right. It led back a short distance in the direction they had come before it veered a sharp left into a new tunnel, narrower than the others she had been through. *How many tunnels and caves are there here? I am more lost than ever.*

Only a short distance into this tunnel the thread led into yet another cave. Even before she entered it M'rain detected the knocking of rock against rock. When she reached the entrance and peered cautiously into it she recognized the source of the sound. A lone man stood with his back to her, a dilapidated grass basket behind him partly filled with black rocks. Even as she watched, the man knocked another piece loose from the seam in the wall over his head, bent to pick it up off the floor, and dropped it into the basket. M'rain noted that he seemed to have more strength than the women she had rescued, although even he moved slowly, as if not fully aware. *Is it the dream-fungus or is he just weak?*

The man lifted his head, about to turn back to the wall and resume his pounding when he spotted M'rain standing in the entrance. At first his face broke into fear. That changed to challenge as he stood up straight, back to the wall, and raised the rock in his hand as if to use it as a weapon.

M'rain stopped her advance, planted her feet firmly where she was and held her hands open to show she had no weapon. "I am M'rain. I am sent to take you to your village, along with three other women I found today."

The man said nothing, only made his stance more secure and held the rock higher.

"I have water." M'rain took the skin from her waist and began to untie the thong that kept it closed. Then, noticing the threatening stance had not lessened, she thought the better of it tossed it to the man instead. "Here. Drink."

The man caught it with his free hand. Then he dropped it as if it might harm him, suspicion suffusing his face, his eyes darting back and forth between the waterskin on the ground and M'rain.

"It is only water. You can drink it. It will not harm you...I will not harm you. Put down that rock. You will not need it."

The man slowly bent to pick up the waterskin, still holding the rock in his free hand and keeping his eyes on her. When he had trouble untying the thong he sent M'rain a long, questioning look and let the rock fall at his feet. He got the waterskin open and sniffed the contents. His nose wrinkled in disgust but, after another questioning look at M'rain, shrugged one shoulder and took a long drink.

M'rain nodded. "See? Only water."

The man sniffed the contents again then tied the skin closed. M'rain reached out to take it back but he held it behind his back. "No." The word came out no more than a hoarse croak. M'rain suspected he had not spoken in a long time, nor had anything to drink since leaving K'kor's cave. "All, right. You can hold it for a while. But you must follow me. I must take you back to your village, along with the other three waiting in another cave." She turned as though to leave.

"No!" The man bent down to retrieve the rock. When his hand touched it he yanked it back with a yelp as though burned. He examined his palm. His expression changed to astonishment mixed with fear as he shook the affected hand and looked at it again. Then, keeping a close watch on M'rain he crouched down and touched the rock with the tip of one finger, only to yank it back again with a gasp. He stared at M'rain, eyes wide. "How?...What?..."

M'rain sent Glick a quick thought of thanks, knowing that this must be his doing. "It is magic. I am sent to take you back. You must follow me. Leave the rock...and leave that basket. You will not need it." When the man still hesitated, his face filled with fearful awe, she said,

"Come. There is food where I take you." She turned her back on him once more, hoping he would not find another way to attack her, and strode resolutely out of the cave, following the thread back the way she had come, back to where she had left the three women sleeping.

She could hear the man muttering to himself as he followed. With the entrance of the cave in sight the man's mutterings became loud enough that she could make out a word.

"T'torkin." A short silence followed, then a shout. "T'torkin! I am T'torkin. I remember. I remember!"

By now M'rain had stepped into the cave. The three women stirred and began to sit up. T'torkin's shouts had wakened them. Their dazed looks turned to joy as they rubbed the sleep out of their eyes. Upon hearing T'torkin repeat his name once more they appeared to have an additional awakening. One by one they spoke their own names aloud, breaking into wide smiles of pleasure mixed with surprise, and repeating them as they hugged each other amid exclamations of joy.

When T'torkin dropped her waterskin M'rain retrieved it and refilled it from the pool.

A new thread of yellow light appeared on the cave floor, once more pulsing with urgency.

M'rain tried to take charge again. "You must all follow me. I will lead you to your home village. But first drink more water. It may be a long journey and we may not find more along the way." When they took no notice of her, continuing to revel in their new-found memories, and in recognizing each other, M'rain clapped her hands for attention. All four heads swiveled in her direction. She repeated her instructions with more force than she intended, which resulted in frightened looks and a scurry to obey. As soon as they had all drunk their fill, M'rain did the same. When she looked behind her as she rose from the pool she saw the four standing silent, huddled close together, uncertainty in their posture.

Before M'rain could tell them to follow her one woman asked, "Are you a god?"

The question gave her pause. "No..." *What am I, really?* She hesitated forming her answer, as much for herself as for her charges. Finally she settled on, "But I am sent by a god."

When they continued to stare at her M'rain knew she would need to say more. She looked at their expectant expressions and wondered how to answer. *What am I?* Though full understanding still eluded her she had to tell them something. She struggled for an explanation that satisfied her own need for truth and would also inspire these four to follow her. "No…. I am not a god. I was an ordinary person, like you. But I am chosen by a god and I am protected by magic. I am sent to take you all home to your village. You do not belong with K'kor." A forceful thought stuck her. "K'kor's magic is false. He has no real magic."

When the expressions of the four did not change she prodded them into action. "Now you must follow me. There is no time to wait. I can answer no more questions." With that, M'rain passed by her charges and exited the cave, knowing without looking back that they would follow her as the others had.

XVIII

P'PUCK COULD NOT stop thinking about the caves, about the stories told by the women who had returned, and most of all about the young woman he had left sleeping. He went about his duties with only half attention. Fortunately this was not a hunt day or he might have found himself at the sharp end of a boar's tusk from his lack of focus. He daydreamed his way down the rows of ear-grass and gourds, missing some of the weeds with his wooden hoe. Since he had chosen to work in a far corner of the gardens by himself no one noticed.

When his stomach began to growl loudly reminding him he had not stopped to eat since early morning he looked up from his hoe and noticed the sun had already sunk half-way below the horizon. If he did not hurry he would even miss the evening meal. He had just begun the trek back to the central fire when one of the young girls came looking for him, a shy smile and lowered eyes letting him know why she had come.

"You did not come for the midday meal. I wondered if something had happened to you. Come. The people are already gathering."

"Thank you, O'ona. I am coming." He laid his hoe down at the edge of the garden while O'ona stood watching from the corners of her eyes. As he strode toward the centre of the village she fell into step, saying nothing but stealing shy glances at him as they walked. P'puck hardly noticed. His mind was on another young woman.

"That was a nice boar you killed." O'ona found her tongue. "We are roasting the second half tonight. I spent the afternoon turning the spit."

They had reached the edge of the circle around the fire. The smell of the roasting boar brought P'puck back to the present. A glance to his right told him that O'ona's eyes had not left him. At her expectant, hopeful look he realized he had been rude.

"I had help with the kill. The others kept him cornered so I could finish it off." He smiled into O'ona's face. "I am sure it will be extra delicious since you took such care at the spit."

O'ona beamed then looked quickly at the ground, a red blush rising to her hairline.

By then they stood in line among the others, waiting their turn to take a portion of the prepared meat and other food. This gave P'puck an excuse to end the conversation and let his attention leave O'ona. He liked her well enough but her flirtations made him uncomfortable. Besides, it would be at least another year before she would undergo the rite of womanhood and be allowed to mate. To make sure she did not follow him, and sit beside him to eat, he caught the attention of one of his hunting friends and strode over to join him.

"I see you have an admirer", his friend teased, a mischievous twinkle in his eyes. "That is what comes of becoming a man. They will all be eyeing you now."

"Hmph. She is far too young for me. She is still a child."

"Look again my friend. Those are not the breasts of a child." As he spoke he made a gesture that spoke of what he would like to do to those breasts. He added a rude laugh as he jabbed an elbow into P'puck's ribs.

P'puck laughed in spite of himself. "And you. Have you made any progress with the elusive K'kila? Hmmmm?" He gave his friend a sideways leer.

"Nah. But you wait. She will change her mind. You will see." He watched P'puck wolf down his food. "Say, what made you so hungry?"

P'puck answered through a full mouth. "Missed the midday meal." He swallowed. "I was working and forgot."

"What? You never forget a meal."

P'puck shrugged, his mouth full again, but offered no explanation.

He debated with himself after the meal. He wanted to go back into the caves, past the safety of the stalactites but his friend kept talking so that it grew dark before he could get away. He would have to put it off to another day. Besides, what if his torch burned out before he could get back? And what if he could not remember the way? The taboo around the caves still had the power to hold him back.

What he really wanted was to be there when M'rain brought back the other women as L'lowen had told them she promised to do. He wanted to see her awake. He wanted to follow her. And he wanted her to see him, to talk to him.

Before he fell asleep, alone in his hut, the one that had belonged to his parents before they both died of a fever, he made the decision to work at the animal pens the next day, close to the entrance of the cave. The spot had been chosen for the pens because they stood in the shade of the trees. All he would have to do was make sure that no one caught him and assigned him other duties before he could steal away. Working there, when she came back he might spot her.

A young, slender woman with long, sleek, black hair and copper skin led the way. She followed a trail of yellow through the maze of caves, confident and sure. He followed her, less confident and less sure. But she had promised him they would not get lost.

As they went he watched her drop a trail of blue, glowing powder on the floor. He carried another sack of it. When hers emptied she took his from him and carried on with its contents.

She did not speak much, indeed had cautioned him to keep quiet. "There really is a monster. We can deal with it but I would rather not." She had told him to bring his spear and had had him fashion one for her as well. He had taken it as a precaution but had not expected they might need to fight a monster. Her words sent a shiver down his spine.

◇◇◇

P'puck woke refreshed. He hurried to fill his bowl with the morning meal of p'pone and meat, and stole away toward the animal pens before anyone noticed. Today would be the day. He felt it in his gut. Just as he knew that the woman in his dream must be the same one he had left food for. *That dream means something. We are destined to meet. And I will go into the caves with her and not get lost.*

He got the animal pens cleaned out and made sure he didn't miss feeding any of the egg-birds there, or the squealers. In between, he kept checking on the cave entrance to make sure he did not miss the woman if she brought more refugees home. He even skipped his midday meal so he would not be held up by anyone or be sent in another direction with other work to do. Instead he plucked a ripe fruit hanging from a branch behind one of the animal pens to sustain him, and drank the water from one of the hard fruits that had to be opened with a heavy, sharp blade.

XIX

M'RAIN HAD TIME to think as she led her charges back through the tunnels and caves to their village. Their initial enthusiasm upon discovering their names had waned as fatigue set in. M'rain kept a slow but steady pace, so they had no time to linger or they would lag behind. Other than the occasional grunt if one stubbed a toe, or a weary sigh, the only sound was the steady shuffling of near silent feet.

M'rain's thoughts went back to her last conversation, if it could be called that, with Glick. While he had not told her all she wanted to know he had agreed to stay out of her mind. The more she thought about it the more certain she became that he had approved of her telling him to stay out. *He needs me. I am the only one who can rescue these people. That makes me the chosen one, whatever that means, whether he likes it or not.* She came to the conclusion that she would not understand why she had been chosen no matter how much she thought about it. *But he needs me. He cannot do this without me. Hah! He even told me he does not know everything.*

M'rain thought they walked for the better part of a day. Even she felt the fatigue of the long trek and her stomach protested loudly when it occurred to her they had not eaten in all that time. In spite of the length of the trek the women kept up the steady, shuffling pace as though in a trance. Conversation had long since ceased.

Even before the group approached the stalactites at the back of the village cave M'rain came to a decision. She wanted food – real food.

113

And she wanted light. And people to talk to. *I am going to go into the village with these people.* Even as she said it to herself she felt her stomach tighten with apprehension. She pushed it back, replacing it with stubborn resolve. *If it is my destiny to rescue all of those prisoners then Glick cannot prevent it, no matter whether I stay hidden or not.*

"I see light."

The excited voice behind her brought her out of her reverie. The moment of truth had arrived. For an instant she thought she might back out of her decision. *No, I must do this. I cannot stay in the dark any longer.* She turned to face the one who had spoken.

"Yes, your village lies just beyond those trees." When she saw the mix of yearning and fear she added, "They wait for you. They will welcome you home."

"Even me?" T'orkin's eagerness seemed to leak out of him. His shoulders drooped and he hung his head. "I am a man. I failed to do my duty to these women."

M'rain did not need to answer. One of the women spoke up.

"We will tell them. You were not in your correct mind. K'kor held us in thrall with the dream-fungi. We will make them understand." The woman looked at M'rain. "They will understand, will they not?"

"I think so, though I cannot be certain. I have not been told - but that is what I believe."

By now the group had passed the first trees. When M'rain scanned the way ahead of them she spied a lone figure approaching in their direction. When the figure spotted the group he stood still, as if expectant, or perhaps uncertain. Then he opened his palms toward them in what M'rain took to be a sign of welcome. The group had come to a standstill behind her. Now they stepped past her and hurried toward the welcoming figure, tentative smiles on their faces.

M'rain hesitated, took a deep breath, and followed, watching warily as the man once again strode toward them. When he got closer M'rain recognized him as the green-eyed young man from her dream. She froze in her tracks, uncertain, now, whether to go forward or to flee. It felt premature to meet him. Somehow it did not fit with what she had seen in her dream. Was it too soon?

She had no time to think about it. After greeting the returnees and waving them on to the village he wasted no time in approaching her. M'rain waited, rooted to the spot. Had she made the wrong decision to come so far, to risk being seen? *Does this mean I will not be able to rescue the rest of the women?*

About two steps from her the young man stopped. They eyed each other in silence. He was the first one to break it.

"I am P'puck. Welcome to my home. I know you must be M'rain. The other women have told us about you. Are you hungry?"

The question caught M'rain by surprise and shook her out of her inertia. "Yes. Are you the one who left food for me?"

P'puck grinned. "Yes, did you like it?"

M'rain found herself smiling back in spite of her misgivings. "Yes, thank you. I was very hungry."

"Are you hungry now? It is almost time for the evening meal. Let me take you there." He turned as if expecting M'rain to follow him. When he looked back and saw that she hesitated he faced her again.

Before he could urge her on she asked, "Will they allow me to leave again if I come?" The surprised expression on his face told M'rain he had not thought of that. "You see, there are others who must still be returned home." When P'puck did not have an immediate answer she added, "My duty is not finished. I must bring all of them back."

P'puck was not given time to respond. Over his shoulder M'rain saw a woman she thought resembled L'lowen and another unfamiliar woman racing toward them. A wizened old man followed close behind at a slower pace.

"M'rain!" L'lowen rushed past P'puck and took M'rain by the arm. "M'rain, I knew you would come back." She moved her hand down from M'rain's arm to take her by the hand, tugging her in the direction of the village. By now the strange man and woman flanked her, edging P'puck out of the way. The woman looked more excited than afraid but the man eyed her with apprehension, although M'rain did not think it was fear. She had no option now but to allow herself to be led into the village. If she had had any doubts about her earlier decision the choice had now been taken from her. L'lowen chattered on as they walked ahead but M'rain heard nothing of what she said. Her attention was on the village and the people in it.

As they emerged from the trees and into sight many pairs of eyes lifted from their tasks and fixed on the group. Those women who had been bent to their work stood up, their hands dropping to their sides, duties forgotten. Those who had been sitting also stopped what they were doing, heads swiveling in M'rain's direction, hands lax. Children who had been chasing each other, laughing, stopped and went to stand, silent and wide-eyed, next to the women M'rain assumed were their mothers. Other than P'puck and the one with her M'rain saw no men. Since the sun had not yet met the horizon she concluded they must still be away hunting.

Birdsong and an occasional animal grunt were the only sounds that broke the silence as she was led into the village. It was as though the world held its breath.

XX

EVEN BEFORE THE group reached the central fire the first hunters emerged from the trees at the opposite side of the village, a small, horned fourleg hanging by the feet on a pole between the two at the front. M'rain had never seen such an animal but she took comfort from the familiarity of the scene. This was just how the men of her own people brought back the large running bird. Behind the hunters the afternoon sun had begun to sink. Dusk would soon follow.

The hunters looked similar to those from her village, as did the women and children. Their skin was somewhat paler, more gold than copper, and their hair varied more in colour from the uniform black of her own people, but they wore simple wraps much like those her people wore, loincloths for the men, and ones that extended over the breasts and upper thighs of the women.

M'rain had trouble concentrating on the questions and chatter as all of the women, and children, had come to crowd around her. Only a few stood back a little, wary, or shy, M'rain did not know which. Others reached out to touch her, as if to see if she was real. Many exclaimed amongst themselves, while others directed curious questions at her. While she understood their speech, just as she had in the caves, they spoke with a cadence she was unaccustomed to which gave her some difficulty.

When the world began to spin and go black strong arms caught her

117

and lowered her gently to sitting on the ground. All chatter ceased. M'rain put her head between her knees and took a few deep breaths to steady herself. When she looked up all but the young man, *what was his name again? Oh yes, P'puck,* had retreated to a polite distance and watched her in silence.

She caught the last of what P'puck said to the villagers, "...needs to eat. She must think us very rude, with all our questions. We should wait until all the men return and we gather around the fire for our meal. Then, perhaps she will tell us her story."

M'rain sent him what she hoped looked like a grateful smile. "Thank you. This is all very strange to me. If you will wait I will tell you what I can...when everyone is here."

P'puck flashed her a grin before facing the villagers again. "See. It is as I said." With a smug look he lowered himself to sit cross-legged beside her. "I will wait with her." He nodded to one of the older girls. "L'lini, fetch M'rain some tea with honey to refresh her." As the girl scurried to obey P'puck leaned toward M'rain, assuming a contrite face that did not quite lose its smugness. "We do not receive guests here. Indeed we did not know others existed. You must forgive our lack of hospitality."

M'rain had no need to respond as L'lini returned and held out a gourd from which steam rose. "Thank you." As soon as M'rain took it from her, the girl stepped back. The women and older children had begun to drift away, back to their chores. Their frequent glances in her direction showed how reluctant they were to do so. The younger children remained, transfixed, at a safe distance, except for the very youngest who had lost interest and toddled or crawled away, back to their mothers.

P'puck, her self-appointed guardian, seemed to sense her need to be left alone. He sat beside her but said nothing more. It gave her the opportunity to take stock of her surroundings. While she had seen a few of the square huts through the trees previously, and in her dream, sitting in the middle of the village allowed her to take in much more. She saw similarities with her home village: the central fire, the huts in an irregular ring around it, the women going about their communal cooking chores. Like at home, these women worked together without speaking more than a few words, each one familiar with her part in the ritual of the evening meal. Those habitual movements helped M'rain feel more at ease.

As the sun began to dip behind the trees to the west the rest of the men returned, some alone, others in twos or threes, a few with game in their hands. Some brought back plants she had never seen before. When the women took them from the men M'rain realized they must be food. She recognized a stack of the broad leaves the food package left in the cave for her had been wrapped in. These were placed in a pile at one end of a raised of platform to one side of the fire. M'rain thought this strange. Beside the pile of leaves stood what looked like huge gourds and ladles. *What are those made of? I have never seen gourds that size. They do not look like the small ones we have ay home. And are those ladles made of wood? Maybe those gourds, too. The trees around the village here are so big. Not like the bushes that grow in the desert.*

By now cooking aromas filled the entire space. Her stomach growled loudly, letting both her and P'puck know how hungry she was.

"The meal will soon be ready. Almost all the men are back. Then you may eat all you wish. I smell fowl, tonight. The fourleg the hunters brought will be roasted tomorrow." Even as he spoke P'puck's stomach seemed the answer her growl with one of his own.

At his comical grin M'rain found herself smiling back. "I am not the only one who is hungry, it seems."

Out of the corner of her eye, M'rain spotted the foursome she had brought back earlier. At least that was who she thought they were. But now they looked clean, their hair shining and wet, fresh wraps covering their bodies. Their bare arms and legs almost glowed now that they had been rid of the grime of the caves. She turned to P'puck. "I am so dirty. Is it possible for me to get clean, like those who came back with me?"

P'puck jumped up, a shamed expression on his face. "Of course. I have been neglectful. Forgive me. Come. I will show you where we wash."

When M'rain made to follow him two men blocked their way.

"Where are you going?"

"M'rain wishes to wash. I am showing her where to do that." P'puck made to walk around the men and carry on but the two would not allow it, stepping in their way again to prevent it.

The old one who had met them at the edge of the trees spoke "She must stay here. We cannot let her leave."

"She will not leave. Let us pass."

When they refused to give way M'rain added her assurance. "Please, I only wish to get clean before I eat. I promise to return and tell my story for everyone." She indicated P'puck with a sideways nod of her head. "P'puck will make sure I do not run away." When they still did not move aside M'rain began to feel uneasy. She decided to challenge them. "Am I a prisoner, then? I, who have returned your lost ones to you?" Her stomach clenched in fear. It took all her will to keep a bold face and not show it.

The men eyed each other.

"She is our honoured guest. Shame! Shame for treating her this way. Let us pass." P'puck's indignation had the desired effect. The first one gave his companion a hesitant nod and stepped out of the way. As they passed P'puck shot over his shoulder, "And do not follow us."

XXI

'PUCK LED HER to the edge of a pool. Fresh water flowed into it via a freshet emerging from a crack in the stone side of the hill, one of a string of great, rocky hills that continued as far as the eye could see. The water exited on the other side of the pool following a crooked gully before disappearing again into the trees behind the village. *These must be the same hills I saw from the other side of the caves.* A small pile of dried grass, beaten to soften it, lay at the edge of the water inside a circle of stones with another stone on top. M'rain assumed it was meant to prevent it from blowing away. Within one of the huge bowls, like she had seen on the food platform and finally deduced were made of carved wood, M'rain saw a substance that looked like wet sand, but of a pale green colour.

She looked at P'puck who stood as if waiting for her to do something. "This is strange to me. My people do not clean themselves like this. What must I do?"

P'puck's look of astonishment made M'rain blush, embarrassed. "We have almost no water where I come from."

"Oh. That must be very strange...Um, you need to walk into the water. It is not deep - only to your chest. Then you take this green soap and scrub your wet skin with it...your wet hair, too. Then you rinse it off...I mean...dip under the water again until all of the soap washes away. Then you come out and dry yourself with this dried grass."

"Oh..." M'rain remembered her dunking in the cave. "Are you

121

certain I will not sink below the surface?"

P'puck held his hand in front of his chest. "Oh, no, it is only this deep. It is quite safe." He seemed the think of something. "While you wash I will get a clean wrap for you." He turned to leave, then hesitated and turned back to speak. "I promised to make sure you would not leave. If I go do I have your word you will stay to share your story with us?"

After a moment's hesitation M'rain nodded. "I am too hungry to go. You have my word. You can trust me."

P'puck appeared undecided for a moment, then gave a quick nod and ran away.

As soon as he was out of sight M'rain tore off the filthy wrap she wore and knelt by the pool. She put her hands in the water, testing its depth. When all she felt was sand sloping gently into the centre, she stood up and placed first one foot, then the other, into the water. The sand felt soft and cool between her toes. She stepped out again to take a big handful of the green, grainy stuff P'puck had called soap, and slipped carefully back into the water until it came to her waist, holding the soap hand above the water. With her free hand she poked up a small bit of the soap onto a finger and rubbed it onto her wet arm. To her surprise bubbles began to form and she detected a fresh green scent coming from it. Where she had rubbed all the grime had disappeared from her skin.

She had not done much more before P'puck returned, out of breath, with the clean wrap. "Go farther in. Duck under the water to get all wet – your head, too."

When M'rain still hesitated he whipped off his loin wrap. "Here, I will show you." Before she could say anything he had plunged in beside her, splashing her as he ducked under-water and came back up, grinning, water streaming out of his hair and down his face. "Ah, that feels good. See? I am in the deepest spot. Come in. Get your hair wet or it will not come clean." He reached for the soap in M'rain's hand, took a dollop and rubbed it into his wet scalp, where it foamed up. Then he rubbed what was left onto his torso and arms. "See? Now watch." Once more he ducked underwater, and a third time, until the water in his hair ran clear. "That's how it is done. Now it is your turn. Hold your breath, close your eyes and get your hair all wet. You can hold your nose if you want – like this."

M'rain took courage from his infectious good humour and slowly lowered herself into the water, pinching her nose tight as he had shown her. With a last wide-eyed look at P'puck she squeezed her eyes shut and let the water cover the rest of her head. Then she levered herself up again and looked for P'puck through the streams of water that flowed from her hair, down her face.

"Here, I will help you." P'puck took the remaining soap from the hand she still held above the water and began to rub it into her hair. Instead of the white foam she had seen in his hair, it came out brown from hers. "Hmmm, I think we may have to do this twice. How long has it been since you washed?" Without waiting for an answer P'puck prattled on. "There, now duck under again until the water runs clean. I will get more soap." Without waiting to see if she obeyed he scrambled out of the pool, grabbed more soap and hurried back in.

M'rain was, by this time, beginning to enjoy the sensation of the water around her. Now confident that she would not drown, she had ducked under, sputtering as she emerged, her hair hanging in her face and making it hard to breathe. She swiped it away and gasped for breath, coming nose to nose with a triumphant P'puck.

"See? Does it not feel good? Here, more soap." Without waiting for her approval he once more rubbed the soap into her hair. This time the foam came up white. "Now, the rest of you." He began to rub her back with the remaining soap but when his hands continued to her front M'rain stopped him, blushing at the new sensations his touch aroused.

"I must do this myself." She glanced up at him, then quickly away.

P'puck seemed to understand as he backed off. "Oh, I got carried away. It is a bad habit of mine. Forgive me." He lowered himself further into the now murky pool, but not before M'rain caught sight of his arousal.

M'rain turned her back to him before rubbing the rest of the grime off her skin and rinsing it all off and out of her hair. By the time she finished P'puck had already emerged from the pool and was busy tying on his loin wrap, looking more subdued.

"Here." He held out some of the dried grass to her. When she got out and took it from him he reached behind himself to retrieve the clean wrap he had brought for her.

By now he had regained some of his composure, as had she.

She took the wrap from him and put it on. "Thank you. Next time I will not be afraid."

His grin returned. "Did it not feel good?"

She managed a smile. "Yes, it did. It feels good to be clean. But now I must untangle my hair. Do you have something with fingers or teeth for that purpose?"

P'puck looked puzzled for an instant then seemed to understand.

"Oh, you mean a comb. Yes." He reached under the dried grass and pulled out a comb of carved bone. "Here." For the entire time she worked with the comb to untangle her hair P'puck never took his eyes off her, his look almost hungry.

M'rain found herself needing to look away. When she finished with her hair she dropped the comb back into the bowl. "I think we ought to go back, now. They will be waiting for us." She walked in the direction of the village, not daring to look back to see if he followed.

XXII

HE ELDERS MADE it clear that their guest was to eat before she would be asked to tell her story, a kindness for which she was grateful. It kept the clamor at bay for a while and gave her some time to collect her courage. This village had so many more people than her own. That, as well as the other differences, still threatened to overwhelm her. Even so, she managed to eat her fill of the delicious food and to drink a bowl of their strange brew. She could tell, from the bubbles in it and the mildly astringent taste, that it would be intoxicating if she drank too much of it but the one bowl helped relieve some of her anxiety. When they offered to refill it she declined and asked P'puck, still sitting next to her, if she might have more of the tea they had given her when she arrived. He jumped up to get it for her.

By the time the evening meal finished darkness had settled on the village, blocking all but the fire and circle of eager faces from her view. This helped, too, as it felt more familiar.

As soon as one of the elders stood all chatter ceased and a hush of expectancy fell over the group.

"My people, we have a guest. This has not happened for many, many years, not since the time before time. We owe this guest a great debt, as she has restored several of our lost ones to us when we had given up hope of ever seeing them again. She has agreed to tell us how she has done this." The elder turned to face M'rain and bowed deeply before sitting down again.

While M'rain had prepared herself to speak, she now wondered if she was expected to stand to do so. She looked around the circle at all the rapt faces, and decided her legs would not hold her if she stood. She remained sitting.

No one interrupted her as she told her tale. Not until M'rain indicated that she had finished did the elder stand once more. "Now you may ask your questions." He held out a stick carved with delicate leaves and animals, sat down again and passed it to the adult to his right. This, too, was familiar to M'rain, although her people used a running bird feather. The holder of the feather could speak and all others were required to wait until they were given possession of it before they had permission to do so. What did surprise her, however, was that even very young children were given an opportunity to speak. In her village speakers had to have passed their rite of maturity.

By the time everyone who wished to had taken their turn the moon had crossed to the other side of the sky. The night was half over, though this did not appear to bother anyone. The youngest children had long since fallen asleep on the ground or in their mothers' laps. When all talk ceased the adults simply scooped up their sleeping children and slipped to their huts. Most of the people had already drifted away when the man who had controlled the fireside discussion, who M'rain now assumed to be the chief elder, approached her. "You will sleep in my hut."

This made M'rain uncomfortable. She could not quite place what it was in his face or tone but for the first time she began to suspect that he meant to make certain she stayed, even though she had told her story. As she walked beside him toward his hut she said, "There are others I must bring back. My work is not yet done. I plan to leave in the morning."

The chief remained silent for a moment. When he spoke his tone was both cautious and conciliatory. "Of course the others must be returned and you are the one who knows how this can be done. But I wish to send two hunters with you to protect you. We will discuss it in the morning. This is too important for a young woman alone." The finality in his voice told M'rain that arguing would not help her cause.

Her stomach clenched.

They had reached the chief's hut and he pulled back the heavy hide that covered the opening into it, gesturing for M'rain to enter.

M'rain grasped at an idea. "In my village it is not permitted for a young woman to spend the night alone with a man."

The chief let the hide fall slowly back in place. He stood for a moment, a slight frown between his brows. "Yes, it is so here, as well. Follow me."

M'rain could tell he wasn't happy with this. It confirmed for her that she needed to tread carefully if she wanted freedom. She strongly suspected Glick would not help her complete her quest unless she was alone.

She did as he asked, doing her best not to show the turmoil she felt. *I must sneak away. But if I cannot...how can I convince them to allow me to go alone? I should not have let them see me. I should not have come here.*

When the elder reached another hut he pulled aside the hide door a little and called softly to whoever was inside. An older woman came out, followed by a man M'rain assumed was her mate. The elder gestured them to one side where he spoke to them so low M'rain could not make out what he said. By the furtive glances sent her way, and the secretiveness, she had no doubt the pair had instructions not to let her leave. When both nodded the elder beckoned M'rain to join them.

"These people will make you comfortable. Sleep well. We will speak again in the morning."

M'rain did her best to smile. "Thank you for your hospitality." She followed the couple into the hut. By the embers of the small central fire contained in a circle of stones in the centre she could make out a layer of reeds on the floor and a few large fur pelts. She thought that must be where they slept. Though hidden in shadow so she could not see clearly, she could tell that several things hung from the walls, some sat on a flat plank attached there. It all felt very different from her home, where the huts were round, and the only fire was in the centre of her village. Did it get that cold at night that people wanted a fire? What few possessions her people had were simply kept on the floor at the inside edge next to the wall.

The woman took a bundle from a peg on one wall and spread it out on the floor on the opposite side from where their pelts lay. Once rolled out M'rain could tell it was another fur.

"This is for you. I hope you will find it comfortable. If you get cold just wrap it around you."

M'rain let herself sink down onto the fur. It was soft and she felt instantly warmer. Her people did not have such things – but then, her people had no need of warm coverings. The walls of their huts held the heat of the day so they never got cold at night as long as they remained inside. "Thank you. I am sure I shall be comfortable." She watched as her hosts lifted one of the furs on their side of the floor, slid down together and pulled it back over them. Imitating them M'rain lay down on her fur and pulled one side over to cover herself.

"Sleep well," The woman called out from the far side of her furs.

"Thank you." M'rain could not help but notice that the man slept closest to her, making her feel even more like a prisoner. *Will he fall asleep? Will he hear me if I try to sneak away? Those women in the cave are starving. If they die it will be my fault.*

XXIII

M'RAIN GOT NO sleep at all. Nor could she find an opportunity to sneak out. Every time she sat up her host moved, so she knew he was listening for her. Even if he were not fully awake any attempt to move aside the hide door would certainly rouse him.

To make matters worse, no matter how much she tried to call Glick with her mind, he gave no sign that he heard her. Had he abandoned her? Had she failed and condemned the women to death by her stubbornness? She had hoped he might be able to help her escape without being seen. Glick's magic might keep the couple asleep. After all, he had done that in the caves. *Maybe his magic only works in the caves. Maybe he cannot help me here.*

When dawn began to light the cracks around the hide door and her hosts rose from their furs, M'rain followed their example. Her anxiety prevented her from feeling fatigued.

"Come, join us as we eat the morning meal." The woman's face was kind, her voice sympathetic. "The chief elder told us you will be meeting with all the elders when we have eaten. You do not want to be hungry. Meetings with the elders can take a long time."

The older woman's soft chuckle and shy smile did little to calm M'rain, but she thanked her hostess and followed her to the food platform where she accepted a bowl of hot mush filled with small dried fruits. While it tasted different than the p'ona of her people, M'rain found it delicious.

"I am N'nansa. My mate is T'tun." The woman took her now empty bowl, refilled it and handed it back. "This is p'pone we eat it every morning."

"And what is the name of the chief elder who brought me to you?"

"He is called T'trint. I am to take you to him when you have eaten." N'nansa glanced at M'rain's empty bowl. "Did you enjoy it? Would you like more?"

"It was delicious, thank you, but I have had enough." M'rain set the bowl on the platform. "Where may I make water?"

"Oh, please forgive me." N'nansa's hand flew to her mouth in embarrassment. "Come, I will show you." She turned and led M'rain to a path behind the huts and into the trees on the side of the clearing opposite the cave. Even before they reached it M'rain could smell the odour of the middens. "Here," N'nasa lifted her own wrap and squatted, relieving herself. While she could not tell if this was to demonstrate what was expected or out of need, M'rain followed her example. She looked around and was pleased to see that the water from the creek which ran alongside flowed away from the village and the bathing pool.

"That is better." N'nansa sighed in relief as she stood and rearranged her wrap. M'rain could not help answering her smile with one of her own. She liked this woman in spite of knowing she would not allow her to leave. The two soon arrived at T'trint's hut, where they found him sharpening a long stick into a weapon.

"I hope you rested well. Did you get enough to eat?"

"Yes, the food is different from what my people eat, but I liked it very much." M'rain chose not to comment on sleep. She was sure it was plain to T'trint she would not have slept much.

T'trint nodded to N'nansa that she could go and turned back to M'rain. "Come, the others wait for us." He led her to another hut, this one bigger than the others, set off to one side, at the edge of the forest which continued behind it, blocking her vision beyond the trees. She suspected this was where the men hunted the strange game.

Inside waited two more elders and two other men M'rain did not recognize, but surmised must be the hunters T'trint had spoken of. All held gourds of a hot drink from which steam curled up into the roof peak. There it joined with the smoke from the small fire in the centre and escaped out the funnel hole in the top. As she and T'trint entered the man nearest the larger gourd – or bowl – M'rain could not tell which now that the door flap had dimmed the light, dipped two more gourds in and handed one to each of them as they sat down. Her magic sight, it seemed, only worked in the caves – or had Glick taken it from her for disobeying him?

A sniff at the contents told M'rain she had not had this drink before, but decided it must be a kind of tea as it did not bubble. She believed it would not cloud her judgment so she did not limit herself. It tasted strong, somewhat bitter. She wondered if it was a wake-up tea because this meeting was important and they all needed to be alert. After a few sips she decided she liked it. Soon she realized it had given her new energy and she no longer felt fatigued. *I must be right. It is a wake-up brew.*

T'trint took his time over the tea before speaking. This only made M'rain more anxious, although she did not think that was the intent. It was the same with her people. Serious discussions must not be rushed. They must be given the time and attention befitting their importance.

When his cup must be almost empty T'trint faced M'rain. "Once again, I wish to tell you how grateful we are that you have returned some of our lost ones to us." He gestured to the others. "These two are elders, F'fant and G'glin, and those are two of our best hunters, D'dros and N'norn."

Each one inclined a head to her as T'trint introduced them. M'rain answered with a nod of her own.

T'trint's voice brought her back to the present. "You have explained that you wish to rescue the remaining captives. But you have also told us that K'kor has gone mad and is prone to violent outbursts. You say he is dangerous to everyone. And we heard from you that the disappearance of some of his women has angered him."

Four heads bobbed agreement.

"We know the caves are dangerous. Our people are forbidden to

131

enter them, lest they be lost or eaten by monsters. The history of our ancestors is clear. The One Who Provides has decreed it and we must obey. Those who disobey do not return."

T'trint halted and M'rain thought he looked both undecided and uncomfortable.

"But you *have* travelled them – and brought some of those who disobeyed back to us. We three," he indicated the two elders, "have discussed this throughout the night. We have decided they were allowed to return because K'kor tricked them, lured them away with lies, so they are not entirely to blame. They have been punished enough and are being allowed to come back to us."

He stopped again, as if trying to find the right words, or to understand something that eluded him. With a puzzled shake of his head he addressed M'rain more directly. "You have not become lost, or been devoured. We do not understand how this can be. But you are not of our people. Perhaps the decree is not meant for you." After another uncomfortable silence he continued. "The law is clear and has never been successfully disobeyed. What you have done is troubling. It goes against everything we have been taught. We have many questions that we find no answers for." He opened his hands wide, not making any attempt to hide his perplexity. The expressions on the other four faces mirrored his.

M'rain took advantage of the uncomfortable silence and gestured to the talking stick in the chief's hand. She dared not speak without permission. Even this gesture was a bold move. She caught T'trint's eye and kept her hand open, as if waiting to receive the stick. He registered surprise, but only for an instant, looked at the stick in his hand, and after a moment's hesitation asked, "You wish to speak?"

"If I may, yes."

T'trint handed her the stick, looking, M'rain thought, almost relieved. *Is he feeling a loss of control? Am I so foreign to him that he is a little afraid of me?* Those thoughts bolstered M'rain's confidence. She decided to challenge the elders on her position - guest or prisoner. She did not even bother to thank T'trint for the stick.

"I have been assigned a quest. As I told everyone around the fire last evening, my quest is to return all of K'kor's captives back home, here. That quest is only half complete." She paused long enough to look each of the men in the eye. "You have told me, before all of your people, that I am an honoured guest. Yet you prevent me from leaving so that I may complete my duty."

T'trint and the two elders lowered their eyes, either to the ground or their hands. All three looked uncomfortable.

Good. "I wish to depart as soon as possible to continue what I have set out to do. I need to do that alone. I have no need of men with weapons. Nor do I have need of food or water. I am protected by magic." She let that sink in before continuing.

When no one met her gaze she decided to press further, although she did not know if what she said was entirely true. She squared her shoulders and kept her voice strong. "If you insist on having these men accompany me I believe the magic will break. And even if it continues to protect me, I believe it will not protect the men with me."

Now the two hunters also looked fearful, though she could see them doing their best not to show it. *Good, I want them to say they do not need to go with me.* "The women I have brought home were, as you know, near starving. The ones still in the caves have little or nothing to eat. K'kor grows more mad every day. He no longer sees to their needs. They must be rescued as quickly as possible. Even now I fear it will be too late for some. I must leave – and it must be now."

Some of her mounting anger leant force to her tone. "So I ask you again, am I guest or prisoner? Will you hold me here against my will or will you allow me to complete my task? Do you wish to see your lost ones restored to you or will you cause me to delay so long they will die before I can help them?"

T'trint met the eyes of his two elders but did not wait for them to speak. He reached for the talking stick, taking it before he answered. "You are indeed a guest, and not a prisoner. I apologize if we have delayed you. We thought it best that we send these men with you to assist you. I ask you to reconsider and accept their help."

M'rain's anger was building. She did not wait to be handed the talking stick. "Have I not yet made it plain that I must do this alone, that I believe the magic will fail if I do not?" She stood, feet planted squarely under her. "I am leaving. Do not follow me. Do not try to accompany me. If you do I will not be responsible for what happens." She whirled around, strode the two steps to the hide door, flung it back and headed toward the caves without looking back.

XXIV

P'PUCK SPOTTED M'RAIN as she burst out of the hut. He had positioned himself back in the gardens within sight of the entrance to the cave, across from the animal pens but also where he could keep the meeting hut in sight. By the time the elders emerged M'rain had already come almost half-way to the cave. Looking back, P'puck could see them begin to follow her. Then T'trint held up his hand and stopped. All three stood watching M'rain's receding back. They looked almost defeated. That gave P'puck a small feeling of satisfaction, making him smile inwardly as he turned to watch M'rain stride into the cave, back straight, head held high. *So she has won. Hah!*

He felt so elated that it seemed as if he shared in her triumph. Hidden by the tall beans in the garden he hurried after her. *Perhaps she will allow me to go with her. She knows she can trust me.* By the time he reached the entrance to cave he had to sprint to catch up before the darkness swallowed her and he'd be lost.

"M'rain, wait."

If she heard him she did not show it. He increased his speed. But before he reached her she hesitated and stood still at the far side of the stalactites inside the cave's mouth. He opened his mouth to call out to her again but something made him hesitate. She stood so still, as if waiting for something – or someone. He slowed to a walk and stopped several paces behind her, watching. When he could stand the silence no longer he called out softly to her. "M'rain?"

This time she heard and turned slowly to face him. "Go back, P'puck."

Had she read his mind? A prickle ran down P'puck's spine. "But I need to go with you. I have dreamed it."

He watched as first puzzlement and then doubt flickered across M'rain's face.

"You have dreamed it? What did you dream? Tell me."

"I dreamed that I followed you through the caves. You followed a path only you could see. We left a trail of something blue I have never seen before as we went."

M'rain went silent for a long time. "Were we alone? The women were not with us?"

"We were alone. But I know my dream is true. I am meant to go with you."

M'rain looked behind her, back into the darkness. When she faced P'puck again she shook her head. "No P'puck. I am meant to do this alone. Perhaps the dream is for a later time. It is not for now." She sighed. "I would welcome your company under other circumstances but I know I must finish this alone – if it is not already too late. Please return to your work." She gave him a feeble smile. "I do hope I shall see you again." She hesitated, as if deciding whether to say more. "I, too, have dreamed, and have seen you...I hope my coming into your village has not changed the course we will follow."

When P'puck shook his head in protest M'rain held up a hand. "I cannot take you with me. Please...go back...now. I must hurry and cannot leave until you have gone."

"Then, you plan to return when all the women have come back?"

"I hope so. Now, please go."

"But you have no food with you?"

"I have need of none. Go."

The finality on her voice told P'puck that pleading would not change her mind. He backed away a step before turning. "My dream is true. You will return – and we will travel the caves together."

Her smile was so sad it almost made P'puck change his mind, but when M'rain turned away from him to gaze into the darkness once more he turned and trudged back to his work.

He spent the rest of the day feeding the animals', mucking out their pens, and hoeing in the garden. But the day passed in a blur, because he was preoccupied with thoughts of M'rain and worried for her safety. *The dream is true. She will return. She must.* But P'puck did not sleep well that night, all hope of having the dream again dashed by his wakefulness.

XXV

M'RAIN WENT AS far into the cave as she dared, the glow of light penetrating its entrance almost lost in the darkness where she sat waiting. Since her special sight had not left her she had some hope that Glick would return and show her where to go. The only indication that time passed was the eventual grumbling of her stomach telling her she had not eaten for far too long.

She called out to Glick a few times with her mind but if he heard her he showed no sign of it. Then, when she had made up her mind to remain here to die, if necessary, he appeared right in front of her. He did not speak, just eyed her, his expression neutral, or what M'rain thought neutral would be on a lizard.

"I am sorry, Glick. Please tell me it is not too late. Tell me I can still rescue the women. I thought they would let me leave. You told me not to go into the village. I am sorry."

Glick blinked once. He made no attempt to respond. Instead he said, *"K'kor is dead. When he tried to cut one of them with his blade they all attacked him. He fell and hit his head. They killed him."* He showed neither anger with her nor sympathy for K'kor.

The announcement shocked M'rain so it took her a moment to sort her confused thoughts and bring them back to her main concern. *"The women? Are they all right?"*

"They live, but they hunger. They fear to leave the cave but that will not last. They know they must find food."

"Then please let me bring them back here."

Instead of an answer a familiar thread of yellow light appeared. M'rain heaved a sigh of relief. *"Thank you."*

"Do not delay. They will separate soon. They will not remain together." Glick winked out.

M'rain almost ran, going as fast as she could without falling, her empty water skin bouncing from her waist. *"Glick, I have no water for the women. I did not refill the skin when I washed."* She hoped he heard her – and that he would make sure to lead her to water once she had the women with her. She knew she ought to have been more mindful and did not deserve an opportunity to fill the skin until after she had reached the women.

She stubbed her toes several times but pushed the pain from her mind and refused to slow down. Her breath came in painful gasps and she was forced to slow her pace long before she heard the sound of voices ahead. As she approached she made out some of the words.

"…which way"

"…lost"

"…gone with the others"

M'rain turned a corner and came upon six women. They stood looking confused and about to go back the way they had come. "Wait. Do not go that way."

Six pairs of astonished eyes turned in her direction. Their expressions soon changed to wariness.

"I am the one who escaped. I can help you." Remembering that the others had forgotten their names and where they came from until they were well out of K'kor's control M'rain asked, "Do you have names? Do you remember your home village? Oh, and I am M'rain." She did her best to offer a reassuring smile, not at all sure they would see it in the darkness. She remembered Glick had told her they saw less than she, but did have some limited sight in the caves.

The women looked from one to the other in confusion, then recognition dawned on each of them as they recalled who they were and spoke their names to each other. After a time, one turned back to

M'rain. "But how…?"

"I am protected by magic."

When the women shrank back from her she added, "Not evil magic, like K'kor. Remember, I was his prisoner, too. His magic was not real."

When the women remained wary she said, "I am sent to take you home, back to your village. Your people wait for you. Remember the other women who disappeared? They are already there, as well as T'torkin. Come. Follow me."

The woman who had spoken whose name was N'ness, sent her companions a questioning look then regarded her again with a weary shrug. "Very well, we have nothing to lose." She took two tentative steps toward M'rain. After a moment's hesitation the others followed.

M'rain looked for a new thread of light but the one she had followed still led away from where they stood instead of back toward the village. It now pulsed with urgency. She stopped, uncertain. Then she understood.

"There are more of you. We must find them as well."

"They are lost."

"Yes, but I will find them. I must take all of you back. Come."

The women hesitated. "You will be lost, too," one said.

"No. I am guided by magic. Come. If you stay you will certainly be lost and die. You must come with me. I must bring all of you home…together."

The women turned to N'ness, who seemed to have taken on the role of leader. When she shrugged again and took a few hesitant steps in M'rain's direction, the others fell in behind, forming a shuffling line.

The thread pulsed more strongly and M'rain's sense of urgency increased with it. The remaining four women must be in danger. Instead of waiting for her followers to catch up she got behind them and herded them forward. "We must hurry. Try to walk more quickly."

Groans and mutters followed her urging as they shuffled forward. One woman croaked, "We cannot. We need water."

M'rain couldn't keep her anxiety out of her voice. Some of her tone of authority abandoned her. "There will be water ahead, I promise you. But hurry. Please."

N'ness shook her head. "Why should we believe you?"

M'rain was unprepared for this. The urgency she saw in the pulsing thread had sent all other thoughts from her mind. She stopped for a moment trying to find an answer that would convince them. "Because I have saved the others who disappeared from K'kor's cave. They are safe back in your home village...and because I escaped from K'kor and have not become lost in the caves...and I told you I am protected by magic...and because I came back for you. I did not get lost."

When the women clustered around her looked to N'ness with doubt on their faces M'rain added, "What choice do you have? You know you are lost and will die if you do not trust me...and if I am wrong you will be no worse off. You will still die. I am your only hope."

N'ness finally gave a hesitant nod. "It is so. We will follow you." Her resigned shrug spoke more clearly than if she had said aloud, "but we will die anyway".

They resumed their slow trudge. No amount of effort to make them go faster had any effect. M'rain knew they were losing what little strength they had but if she could not keep them moving all was lost.

XXVI

S CREAMS PIERCED THE silence of the tunnel and echoed off the walls. The sound sent a shock through M'rain that raised all the hairs on her body and made her feel suddenly chilled.

The group of women froze in their progress and clutched at each other. M'rain heard one whisper, "Monster". She shook off her own fear. "Wait here," and ran ahead as fast as she could. The thread took an abrupt turn to the right. M'rain's headlong sprint caused her to run smack into the remaining four women and stumble to her knees, skinning them both.

As she scrambled to her feet she saw them huddled together, shrinking away from a huge beast blocking the entrance to a new cave. A glance at the monster told her there was something familiar about it. It bore more than a passing resemblance to Glick. She hurried to place herself between the women and the monster. *"Glick?"*

The answer came instantly, the tone a combination of amusement and reproof. *"Of course. They were about to get even more lost. There is a pool in this cave but the water in it is not safe to drink."*

"Oh. Can you show me where I can find safe water? If the women do not get some soon they will not be able to keep going."

"Hmph. You might have thought of that before enjoying yourself in the village."

M'rain had no patience for more recriminations. *"You have already made that plain and I have done my best to atone. Now stop punishing these women to make me feel worse. You may be as angry with me as you wish but we must get*

143

these women back where they belong." As an afterthought she added, *"And some food would be welcome as well."*

Her indignation had the desired effect. The thread of light, which had stopped where she stood, resumed, not ahead, but back in the direction from which she had come, where the others had been told to wait.

The four women who witnessed the silent stand-off watched from the side in awe. When Glick reduced to his normal size and disappeared their awe grew. M'rain had seen their reaction from the corner of her eye and now turned to face them.

"The monster has gone. Follow me." She gave them no time to question her, but strode past them and followed the thread back to the waiting group. When she reached them she turned and waited for the four to catch up. Once all of them could hear her and had gathered close enough to see her she held up both hands to command attention and raised her voice. "You see, I have banished the monster and brought you all together." She caught N'ness's eye. "You see what I have done. Do not question me again. Now follow me. I know where to find water and food." She walked past them into the cave where Glick had told her she would find what she sought.

The women followed after her in silence until they had all entered the small cave. A trickle of water made its way down the back wall and pooled in a depression in the floor before spilling its banks and disappearing back into the darkness of another tunnel. To one side stood the expected pile of fungi.

"There, you see – water - as I promised." The women rushed forward. The pool was too small to let all of them drink at once but they waited their turn without speaking. M'rain recognized the behavior. K'kor had trained them well, it seemed.

When they had drunk their fill M'rain indicated the fungi. She decided to test the magic. Surely Glick would not withhold it just because he was still angry with her. "If you imagine your favourite food as you eat this it will become that food in your mouth. See?" She popped a piece into her mouth and made a show of pleasure, hoping they could see her expression.

At the strange looks from the women she added, "It is part of the magic."

Hunger overcame caution. First two, then the rest, reached for the fungi and put it in their mouths. Soon exclamations of delight could be heard as they reached eagerly for more.

While they ate M'rain filled her water skin at the pool. The moment of peace gave her some time to reflect. *Glick still needs me. And he has not taken away his magic.* She turned her head to watch the group over her shoulder as they exclaimed over their food. *They believe me, now. And I know I can finish this. And this time Glick is not putting them to sleep.*

With renewed confidence she rose and approached the pile of fungi, hoping there would be some left for her. To her surprise she noticed that it had not gone down much. *Glick must be replenishing it.*

The women parted so she could reach the food. *Will the magic still work for me?* She popped a piece into her mouth, thinking of the fowl she had eaten in the village and closed her eyes in relief. *"Thank you, Glick. I am glad you're no longer angry."*

When it looked like everyone had eaten enough the pile dwindled. M'rain ate the final piece before addressing the group. "It is time to return home. Follow me."

Food and water had revived the group considerably. They kept up with M'rain's increased pace with little difficulty. Their moods had also improved. M'rain could hear them chatting behind her for the first stretch. While they kept their voices low their tones conveyed an air of optimistic expectancy.

When they had gone some distance and the pace began to flag the thread of light led into another small cave where they could refresh themselves with more water. The women took advantage of the pause to question M'rain.

"Who are you?"

"How do you not get lost?"

It reminded M'rain that only she could see the thread of light. "I am guided by magic. The magic tells me where to go."

"Are you certain we will be accepted back? Are the others really there, now? Perhaps they are dead and this magic is false." This came from a different woman.

While the renewed doubt irked M'rain she bit back her retort. *K'kor has tricked them. No wonder they mistrust magic. I doubted Glick, too.* She took a moment to think before answering. "What is your name?"

"S'sala."

"S'sala, K'kor made you forget your name with the dream fungus and with his evil – all of you forgot your names until he was gone. Now you know your names again. That means his bad magic is broken."

The woman narrowed her eyes and studied M'rain from behind lowered lids, her expression intent, still hesitant but listening. The others clustered about, similar doubt beginning to flicker across some faces.

"I have saved you from the monster. I have brought you to food and water." M'rain halted. Slow, hesitant nods told her the women thought about what she had said.

"Everything that you have seen and heard from me has shown me to be truthful."

The women eyed each other, nodding again.

"So I tell you once more. Your friends are safe in your home village. I have been sent to take you there as well. Magic guides and protects me so that I am able to do this."

M'rain paused. "You have followed me this far. Before this day is done you will be home." She shrugged. "You will see the truth of all I say." She turned and led back out of the cave, knowing the women would follow, whether they believed her or not. The alternative was certain death.

The thread of light glowed clear, with no urgent pulsing, but M'rain kept a steady pace. *I want this to be over.* Thinking of the village brought a flash of memory - P'puck's grinning face as he splashed her at the bathing pool. It helped lift her mood. But having to speak about her magic made her wonder, again, what kind of magic K'kor had had and how he had come by it. *I will ask Glick. Perhaps he will be willing to tell me.*

XXVII

S SOON AS P'puck turned back from M'rain and the elders caught up with him T'trint sent him off with a group of hunters. *He knows I want to follow her. He is making sure I stay away from the cave.* The need for concentration on the hunt kept his thoughts away from M'rain until an end of the pole with the fourleg suspended from it rested on his shoulder and that of his companion as they all trekked back to the village. With the danger behind him he could let his thoughts roam where they willed – and they willed to roam to M'rain.

The knot of anxiety returned to his stomach as he worried for M'rain's safety – but not only her safety. He wondered what she thought of him, whether she shared his attraction. *Will she stay in the village when all the women have been returned?* His musings took him back to the bathing pool, to M'rain's luminous black eyes, to the bright drops of water that fell from the ends of her ebony tresses as she combed out the tangles, to her delight when she discovered she could remain safe in the water – and to his arousal. *Had she noticed?* Just the thought set his face burning again in embarrassment. But since he walked at the front no one noticed.

As soon as the hunters had all emerged from the trees and crossed the short distance to the central circle, two women separated from the others working together to prepare the evening meal and took the carcass from P'puck and his partner.

"Ah, good hunting, I see. This is a big one. We will feast well tomorrow with enough left to smoke and dry for later."

P'puck gave the ritual nod of acknowledgement and followed the others in his party to the bathing pool.

A girl sidled up to him. "You had a good hunt. That is a fine beast."

P'puck gave her a distracted "Hmm," before turning his head to recognize O'ona walking beside him. He almost shot out an irritated retort at having his daydream interrupted but bit it back just in time when he saw her innocent gaze fixed on him with such admiration and hope. He cleared his throat and managed a polite, "Yes, thank you O'ona. It was a good hunt."

Something in his tone must still have been off because O'ona's face fell and she hung her head so he could not see her expression any more. "I must attend to the greens. The others will be missing me." She stepped aside to let him move ahead and hurried back to where the other women worked, head still down.

P'puck watched her over his shoulder with a pang of guilt. *Poor girl. It is not her fault my thoughts are on another. She is pretty – and sweet natured. I should not have been gruff with her.*

When he joined the others at the pool he said nothing. One of his companions noticed his uncharacteristic silence. "Hey, P'puck." He splashed water into P'puck's face. "What is wrong with you?"

"Must be a girl," another teased.

"I have seen that pretty little O'ona making eyes at you. You could do worse."

P'Puck did his best to laugh. "No, O'ona is pretty but she will need to cast her eyes on another."

He felt a jab in the ribs, "All right, who then?"

P'puck shook his head. "You are mistaken. There is no one. I am tired, that is all." He jerked his head in the direction of the village as he climbed out of the water. "Come, I am hungry and I smell that boar that was killed yesterday."

He dried himself off as quickly as he could, wrapped his cloth around his waist and strode in the direction of the fire, leaving the others no choice but to follow.

Soon everyone sat around the fire absorbed in their food and sharing news of the day, leaving P'puck alone with his thoughts. He took his meal to the edge where no one else sat, ate as quickly as he could, and snuck away to the cave to check for signs of M'rain's return. Full dark had fallen before he admitted she would not come this night and made his reluctant way to his own hut. Restless dreams of danger and being lost left him irritable and tired when dawn told him to prepare for the day's work.

XXVIII

THE PERPETUAL DARKNESS in the caves robbed M'rain of all sense of time. She had no way of knowing how long she and the women had been walking so when a pale circle appeared at the end of the thread she followed she could only guess if it was morning or evening. At midday the sun would have shone much brighter and further into the cave. One thing she did know – this was the end of her quest, her journey.

Soon she heard a babble of excited voices and saw silhouettes limned in the entrance of the cave. That banished any thoughts other than her relief that her charges had reached home and would now be welcomed and healed.

In all the excitement no one took notice that she followed the group slowly into the village, or how dirty, and exhausted she looked.

M'rain watched the villagers from the edge of the central circle for a while, satisfied her charges were being fussed over and drawn in. As she passed by the food platform she could tell by the smells it must be morning. The men had already gone on the hunt, or to their other duties, and most of the food had already been cleared. She had walked an entire day, no, more than a day.

Part of M'rain was glad that they took no notice of her. It allowed her to slip past them to the pool to wash herself. Another part of her felt let down. Now that their lost ones had all been returned it seemed they had no more need of her. As she sank into the cool water it occurred to her that she ought to be ravenous. Yet her appetite had flown. Food held no appeal. The pit at the bottom of her stomach needed something other than food – something she had to do without.

Feeling empty, void of any emotion, she washed her skin and hair until all signs she had ever been in the caves drifted out into the creek that led away from the pool. Then she let herself sink in up to her neck. *These are not my people. I do not belong here.* Even gloomier thoughts followed. *But I am not the girl I was before. I do not belong with my own people any more either. They will not understand me, now. Even there, I will be a stranger.* The weight of that revelation broke something inside her, something she had kept locked away ever since accepting that she would never go home unless she rescued K'kor's prisoners. Fat tears slipped down her cheeks, unheeded, and dripped down to mingle with the water lapping her chin. She was hollow – no thought of past, none of future, no awareness of the present.

She had no idea how much time had passed when voices drew her back to awareness. Someone called her name. Someone far away.

Closer now, louder.

"M'rain!"

Why did it sound so urgent?

"M'rain, are you all right?"

Hands grasped her arms just as she took a breath, choking on water, and held her steady while she coughed and gasped. When she opened her eyes they met the frightened gaze of a woman who was holding her up. That one shook her arm gently, as if to wake her, or get her attention. At the edge of the pool stood the women she had just brought back, plus a few others, watching with anxious expressions.

"M'rain. Please. Are you all right? You were sinking."

It took M'rain a while to shake the lassitude she felt and to focus on the woman speaking, and even longer to recall her name from her previous stay in the village. S'seta, it was.

"You were sinking," S'seta repeated.

"Was I?"

"You looked asleep. I thought you would drown – you almost did drown."

"Oh..."

"Come, let me help you out. You need to get dry. We were looking for you." As they stepped out of the pool S'seta shook her head at M'rain's skin. "Oh, you have been in too long. Your skin is all wrinkled. Come. We must get you dry and warm."

Out of the water the cooler air hit M'rain and she began to shake. She felt herself being vigorously rubbed all over with the dry grass. Another voice said, "She needs food, too. She must be hungry. We should have looked for her sooner."

M'rain soon felt a clean wrap being wound around her.

"Yes, perhaps that is what made her weak. Perhaps that is why she fell asleep in the water."

When another woman M'rain did not recognize saw that she was still shivering she pulled a fur from a basket behind the ring of stones that held the drying grass. The woman unfolded it and wrapped it around M'rain's shoulders. Soon she felt herself firmly supported as S'seta and the other, whose name she did not recall, guided her back to the centre of the village.

As soon as they reached it M'rain was lowered to sitting at the edge of the circle closest to the food platform. She found herself with a bowl of cooling morning mush laced with honey in one hand and a spoon into the other. She struggled to remember what it was called. *P'pone...yes, I think that is right...p'pone.*

"Are you able to eat? Should I feed you?...Here, drink some tea. It will warm you." A strong arm supported her shoulders and M'rain felt the rim of a warm gourd at her lips. As she drank the hot, sweet liquid she felt some strength return and her shaking subside. She managed a weak smile for her attendant and reached for the bowl and spoon, which someone had rescued from her before she dropped them. "I can eat, now. Thank you."

The villagers gradually eased back into their daily routines, but not without frequent glances in her direction to make sure she did not disappear again. When she had eaten her fill S'seta returned and asked if she would like to lie down in one of the huts and rest, an offer she gladly accepted as it allowed her some peace from their curious eyes. Before she entered the hut she thought to ask after the welfare of the latest group she had brought back.

"Oh, they have all eaten and bathed and are now resting together in that larger hut. Do you want to join them?"

"No - no thank you. I only wanted to know how they were."

"They are very happy to be back. May I wake you to join us for the evening meal? They will join us as well and can all share their stories."

"Yes, I would like that."

"Good." S'seta held aside the skin that served as a door and gestured that M'rain should enter. "I will come for you, then."

As it fell back down behind her M'rain spotted a fur on the ground and sank down onto it, wishing for the oblivion of sleep. Yet, that was denied her. All that came was a return of the great sadness she had felt in the pool and loneliness far heavier than at any time in the caves. Then, she had clung to the hope that she could return home. Now, she knew, even if she could return, it would no longer be home. She had no home, and no one. She belonged nowhere. She curled into fetal position, dry eyed, unable even to weep. Even Glick had abandoned her it seemed, now that he no longer needed her.

XXIX

P'PUCK WAS GLAD the men did not include him in the hunt that day. He knew he would not be able to concentrate and might put the others in danger. His skill was poor at the best of times. Instead, today he had been assigned to the animal pens, to cleaning them and feeding their inhabitants. He liked this solitary work as it gave him time to think. This had been so even before the women began arriving back from the caves. He valued these times of solitude away from the jostling, ribbing, and raucous play of his boyhood companions and, later, as he grew older, the constant camaraderie of the men when he joined them at the hunt. He did enjoy the good-natured teasing and babble of the men when he was with them, but his days working in solitude refreshed him more than their company. It also left him time to think about his next creative attempt. Carving the small, hard tree nuts was a favourite pastime and one that made him popular for the beautiful gifts he bestowed.

Today, though, he forgot to feed the tame squealers after he cleaned out their pen. When he opened the gate to leave their enclosure they let him know it with loud squeals of protest. Upon his return he noticed he had also left the wooden fork, used to clean their manure, lying on the ground instead of hung on its peg on the wall. *Stupid. Not paying attention, are you? Wake up.*

As he left for the second time one of the older children arrived to bring him some food. "Did you hear? They are back – all of them. All the women have returned."

P'puck sucked in an excited breath. "And the other woman, M'rain? Has she returned as well?"

The boy frowned, trying to remember. "I did not see her with the others."

"Are you certain?"

The boy shrugged, "Perhaps...I do not know." With another disinterested shrug he turned to leave, his nose wrinkled in disgust at the reek of animal manure still steaming on the pile behind P'puck.

P'puck watched the lad run back into the village until he was no longer visible. He stood, filled with indecision. *She has to be with them. Surely she did not leave already.*

Knowing his duties would be considered more important than asking after a strange woman's whereabouts he reluctantly returned to his work. As he picked up the woven basket used to gather the fowls' eggs he managed to remember to put some soft grass padding in the bottom. He had placed only the first egg in the basket when a thought stopped him in his tracks. *What if she did not even come back with them?* He had to shake himself to bring his attention back to his task.

Some of the fowl laid their eggs near their wooden roosts on an outside wall of the animal pens, but many chose to hide them in the grass, behind clumps of dirt or in bushes. They never went into the darkness of the caves, for which P'puck was grateful. Many times he had wondered why they didn't disappear into the forest. *Perhaps it is because we feed them. Or perhaps they sense the caves hold danger.* They could not fly high because the people kept their flight feathers clipped.

He set aside the basket of eggs and reached into a larger one sitting on the ground next to the wall. This one had a secure lid on it. He lifted the lid and pulled out a wooden scoop filled with grain which he scattered in a wide arc on the ground. It brought the fowl close, clucking in satisfaction as they pecked at their food. *Not clever are you? You know you ought to feed them before looking for the eggs. Then they would leave you alone.* He gave his head a shake, viewing the scratches on one hand from a hen that had not been happy about having her egg taken from her, before making his way to the corral where the wool-beasts grazed. Half-way there he remembered he ought to have brought the gourd to collect their milk in and had to go back for it. Three of the female wool beasts had recently given birth. Their milk was a rare treat. The village women would add it to the morning p'pone. The two older female wool-beasts had already been trained to allow their milk to be taken but P'puck knew he would have some trouble with the youngest. This was her first birth. As he returned with the gourd he decided to keep the new mother close by while he milked the other two so she could watch.

XXX

P'PUCK'S ELATION ON learning that M'rain had, indeed, returned with the rescued women proved short-lived. As he watched her emerge from the hut where she had been resting his heart sank. This was not the strong, determined young woman he remembered. Instead, the woman one of the villagers led to the platform laden with the evening's meal seemed no more than a shrunken shadow. Her head drooped, so that the raven hair he had so admired hung to each side, hiding her face. Her shoulders slumped, her arms hung limp at her sides, and her feet shuffled, scuffing up dust as she crossed the circle.

What had happened to her? Was she ill? Was she a prisoner again? Why did she look so weak and forlorn? Or worse – was she dying?

P'puck abandoned his intention to greet M'rain and offer to sit beside her as they ate. Indecision held him back. Perhaps she would no longer welcome his company. But his eyes never left her as her companion helped her take some food and find a place in the circle to sit. As he got his own meal he noticed that the usual evening babble seemed subdued. This time of day was normally filled with raised voices, banter, and laughter. Tonight even the children made less clamor than usual. It was as if M'rain's melancholy had brought a pall that spread over the entire village.

P'puck chose a spot opposite M'rain so he could watch her as he ate. She only picked at her food and needed to be reminded to drink her tea. P'puck's stomach churned with anxiety. Something was dreadfully wrong. Much of his own meal also went uneaten.

M'rain showed little interest as the women who had just returned with her began their story. That was, until one of them, introduced as N'nori began to recount their last encounter with K'kor. P'puck watched her head come up as she fixed her gaze intently on N'nori's face.

P'puck, too, found himself drawn into the tale, his gaze moving from one to the other as the other women filled in when N'nori faltered.

"We were so afraid," she began. "First, some of the group split off from us and disappeared. When they did not return for the evening meal we began to wonder if K'kor had killed them..."

"Yes, especially after telling us to eat that man...what was his name...M'malk..."

"...he...K'kor made us cut M'malk up...and cook him." The woman shuddered and put her hands over her face.

"Then he left, and we...we were hungry..."

"...but we could not eat him...we...could not..."

"...K'kor did not come back..."

"...We began to talk together." N'nori had taken up the tale again. "Finally we all agreed to leave the cave. If we were lost and died what would it matter? We would die if we stayed, as well..."

"...so we all left together and started to look for a way out. We had only gone past two caves when we saw the blue glow. We stopped to listen and heard strange noises coming from that cave...like a monster, or...something..." N'nori paused, a far-away look of horror on her face.

"...It was terrifying, like growling and scratching and..."

"...and then we heard screams...not screams like we would make if we were afraid. These sounded...there are no words..."

"...mad, that is the word." N'nori's hands fluttered in front of her as if to ward off something she could not see. "The screams were mad...high and then growling low...then strange laughter..."

"...We began to go back the way we had come but it was too late..."

"...He...K'kor...he came out and he saw us..." N'nori buried her face in her hands, shoulders shaking. One of the village women put a comforting arm around her and stroked her shoulders.

After a brief pause, during which the only sound was the call of birds from the forest, incongruous with the tension in the circle, another captive continued the broken story.

"He was all blue, and he glowed...but...underneath we could see the sores, with blood and puss showing through the blue...and..."

"...It was the powder, you see, the powder he said proved he had magic power..."

"…but we did not know that...not then...not until later..."

Every time one woman faltered in the telling another took it up. The horror emerged haltingly, piece by hideous piece.

"...He did not even seem to know who we were. We were too afraid to run...and had nowhere to run to...and he held that blade he used on M'malk."

"He charged at us, waving it, screaming..."

"...and his eyes..."

"He backed us into a hollow in the tunnel..."

"…We had no choice…"

The last had been no more than a whisper. Yet not one person listening needed to hear it again. It seemed the whole world had stopped breathing.

"...I pushed him away and he fell...and...we all...we...killed him…"

"...no choice..."

"...we kicked him...and stomped on him...until he was dead..." N'nori, who uttered this last, lurched forward and emptied her stomach on the ground in front of her, gagging as the last of the bile caught in her throat.

A long pause, during which no one spoke or moved, seemed to hold time still. Finally, a village woman seated beside N'nori seemed to waken as if from a trance. She sucked in a breath and reached for a gourd, which she brought to N'nori's lips.

That broke the silence. In between quiet murmurs and shared looks of horror and concern, gourds were replenished. One woman, S'seta again, rose, left, and returned moments later with the foaming brew that was kept for celebrations. She went around the circle filling gourds for everyone who wanted it. The elders made no objection, holding up their own to be filled along with all the others.

As the brew helped lift the dark mood the elders encouraged the rescued women to tell the rest of their tale, including how they came to separate, and of their rescue by M'rain. By the time they finished full darkness had fallen. Sober and quiet, the people began to depart for their respective huts.

When P'puck spotted two women guiding M'rain to one of the huts he knew he had lost his opportunity to speak with her this night and reluctantly made his way to his own small hut.

Sleep eluded him. He lay on his back, staring at the smoke hole in the top of his hut, disappointed, worried for M'rain, and unable to decide what to do, come morning.

XXXII

B Y THE LIGHT of the moon passing over the hole P'puck knew night had passed the half-way point. At dawn he would be expected to rise and get ready for the hunt. He turned with a sigh onto his side and closed his eyes.

"I thought you wanted the girl."

P'puck's eyes flew open and he sat bolt upright. "What?" He looked about wildly until a sliver of moonlight revealed the shape of a greyish lizard the size of his hand.

It blinked one eye slowly at him, the other being on the dark side of his head. *"Yes, I allow you see me."*

The satirical tone confirmed what P'puck had already guessed. His whisper came out in a hoarse squeak. "You are Glick!"

"Well, you are a clever one."

P'puck bit back a retort, recalling what M'rain had told him about Glick's acerbic wit, and waited.

"So you want the girl."

"Yes, she is –"

"Stop talking. We will be heard. Here. Use your mind."

"I do not_"

"Your mind, stupid boy." Glick blinked again, twitched his tail rapidly from side to side in agitation, and turned to fix P'puck with both eyes. *"Never mind, just listen."*

P'puck nodded, not knowing what else to do. It pricked him,

though, to be called a boy. He decided he did not like Glick, but then M'rain had not really seemed to like Glick either, if he remembered correctly.

"She will not be like other mates."

P'puck nodded again, interest replacing some of his anger. Where was this leading? What was this talk of mates?

"She will never obey you."

When Glick seemed to be waiting for a reaction P'puck took a deep breath, trying to remember what M'rain had mentioned about the mind speech she had with Glick. He made himself take another calming breath and tried to send a thought. *"I know."*

"Hmph, not bad. Next time use less force."

P'puck allowed himself a small smirk of pride. When Glick spoke next, P'puck thought he detected a note of amusement.

"Are you a leader or a follower?"

"What?"

"Do not shout! That hurts."

"Forgive me...what? I...do not know."

"Can you let her lead?"

"I..." P'puck, unprepared for such an odd question, had no answer. Finally, he said, *"I need to know what that means...that is, if it is M'rain we are discussing."*

"Hmph. Perhaps you are more clever than you look. Of course it is M'rain I am talking about. She has more work to do."

The image of M'rain, dejected and silent that evening, popped into P'puck's mind. *More work? Has she not done enough? Has it not almost destroyed her?* He eyed Glick, anger building. But before he could blurt a furious retort he caught a sense of power emanating from Glick and watched as the lizard changed colour, becoming deep, fiery red. His eyes, though, remained orange. The change silenced the young man just in time.

When P'puck calmed himself Glick's colour returned to normal. *"Think, boy. Have I not kept her safe and led her here? Now...why do you think I have come to you?"*

P'puck decided silence might be more productive than a retort and sat back to wait for more.

"So...how much do you want her?"

Back to the original question. P'puck thought Glick must believe he could figure out what he meant with it. *Does he mean to give M'rain to me? No, or he would not ask if I wanted her to obey me. But he wants to know if I will be a leader or follower...no, perhaps he is asking if I will follow M'rain...if I can allow her to lead in the work she must still do. Yes, that must be it. Perhaps we can be together if I can allow her to lead.* A hopeful elation began to rise. Perhaps this meant that they could be together. But...could he be second to her...to a woman...even one such as M'rain?

P'puck watched Glick, who seemed to be taking a nap, curled up, eyes closed, tail over his nose. P'puck almost nudged him to wake up, irritated that he could lose interest so easily in something so important.

Instead, one eye slid half-way open. *"Well?"*

"I need to know more. What are you suggesting?"

"Good, you are beginning to think....She will never follow. She must lead in the work, at least for a time. But even after, she will never follow."

It was becoming clearer but P'puck still did not understand it all. He wished Glick would stop being so cryptic. Could he not explain things in a normal way? After some deep thought he decided to proceed slowly. Perhaps the right questions, or the right answers, would make Glick offer more information.

"So, you have more work for M'rain...but you do not want her to do it alone. You think I can help her...but she must be the leader...and I must follow her."

"Perhaps you are not as dull as I thought."

"But what has that got to do with me wanting her?"

"The work requires two."

By now P'puck had learned that he needed to think before blurting out more questions. What was Glick getting at? The work needed two people?

"Please explain."

"It needs one from both peoples – M'rain from her people and another from this one."

"And M'rain must be the leader?"

P'puck detected a note of approval in Glick's answer. *"In this, yes."*

"Only in this? What about other things?"

Glick became cagey again and P'puck sensed he was being toyed with.

"Do you want her?"

"Stop these riddles. I have already said I do."

"Even if she will not obey you?"

Glick gave P'puck one of his slow blinks again, making P'puck give an exasperated sigh. *"What do you mean? I have said I will follow her lead with the work, whatever that is."*

"And when the work is complete, what then? She will not be an ordinary mate."

At the word "mate" again P'puck's heart took another lurch. Was this not what had filled his dreams ever since he had helped M'rain bathe in the washing pool? But what was Glick telling him? That it was possible? But what did it mean, that she would not be an ordinary mate? That she would never obey him? He knew some women were not always obedient to their men. But life in the village followed so many routines that there were not many decisions to disagree about. Everyone understood their duties. When Glick spoke again P'puck got the feeling he had read his thoughts.

"If you choose to follow M'rain your life will not be like that of other men. Nor will hers be like that of other women – here or in her home village."

That made P'puck sit up and pay closer attention. Did Glick mean to say that M'rain would be able to go back to her own people? And would he be able to go with her? As the implications of that sank in P'puck's excitement grew. He had always wanted more, something new to see and learn. Was Glick offering him a chance at adventure...and even that he might have it with M'rain by his side...as his mate? His mind whirled with the possibilities.

"You are catching on."

This time P'puck sensed none of the sarcastic tone from Glick's previous remarks.

A sudden thought dampened P'puck's growing excitement. *"But does M'rain want me? Will she have me?"*

"That is something you must ask her yourself. But not yet. She has other decisions to make first."

P'puck squeezed his eyes shut and made himself slow down to think. *"But she needs me to help her with her work. That is what you meant, is it not? If I can allow her to lead - if I will not expect her to obey me, follow me."*

But Glick had gone and P'puck found himself talking to empty air. His emotions ran from elation, to hope, to anger that Glick had read his thoughts without permission, back to annoyance that the lizard had vanished without answering him, finally settling on elation and hope.

M'rain had mentioned that Glick was difficult. Now he understood. The talk with Glick reminded him of the dream he had had. This was not exactly the same, but it helped him understand more of it. *In the dream we followed a thread of light. Is that the magic M'rain wields – light in the caves? Is that why she does not get lost?* P'puck was more intrigued than ever. *I must find a way to speak with M'rain – without being watched or overheard.*

XXXII

WHEN M'RAIN REQUESTED to be left alone for the night she learned that the hut she had rested in belonged to S'seta. At the request for continued solitude S'seta offered to spend the night with a friend and told M'rain the hut was hers as long a she wished it.

"Thank you, but it is only for this one night."

S'seta acknowledged this with a short bow and backed out of her hut, leaving M'rain in darkness with the closing of the door-skin. She felt somewhat stronger, now, after the food and after hearing how K'kor had died. Knowing no one need fear him anymore was a relief. Yet none of it had any effect on her desolate mood. *How can I feel so empty and so heavy at the same time? What is the matter with me? Why can I not rejoice that the women have all been returned to their homes?*

With no answers, and none likely to come, she lay down on the fur and curled up on her side. And still, even now, in spite of her fatigue, sleep would not come. She lay there; eyes open, mind blank, heart empty. Even a wish to die was more than she could manage.

"Feeling sorry for yourself?"

At the familiar voice in her mind M'rain sat up, looked around and found Glick on the ground beside her. *"Glick? I thought you had gone."*

"So that is what you think of me."

"I have completed the task you set."

"And so you thought I would abandon you."

For the first time M'rain thought she detected a note of hurt in Glick's tone.

"You have no more need of me."

"Do you not wish to go home, to your people?"

The question startled M'rain. Would he actually send her back – show her the way? She had given that idea up, for more reasons than that she believed he would refuse. She answered slowly, making sure he understood her hesitation.

"I do not think I can. I am no longer one of them. I am too changed. I will be a stranger there." After a moment she added, *"I belong nowhere."*

The finality of that statement made her hang her head and bury it under her hands against pulled-up knees. For the first time since she had had that thought, she was able to weep. Sobs wracked her body, though she uttered almost no sound.

In time her grief wore itself out and when her sobbing subsided enough for her to hear again, Glick said, *"Perhaps not."*

He waited a moment and added, *"Or perhaps you do."*

M'rain lifted her head to look at Glick and wiped her arm across her eyes to rid them of the lingering tears so she could focus on him. His tone had held none of the usual sarcasm or mocking, and now, as she eyed him, she thought his posture looked sympathetic, though how she could tell she would not have been able to say.

"What do you mean?"

"Perhaps there is a place for you – in both villages." When M'rain only gave him a blank look he continued. *"I have more work for you."*

M'rain began to shake her head, returning anger bringing back some vigor. *"No, I have no more strength. And I will do no more for you. No."*

"What if you need not do it alone?"

That made M'rain even angrier. *"Not alone? Have you found another chosen one to do your bidding until she drops? Will you use up another?"*

When the amused tone crept back into Glick's tone, telling M'rain Glick was once again enjoying her discomfiture, she almost slapped him. But what he said made her hold back her retort.

"No, not a girl, this time. A companion for you. Someone who is eager to

venture out with you."

"Companion? There is no one eager to go into the caves. It is forbidden. And I have no wish to be responsible for another in those caves – ever again."

M'rain could have sworn she heard Glick chuckle.

"I see you have become stronger. Good. You will need that strength."

"No, I will not." M'rain's anger rose again, causing her to raise the volume, *"because I will not be your servant any longer."*

"That is a shame. P'puck will be disappointed. He is counting on an adventure."

"P'puck?"

"He fancies you."

M'rain shook her head, memory taking the edge off her fury. *"No. He was kind to me, but his life is here. I even remember another young woman showing an interest in him – and she is pretty."*

"He is not interested in her." After a pause he added, *"It is you he fancies...you remember the bathing pool?"* The last was said in a sly tone as Glick gave her a sideways blink.

M'rain blushed. Yes, she had noticed. She had even secretly been pleased. But she had forgotten the incident until Glick reminded her just now. She thought this over before answering. P'puck had completed his manhood rite, she knew. That made him old enough to choose a mate. *"But you said he wants adventure. Perhaps it is not me he desires, but that."*

"He desires both."

"Explain...and also explain how this fits into your plan for work for me? This time I want answers before I agree to anything...And what if he becomes my companion and I decide I do not desire more with him? What then?"

"He will be disappointed."

A thought hit M'rain like a bolt of lightning. *"You have already promised this to him!"*

"No...not all of it."

"Aha, I knew it. You have shown yourself to him, made him expect things that may not be."

"I have made no promises, only asked questions."

"What questions? What is he expecting?"

"An adventure."

"More than that, I think. What have you said to him? What adventure and what does he expect from me?" Another thought struck her. *"You have not told him I will be his mate, have you, or that I wish this so-called adventure...have you?*

"No."

"Then what have you told him?" M'rain's anger had peaked again and she was practically shouting at Glick with her mind.

Glick flinched only slightly, leading M'rain to suspect he had exaggerated his pain when he taught her the mind-speech.

"There is no need to shout. I have merely told him he is needed for some work the two of you must do together....Oh, and that you will be the leader. I know better than to expect you to allow him to tell you what to do."

When M'rain merely glared at him, waiting for more, he added, *"He has agreed and will do as you ask."*

"Even if we disagree?"

"Yes, even then – at least where the work is concerned." Glick chuckled again. *"I expect you will not always agree. It is not in your nature."*

"You bear the responsibility for my current nature. I was happy enough with my life until you stole it from me."

"Perhaps I have helped you discover the nature you always had."

"And P'puck does not know my nature." M'rain's morose mood returned. *"He will not want me when he discovers it. Nor will any other. You have seen to that."*

"He knows. He is aware that you are not like other women. It is what draws him to you."

That gave M'rain pause. Suspecting that Glick had played a bigger part she challenged him. *"What did you tell him about me?"*

"Nothing he did not already suspect."

Knowing she would get no more out of Glick on the subject of P'puck she went back to the other problem - the task Glick had for the two of them. But by the time she had her question ready he had disappeared. She would learn no more until he decided to return. She let out a loud sigh.

Dawn had begun to creep down the smoke funnel and around the door. M'rain also realized that her mood had lifted considerably, that she looked forward to the day, and to discovering more about P'puck and what lay ahead for them. Perhaps her life held some promise after all.

XXXIII

T HE AROMA OF the morning p'pone and pungent tea greeted M'rain's nose as she emerged from the hut. She spotted a group of men leaving for the hunt. Others, mostly singly, headed in different directions, some with tools in their hands. She recognized a few of the tools as ones used for the gardens. *I wonder why my people do not grow food. Perhaps it is for lack of water. It would be wonderful if I could bring them some of this food, let them taste it.*

S'seta spotted her almost as soon as she headed toward the food platform and hurried over to greet her. "You look better this morning. Did you sleep well?"

M'rain thought about that before answering. In fact she had not slept at all but she did feel better. "Thank you. I do feel much better."

"Are you hungry? We have not cleared away the morning meal yet."

"Yes, I am famished. It smells wonderful. And that tea will wake me up, I think."

S'seta grinned her agreement and led the way to the food platform, where she handed M'rain one of the gourds used to hold the p'pone. With a nod at the huge wooden bowl, indicating M'rain should help herself, S'seta grabbed a smaller gourd and filled it with steaming tea. "Honey?"

"Oh, yes, please. We do not have honey where I come from. I like its sweetness."

S'seta gave her a puzzled look. "No honey?" She flashed M'rain another grin. "I do not think life would be bearable without honey."

Infected by S'seta's exuberance M'rain could not help but smile back. "Now that I have tasted it, I think I agree. But if you do not know a thing exists you cannot miss it."

S'seta's brow wrinkled a bit at that. "Yes, I suppose that must be so." Then her eyes widened. "But do you have foods that we do not know of? Are they also delicious?"

"Oh, yes. One of my favourites is a bird called a Running Bird. It has wings but they are so small it cannot fly...but it runs very fast. It is delicious when roasted over a spit like you do the fourleg. And it has huge feathers on its tail which we use for many things, like ceremonial head decorations."

"A bird that does no fly? How odd."

"You have things that are odd to me, too. If you came to my village I think you would see many things there that seem strange to you."

S'seta grew quiet, seeming to think that over. When they sat down together so M'rain could eat, S'seta said, "I am not sure I would like that. It frightens me to think about going through the caves. They are forbidden." She smiled again before adding, "And I would miss honey too much."

At a stern look from one of the older women S'seta rose abruptly. "I must return to my duties. If you need anything anyone here will be pleased to help you." With another brief flash of a smile she walked away, leaving M'rain to ponder what she wished to do. And where honey came from. *Now that is one thing my people would surely enjoy. Glick said I might go back. Perhaps I will ask to take some with me.*

M'rain kept an eye out for P'puck but he was nowhere to be seen. She wanted to compare what Glick had told her with what P'puck had heard. And she needed to find out what his feelings were about their so-called partnership if he accompanied her back into the caves. She knew that anything Glick suggested would involve the caves. Would he really agree to follow her lead? Did he really fancy her?

That last question gave her some trouble. She liked him well enough. He was friendly, nice to look at, and seemed intelligent. But until now she had not thought of him as more than a possible friend. She had not given any thought to the idea of anything more at all. In fact, she had not thought of her future much since being captured, other than longing to go home. And now that was no longer possible – at least not in the way she wished.

So much had changed. Most of all, she, herself, had changed. As she thought about that she realized she had set out from her home still a girl. That could no longer apply. *I am a woman, now. But I have not undergone the rite. Perhaps the rite of womanhood no longer holds any meaning for me. Perhaps none of the rites have any meaning for me. So what does that make me?* No answers came, but somehow that no longer made her despondent. *Glick says I still have work to do, that I still have a place. And, it seems, I may not have to do it alone - Curse Glick. I need answers.*

When she grew tired of all the furtive looks from the village women and children she decided to find some solitude at the bathing pool. But this was not to be. Apparently S'seta had been assigned the task of keeping an eye on her because, as soon as she left the central area, she called out to her.

"M'rain, wait for me. I am in need of bathing as well." M'rain stood still, allowing S'seta to catch up. "S'seta, I have rested and eaten. You need not be concerned for me anymore. I thank you, but I have no need of someone to watch over me."

When S'seta hesitated, looking uncomfortable, M'rain added, "I truly need some time alone. I have been in the caves alone for so long that I have grown accustomed to solitude and being around too many people has become more difficult."

S'seta still looked undecided.

"Please, S'seta. I promise I will be all right, and I will join you all for the evening meal. You have my word."

"Very well."

M'rain took a few steps away and turned back to send S'seta a reassuring nod and smile. She watched a very reluctant S'seta return a small wave and turn slowly back toward the village's centre.

I suppose I cannot blame them. I disappeared once and almost drowned once. Now I must take care not to fall asleep in the water. That thought made her smirk and give her heard a tiny shake.

XXXIV

THE FIRST THING P'puck did when he and the other hunters emerged from the forest was try to spot M'rain. When he found her what he saw made him smile. *So, she likes children.* M'rain sat outside the central circle in an open area surrounded by several young children. They seemed to be showing her how to do something with the thin, flexible branches used for weaving baskets, a skill every child mastered by their sixth summer. While M'rain worked the children almost hid her from view, heads bent over her, intent. But when M'rain held out her efforts for them to see they stood up hooting with laughter, shaking their heads, some jumping up and down with apparent glee. This allowed P'puck a glimpse of a grinning M'rain, shaking her head ruefully as one child took her work from her and sat down to demonstrate again. He watched M'rain reach for the project before the children once more hid her from view.

P'puck had no more time to watch. The women came to collect the small game the hunters had caught and then sent the group off to wash in the pool.

Later, everyone lined up at the food platform to get their evening meal, a mix of savoury fourleg meat and edible roots sweetened with dried fruit and accompanied by the usual tea. Another item caught his attention, making his mouth water in anticipation.

The women only made this treat a few times a year, when the wool-beast milk was most plentiful. They mixed the milk with honey and finely ground p'pone flour. Then they flattened it onto greased, heated stones until it hardened into small flat discs. *I hope there are enough that I can eat two.*

He spotted M'rain not far behind him in line and gave away his place to stand beside her. He brought her attention to the rare treats. "See those? We call them honeyed p'pone cakes. We do not have them often. I wonder if they made them in your honour. They are my favourite food."

"What are they made of?"

"Milk and honey and p'pone. Only we leave out some of the water we usually boil it in so it is thick. Then we bake it on hot stones."

M'rain gave him a puzzled look. "What is this milk? Is it not needed by the mothers for their babies?"

It was P'puck's turn to be puzzled. He thought about it for a moment before answering. "Did you see the beasts at the back of the village that have a lot of fur...like some of the sleeping furs we use?"

M'rain frowned in thought. Then she pointed. "You mean the beasts over there – with the young?"

"Yes. When they have young they have more milk than their babies need. The babies eat grass almost as soon as they are born. So we take some of the milk from the mothers to add to our food. It makes our morning p'pone much more delicious."

When M'rain seemed to be struggling to understand P'puck asked, "Do your people not have animals that give them milk?"

M'rain gave a slow shake of her head, a look of mild awe on her face. "There is much you have here that we do not."

Food and tea in their hands, they drifted over to the edge of the circle and sat down. Before taking her first bite M'rain gave a furtive look over her shoulder, leaned closer and said softly, "We must speak. We have much to discuss. And we must not be overheard."

She bent casually over her food and took a scoop of the stew. "This is delicious. I have never tasted anything like this before." She gave S'seta, who had just joined them, a bright smile. "My people do not have fruits and meats like this. Our food is wonderful, too, but very different – and less plentiful."

S'seta returned her smile. "I am happy that you like our food. I see that you have one of the honey p'pone cakes. I hope you like it, too. We do not have them often. We made them to celebrate your return."

M'rain bowed her head. "I am honoured." After another spoonful of the stew she asked S'seta, "What do you call that drink that foams and prickles the mouth. I believe it is made from seeds you grow."

"Oh, you mean the b'birra. It is made from the same grain as the p'pone. We use it only for celebrations. It makes us happy." S'seta giggled. "Do your people have a drink that makes them happy?"

"Yes, it is made from the prickle plant fruit. We only use it for certain rites, like the rites of womanhood and manhood, or when a special baby is born. Then we dance around our fire all night and sleep most of the next day."

When P'puck saw her grow quiet and serious he joined the conversation. "Do you miss your people? It must be hard to be so far from home."

"Yes."

When M'rain said no more P'puck seemed at a loss to keep the conversation going.

S'seta took it up, instead. "But you know how not to get lost in the caves. You can go back, now."

"I miss my people, yes, but I do not know if I would be happy there anymore. You see, I have changed so much. They will not know me now."

"Then, stay here. We would welcome you, I am certain of it."

"Yes, and I thank you, you have all been kind. Perhaps, in time, I will know what I must do."

A low drumming sound came from across the circle. P'puck reached over and put a light hand on M'rain's arm, to let her know the storyteller was about to begin and they must be still. At the contact he felt a jolt, pleasant but unfamiliar. He found that he could not break the contact. Then, as he met M'rain's eyes and they both looked down at where his hand rested, Glick appeared on the ground between their knees.

"They cannot hear or see me. They will sleep until I release them." Glick held them both in his gaze, and blinked once. *"When all have entered their huts I will see that they remain asleep until morning. Then, M'rain, when all is quiet you must go to P'puck's hut. Wait for me there."*

Glick winked out. P'puck pulled his hand away, although with some reluctance, and looked around the circle. It was as though nothing had happened. The drumming continued its low thrum as the storyteller made himself more comfortable and leaned forward to begin.

"In the time before time..."

It startled M'rain to hear the familiar beginning. She sat straighter and leaned forward so she would not miss any of the story.

"...long before memory, longer than the names we recall, whose stories we remember, the One Who Provides..."

So the spirit has a different name here – but almost the same...

"...gave us this land for our home. He showed us how to find food - how to hunt, how to find the fruit on the bushes and trees, and which plants and roots were good to eat. We learned how to grow other foods, keep the other beasts and the birds that give us their eggs. All these things were gifts from the One Who Provides. We lived in peace and health and wanted for nothing. Only two things were required of us – that we use our time wisely so that we continue to have enough – and to stay out of the Great Caves. The One Who Provides warned that the Great Caves are ruled by an angry spirit. Those who disobey and enter the caves do not return. They are swallowed by them, or by the spirit in the caves. To this day the caves are forbidden to us.

"But once, still in the time before time, some disbelieved. Those few convinced others. The group grew. The disbelievers decided to enter the caves. They lured many more to follow them with promises of power and riches. Into the darkness they went. The people who remained begged and wept but the disbelievers did not listen. The people who remained waited and waited until all who lived to remember died. But the lost ones did not return. Those who remained behind no longer remembered the lost ones. The spirit of the darkness, of the caves, swallowed them up – all of them.

"The One Who Provides gave no answers when we pleaded to know what became of the lost ones. He was angry and refused to speak to us. He has not spoken to us since.

"We who remain outside the caves obey. We do not enter the caves, and so we continue to live in peace and health and our numbers grow."

The storyteller paused, took a drink from his gourd, and settled himself to continue. The drumming changed rhythm and became more insistent.

"We believed that the story would end there, and all would be well with those who remained. And for time upon time, it was so."

He looked around to make sure he had the attention of everyone there. All eyes fixed on him, rapt and eager. The drumming increased.

"Then, in our time, something changed. Again, one was born who disbelieved, who chose to disobey. As in the time before time, this one raved about riches, about magic, and spoke of stealing the power of the spirit of the caves and making it his own. He was handsome, and spoke with great eloquence. He told of entering the caves and of returning. He told of discovering rocks that burn longer than sticks. He convinced some that the power of the caves was in the burning rocks. He promised it would bring all who followed him riches. In time he held some men and several women in thrall, as if controlled by an evil spirit. No talk from the elders could reach them. No medicines could break the spell they were under. One night, when we slept under the night sky, K'kor lured them away.

"They did not return. We did not understand how this could happen again. Had we angered the One Who Provides? We did not know. We still do not know. But we do know that the One Who Provides took pity. He found a stranger, one who does not get lost in the caves, one who found those who were lost, broke the spell of the cave spirit that held them, and led them back to us."

He turned and found M'rain, meeting her gaze as the drums died to a low thrum once more, and said softly, "And now that one is among us. We are grateful. And we honour her. Her story will remain a part of our story for all time, until there is no more time."

XXXV

M'RAIN ACKNOWLEDGED THE honour with a solemn bow from her sitting position but kept silent. She did not know if more was expected but had no idea how to react otherwise.

Since the storyteller merely responded back with a head bow she assumed it was enough.

By now dusk had given way to night. People rose, returned their drinking gourds upside down, so the bugs would not rest there, to the food platform and wandered off to their respective huts. To M'rain's relief no one seemed inclined to speak to her. She wondered if that was Glick's doing, too. S'seta followed her friend, giving no indication she wanted to come back to her own hut, so M'rain returned there alone, for which she was grateful. It would be easier to leave to meet P'puck and Glick that way.

Soon, now that full darkness covered the village, its inhabitants slept in complete silence, just as Glick had promised. M'rain slipped out of the hut and made her way to where she knew P'puck would be waiting. As she approached she spotted his silhouette, sitting, fully awake, in front of his hut. He noticed her long before she reached it and raised a hand in greeting. Then he rose and held open the skin door until she reached it and entered.

"I do not suppose Glick has deigned to show himself yet." M'rain was still not happy about Glick's announcements. Nor did she want to give P'puck the impression that she favoured him and was pleased Glick had chosen him to accompany her.

Before P'puck could answer a small orange glow grew into the outline of a lizard. If M'rain's remark had irked Glick he did not show it. *"We will use silent speech. I will keep my body lit up so we can see each other."* He turned to P'puck. *"And you will practice control as you speak. I will not have shouting. Understood?"* When P'puck merely nodded, a slightly stunned expression on his face, Glick repeated, *"Understood?"*

"Uh, yes, understood."

"Good. Now listen. I do not wish to waste time."

By now M'rain had seated herself facing Glick. P'puck hurried to do the same. But M'rain was not ready to be merely obedient. *"I will listen. But that does not mean I agree to your plan, or that I will follow your instructions."*

P'puck raised a startled eyebrow at her, as if surprised she would speak back to such a powerful being. M'rain ignored him, thinking to herself that if he was to accompany her he would need to learn to deal with Glick as well. Glick was not the One Who Gives, only one of his guardians, and not a very nice one, at that.

Glick's response felt like a mix of amusement and chiding, although he said nothing about it. He fixed both eyes on M'rain. *"You know the story of how your people came to live in the desert. Now you have also heard the story of this people. You needed to hear it. That is why I had the storyteller recite it tonight."*

When both listeners raised eyebrows he huffed, *"Ye, I did that. Did you think it an accident that he chose this night to tell the tale of your people?"* Glick glared at M'rain first, then P'puck, before settling himself once more. Addressing M'rain again he said, *"Do you understand, now, that your people are kin to these people here? That is why you understand their speech."* He turned to P'puck. *"And do you see, now, that not all those who left died? That M'rain is descended from those who passed safely through the caves and learned how to live in that new world?*

P'puck's wide-eyed surprise, mouth half open, gradually gave way to a slow nod of realization. *"They did not all die. Some made it through alive."*

"Yes. The One Who Provides — or One Who Gives - took pity on them. And

now the time has come to be united once more."

M'rain leaned forward, all anger forgotten. "*Are we to bring all my people here, then? Am I to bring them all back?*"

"*No. Do you really think all your people will give up all they know to follow a young woman because she has a tale of wonder? Do you really think they want to give up the life they know for one they know nothing of – to follow you into the forbidden caves on your word alone?*" Glick's tail lashed back and forth in agitation.

This time P'puck interrupted. "*But you said we are to travel through the caves. To what purpose?*"

Glick turned to P'puck. "*If you listen instead of interrupting you will learn it.*" Then he seemed to realize he had been rude and added, "*It is a good question.*"

He settled again, wrapping his tail over his front feet and blinking once. "*Yes, you will become the travellers. You will learn how to go from one end of the caves and through to the other without getting lost. You will teach your peoples about each other and bring gifts to share, one from the other. As the people come to accept this others will wish to learn how to travel the caves safely. But they will be few. The caves are dangerous and will remain so for those who do not respect them. Only those who are very careful and very brave will be able to travel back and forth.*"

He turned to fix on eye on M'rain, his tone clearly amused this time. "*One of the first gifts you will bring is honey.*" When M'rain smiled in delight he added, "*I knew you would like that idea...and no, I did not read your thoughts. I overheard you talking to S'seta.*" He paused and when neither M'rain nor P'puck spoke he said, "*Now you may ask questions.*"

M'rain sensed his approval when both she and P'puck remained silent for a few moments. She knew he liked it when she thought things through before speaking, that he saw it as a sign of maturity and self-control. She was secretly pleased that P'puck seemed to have that control, too. When she met his gaze he seemed to be waiting for her to begin, giving her a tiny nod, as if to tell her to go ahead. But she also saw the excitement in his eyes, and knew he was eager to hear more. She had to acknowledge that she, too, had begun to see possibilities in what Glick had told them. "*Does this mean that all the travellers will be given the magic sight? And will the magic threads of light always be there to show the way?*"

"No, and I will only show you the way once. Then the magic will be taken away - even from you."

P'puck, clearly perplexed, blurted the next question. *"But how will we not get lost if we are not given the magic? How will we know where to go?"*

"Did I not say you would learn what you need? And that the caves will always be dangerous?"

"So, how...?

"I will teach you what you must learn. And you will teach others. Magic will no longer be needed."

He turned to M'rain. *"You remember the blue dust?"*

"Yes, the dust you said made K'kor go mad and caused his illness. You made me wash it off. You said it would make me sick."

"Yes, yes, but only if you leave it on your skin." His tail lashed once before he continued. *"You remember that it glowed, that you could see it in the dark?*

M'rain gave a slow nod, waiting for more.

"You will gather it and use it to make your own line of light, one that everyone can see and follow."

Now it was P'puck who challenged Glick. *"Then why do you need both of us for this first journey? I want to go, but I need to understand."*

Glick closed his eyes half way and kept them that way a while. When he answered M'rain could not tell if he was pleased or angry

"Travelling the caves is, as I said, dangerous. It must not be done alone - ever. But there is more." He opened his eyes again.*" M'rain, you remember the rocks that burn, and that K'kor said they did not need wood if they had these rocks."*

"Yes, he said those rocks would make him rich."

"Indeed, and this is not far from the truth. But the time for that is not now. That will wait for later."

"Later!"

"Do not shout."

M'rain's anger had risen again. *"If you want us to do your bidding we need to know."*

"No, some things are not important now. One day those rocks will help your people. But that time is a long time away. It can wait."

P'puck chimed in. *"I want to know, too. Why must we wait?*

"Because I decided you do not need to know everything all at once."

M'rain turned to P'puck and shook her head at him, saying aloud, "That is how it is with Glick. He likes to play games. But we do not need to play along. Let us find out more about our current situation. I want to see my people again, and the idea of sharing between our peoples appeals to me. What about you?" M'rain knew speaking aloud would infuriate Glick. She was pleased to see that P'puck caught on.

"I see. Well I do want to see your people and to learn the ways through the caves. Perhaps we will learn about those black rocks on our own. Perhaps Glick will not be needed for that."

Glick lashed his tail in fury and disappeared.

"He will be back." By now the first thin light of dawn lit the hut just enough that M'rain could detect the concern on P'puck's face, in spite of the dying embers that no longer illuminated the hut. She sent him a reassuring smile. "He needs us."

190

XXXVI

"I HAD BETTER get back to where I am supposed to be sleeping." M'rain stood up, a tired groan escaping her. "I wonder when I will ever sleep again."

P'puck quickly followed suit and hurried to the door, hesitating before opening it. "When will we talk again, do you think? We have so much to discuss."

"When Glick deigns to see us again." Seeing P'puck's disappointment she added, "Or at the evening meal, whichever comes first. But now I will beg to be allowed to sleep the rest of the day. I will say I am worn out, which is true."

"Yes, we will eat together...perhaps get to know each other better...since we will be travelling together..."

"Good, I will see you then. I do not expect Glick will come again before nightfall."

P'puck held aside the door and M'rain made her way back to S'seta's hut. As she walked she recalled P'puck's immediate acceptance of Glick, his quick comprehension of what Glick was saying, and his eagerness to hear the plan the lizard had presented. But what pleased her most was that he had fallen in with her so quickly when she had spoken aloud. He must have known Glick would be angered, and, as P'puck did not know Glick as well as she did, must have been at least a little worried about what Glick might do to him. *He trusts me, and he has chosen to take my side.* With that thought she entered the hut, curled up on the sleeping fur and fell into a dreamless sleep.

She woke to P'puck scratching at the door and calling her name softly. When she opened her eyes and remembered where she was the aroma of meat on a spit told her it must be time for the evening meal. She had slept the entire day. *Was that Glick's doing...or was it only my exhaustion?*

When she pushed aside the skin door P'puck's infectious grin greeted her. "So, sleepyhead. You got some sleep after all it seems. I, on the other hand, have been hunting all day."

M'rain tried to hide her own smile behind her hand but it came through in her voice. "So you want pity from me, do you? You will wait a long time."

P'puck laughed. "No, just food. Come, before the best parts are all gone." He led the way to the food platform, looking over his shoulder once to make sure she kept up. "Roast jumper tonight. One of my favourites."

Now she made no attempt to hide her smile. "I suspect you have a lot of favourites. I have seen you eat."

P'puck laughed. "Guilty. Eating is one of the best pleasures in life."

As M'rain accepted one of the big leaves from P'puck she felt some of the heaviness lift from her spirit. *If I must enter the caves again at least I will have a cheerful companion.* Feeling lighter than she had in a long time, she loaded her leaf and followed P'puck to the spot he had chosen to sit and eat. When she had swallowed the last succulent morsel of jumper she met P'puck's gaze. "I think you are correct. Eating is one of the best pleasures in life – especially when the food is this good."

P'puck rewarded her with one of his wide grins. "That is one thing we agree on then. I will take that as a good omen."

"Omen for what?"

"Er...for our journey, of course." He blushed deep red and quickly looked at his hands. "Um, since we will be travelling together...do you not you think it will help if we agree on some things?"

Seeing that he kept his eyes lowered and refused to meet hers confirmed for M'rain that there was more to this than P'puck was letting on. She decided to test him a little.

"I have not yet agreed to travel at all, let alone with you."

"But...?"

The confusion and dismay on P'puck's face made M'rain relent. "But I do want to bring some honey to my people. And I suppose Glick will have his way, no matter what I want."

P'puck's expression became hopeful once more. In an earnest voice, coloured with some doubt, he asked, "You do want a companion do you not? Glick thinks I ought to be the one..."

M'rain lost the will to tease P'puck and sobered. "Yes, I know we must go. And your help will be welcome. But it will be a difficult journey and you know nothing of the caves."

P'puck nodded. "That is why Glick told me I must allow you to lead, and must not let pride make me resist your guidance." He looked once more at his hands and, his voice low, said, "M'rain, I will not get in the way. I know you are not meant for an ordinary life, that you are strong and must lead in some things. I have no desire to change you. I accept you will never fit into the role set for other women."

"Good."

After several moments of uncomfortable silence M'rain asked, "Why do you wish to come with me?" It pleased her that he took his time to answer.

"I have always felt there was more than the life we lead here. I knew the caves were forbidden, but I had listened to K'kor speak of adventure and his claim that he had been into the caves and returned. There was something about the caves that called to me. I did not like K'kor and had no wish to follow him. And when K'kor did not return, nor all his followers, I thought it best to stay out of the caves. But I still wanted something more...something I cannot explain in words. Then, when the women began to return, my curiosity grew. The call felt stronger. That is why I ventured so far and left food for you while you slept. I had so many questions...but then you left and I had to wait for answers." He stopped and gave her a shy, sideways look. "And I like you." He looked away again, seeming to search for courage before continuing. "Then, when you came into the village...and I taught you how to wash yourself in the pool...when I saw your hair shining and dripping..." His voice trailed off.

M'rain did not know what to say, so she kept quiet and waited.

After a time he glanced at her again and back at the ground. She could barely hear his whispered, "You are so beautiful..."

That left M'rain speechless. She had no idea how she felt about his declaration. They sat that way for a time until S'seta approached them. "I am going to the pool, M'rain. Would you like to join me?

M'rain jumped up, grateful for the reprieve. "Yes. That will refresh me. Thank you." She followed S'seta without glancing back at P'puck. She needed time to think.

XXXVII

*W*AKE UP. IT *is time to meet."* Glick sat in front of M'rain's face, tail lashing impatiently behind him.

"Hnh..." M'rain sat up in the dark hut and rubbed her eyes.

"Come. You are wasting my time. P'puck is awake and waiting."

That annoyed M'rain. *"You woke him first? I thought you made me the leader."*

Glick ignored the complaint and blinked out, leaving M'rain to gather her wits and make her way to P'puck's hut. Her path took her past the food platform. The large tea gourd still had some cold tea in it so M'rain helped herself to a drink. She started for P'puck's hut, then turned back to fill another gourd with cold tea for him. *He had best not expect me to do that all the time.* Then she chided herself for the thought. *No, that is not likely. He is more likely to serve me, if what he has done so far is any indication.*

As she approached she saw that P'puck already sat waiting outside his door. He waved as soon as he saw her and rose to hold his door open.

"Here, I brought you some tea. Cold, but I thought you might want some."

P'puck raised one surprised eyebrow as he accepted the drink. "Thank you. Yes."

In spite of the warm night P'puck had a small fire lit, mostly glowing embers, in the centre of his hut, which gave just enough light to see movement and shadows. It had burned down so far that only the smallest curl of smoke rose to the funnel pot in the roof. Next to the fire lay Glick, curled in sleeping position. That did not fool M'rain. To annoy him she let on that she did not see him and continued to address P'puck in a low voice.

"Did you get any sleep? It is early night yet, as the moon is still well behind the forest."

P'puck caught on and fell in with her. "Yes, some, but if I do not get more I will be useless for the hunt in the morning."

M'rain could just make out his mischievous grin.

Glick began to glow orange. His tail lashed twice and he turned his eyes on the pair. *"You are wasting time. If you are clever there will be no need to hunt tomorrow."*

That caught M'rain's attention. A look at P'puck told her Glick had his attention, too. Without a word they both sat down facing the lizard.

"At dawn you must request a meeting with the elders. You will tell them that you wish to leave as soon as you have your supplies ready. That you will travel the caves, bring gifts to M'rain's people, and return. Tell them this is the will of The One Who Provides – or Gives – whichever name you choose."

"And I suppose they will agree without protest." M'rain could not keep the skepticism from her voice.

"They will protest but they will be too curious to forbid it. They have seen that the caves can be travelled. That some can return. They know you are the one who has done it. When you tell them that your people are the same people who left in the time before time they will be too perplexed to forbid you."

After a questioning look at M'rain, P'puck asked, *"What supplies must we take? How long will our journey be?"*

Glick turned one eye on P'puck. *"Only as many torches as you can carry, a large waterskin each, four large, empty skin sacks, two small gourds of honey and one small sack of the crisp-fruits that are just ripening on the trees. Both of these food items are for gifts."*

P'puck blurted, *"No food? What shall we eat?"*

M'rain answered aloud, "Food is not needed. There is food along the way. It looks terrible but it will sustain us."

"*This time only. After this journey I will no longer provide the magic that gives the food.*"

It was M'rain's turn to react. "*What do you mean? Will it not always be there? Will you not always help us with your magic?*"

"*No.*"

M'rain's head swiveled to meet P'puck's eyes, and then back again to Glick. Her tone gave away her confusion. "*But how will we travel the caves without protection?*"

"*You will not need it. I will teach you what you need. You will teach those who follow. Magic will no longer be needed.*"

Now alarmed, M'rain blurted out, "*Not needed...but...surely magic will not disappear. And what of you? What will happen to you?*"

"*My usefulness will have ended.*"

This time P'puck pressed Glick. "*What do you mean? What will you do when your usefulness ends? Where will you go?*"

"*I will end.*"

The complacency in his tone brought M'rain up short. Did Glick want to die? Could it be that he was he here against his will, just as she had been? And how could he sound so uncaring about his own end? She remembered her own near death in the pool and what had brought her to that state. It made her begin to see Glick in a different light. Was he unhappy to be here?

"*Glick, what are you saying to us? Do you want to 'end'? Do you not like being here? Are you saying you will die?*"

"*No one dies. We end. We rest. That is all. I have guarded the caves for time upon time. I will welcome my end. I will welcome my rest.*"

"*But...*" M'rain pressed, now thoroughly puzzled, "*What do you mean, you will end but not die? How can that be?*"

"*I told you, no one dies. We end, and we rest.*"

"*Even us?*"

"*Of course.*"

"*I do not understand. What is this end, and this rest?*"

"*You are not ready to understand. Some mysteries must remain.*"

M'rain and P'puck exchanged glances. She knew Glick would say no more, so she gave him a slight shake of her head to tell him not to press the lizard on it.

Glick eyed them both, one at a time, and then settled himself facing them. *"So, now you must learn how to travel the caves without magic."*

M'rain glanced at P'puck to gage his reaction. She was pleased to see that he looked more eager and attentive than afraid. When Glick gave his tail an impatient swish she returned her full attention to him.

"You remember I told you that you will need empty sacks?"

"Yes." M'rain and P'puck answered in unison.

"I will lead you to the cave with the blue dust that glows. You will fill the sacks with the dust. Each sack will need a small hole in the bottom tip, with a thong to tie the hole shut when you are not using it."

M'rain knew enough to remain silent but P'puck's eyes grew wide and he nodded rapidly. *"To create a trail! You mentioned this earlier."*

Glick shot P'puck a baleful glance that made him sit back again to listen. *"Yes. And you must take as many torches as you can carry. You will leave these at regular intervals along the trail. They will provide light for those who follow who do not have M'rain's magic sight."* Glick fixed P'puck with a glare. *"M'rain has told you of her magic sight. I have the power to grant it to one more. Have you the courage to accept it?"*

M'rain was glad to see that P'puck did not leap at the chance, but gave it a moment's thought first.

"M'rain has told of the pain. But I think the sight will be useful...and it will mean we will not need to use the torches and can leave more of them behind. Yes, I accept." He sat up straight and squared his shoulders. *"I am ready."*

"Good. Now touch my eyes with your two first fingers. Then place those fingers on your own eyes. Touch them both at the same time or you may change your mind."

"I will not change my mind."

M'rain watched P'puck, who looked afraid but determined, and shuddered remembering her own pain. But at that time she had not known what would come. P'puck knew what to expect. She had to respect his courage.

P'puck reached trembling hands down to Glick and touched each eye with a forefinger. He hesitated only a moment before he lifted his fingers to his own eyes, touched both at the same time – and screamed.

XXXVIII

GLICK SEEMED UNPERTURBED by the scream. He waited, relaxed and silent, until P'puck pulled himself together and opened his eyes. He chose M'rain as the first object of his new sight. *"I can see you clearly, although your colours are different, almost different depths of the same colour."*

When Glick responded with a simple, *"Yes,"* P'puck clapped his hands over his mouth. *"Did I wake the whole village?"*

"No, I was prepared."

M'rain thought she detected an amused smugness in Glick's tone. *Of course he was.*

"Now I know why you told me I might not have had the courage to touch the second eye if I did not do them both at once. I fear you were correct."

The lizard gave him an appraising glance. *"You knew what would come. You showed courage."*

P'puck straightened at the small compliment, his ready smile returning once again. It made M'rain curious. Was he really that uncomplicated? What would the coming journey bring?

As if reading her thoughts Glick spoke again, once more his curt self. *"Dawn approaches. It is time to make ready. You must make torches. There are not enough in the village."*

"We do not often need torches here."

"The cave travellers who come after you will need them, always." With that, Glick blinked out.

201

With Glick's disappearance P'puck's new sight also faded. At his exclamation of dismay M'rain shrugged. "I am surprised it worked here. I think he meant only to show you. Mine only works in the caves. I am certain it will return there."

M'rain looked at P'puck, and rose. "Show me how to make torches here. We use them, too, but I expect you make them differently."

P'puck had already reached the door and held it open. "This way. We need branches and grass."

P'puck showed M'rain how to wind the grasses tightly around the branches, leaving just enough space for some air. Then he gathered as many as he could carry, with M'rain taking the last few, and led her behind one of the huts at the back of the village, just behind the squealer pens. There he showed M'rain how to soak the torches in warmed grease. "They will flare at first, but then keep burning more slowly."

"Our method is similar, but we do not have branches so we weave grasses very tightly to make handles. The rest is the same. The handles burn so slowly that we stop the flame and reuse the same one for new torches. I think that will not work with these branches."

"No, you are right. We do not use the same ones again. When they have stopped burning we add them to the cook-fire."

The door to the hut was flung aside, limning one of the elders in the early morning light. "What do you think you are doing? The men are ready for the hunt and you waste time making torches."

Before P'puck could protest M'rain broke in. "P'puck will not be joining the hunt today. We prepare for a journey back to my people."

At the unexpected, audacious pronouncement the elder took a half step back, eyes widening as if he had been struck.

Before he found his voice M'rain added, "We wish to meet with the elders as soon as we have eaten. Then we must collect the remainder of our supplies and be on our way. We do not need much. I will explain when we meet."

When M'rain thought about it later she wondered why the elder had not protested or scolded her for her boldness. Perhaps it was the authority in her voice – or perhaps Glick had something to do with it. In any case, the man had huffed, turned around, and gone in search the others.

After the morning meal she and P'puck found themselves facing three irate elders.

"We cannot allow this. It is forbidden. If we let P'puck go others will follow. You know what happened to K'kor and his followers." T'trint jabbed an angry finger at M'rain. "If it had not been for you, for your magic, they would never have returned. They would be dead. That is what will happen to those who choose to disobey."

M'rain countered. "They will not attempt it as they know it is only I who has the magic. It is only I with whom the spirit lizard speaks. And Glick has assured me that it will remain so, until the trail is set and the way taught."

"No, we will not allow P'puck to leave." At vigorous nods of agreement from the other two elders T'trint added. "You may go. Then perhaps our lives will return to normal."

That brought looks of concern from the other two. "But she is our honoured guest. Look what she has done for us."

T'trint drew himself up, his face reddening in anger. "Yes, and now she wishes to lead us all into danger. I am not fooled by her."

P'puck could no longer hold his silence. "I will go, whether you allow it or not. It is my destiny. I, too, have spoken with the spirit lizard. Glick has commanded it. You cannot prevent it."

"Then you will go empty handed."

M'rain held up a hand for attention. "We will go. It is decreed. But we will take very little." She listed what Glick had told them to take. "Surely you would not deny my people a taste of your honey and crisp fruits. They will be grateful and take it as a token of friendship."

While she could see T'trint becoming ever more entrenched, the other two looked thoughtful and now nodded slowly.

"T'trint, I see no harm in this. It takes nothing we need. Let it be a test. If they disappear and never return we will know you are correct. Then we will have evidence to tell our people of the dangers of the caves once more, not only through the old stories, but in our own time."

His partner piped up. "A sack of honey and some fruit is a small price to pay for the knowledge we may gain. Since P'puck is determined to go we cannot keep him here. Would you imprison him? How? We cannot spare a hunter to watch him. We cannot keep him tied up. Let him go and we will see what happens."

T'trint sent his partners a scorching glare but they did not back down. "Very well. You will see. They will not return. Their loss will prove that I am correct."

M'rain rose. "I thank you all. We will gather our supplies and leave as soon as we are ready." She turned to P'puck, who had risen with her. "P'puck, will you show me where to find what we need?"

He gave her a short nod then bowed from the waist to the elders. "Thank you. We will see you when we return." This time M'rain held the door and the two strode out, not looking back.

XXXIX

B Y THE TIME the sun reached its zenith the pair had gathered what they needed, entered the outer cave and begun their trek into the darkness. It had not taken them long to find and organize their supplies. But when P'puck had offered to carry more than his share of the weight M'rain had refused.

"You will need your strength and endurance as much as I. And when we fill our sacks with the blue dust we will both be burdened to the limit of our strength." At P'puck's fallen expression she had softened. "I thank you for your concern but it is not needed. I am stronger than I appear." She gave him a companionable cuff on the arm to take the sting out of her words and was rewarded with a relieved grin.

As soon as they walked past the last fading light that filtered into the cave from outside P'puck let out a long, relieved breath. "This is a wonder. I can see everything. The magic sight..."

M'rain smiled at his awe. "Yes, I had the same reaction when Glick gave it to me."

She had no sooner said this and taken a few steps further into the cave than the thread of light M'rain expected appeared. By the time her stomach began to let her know they had passed the time for their midday meal it led into the cave with the glowing blue wall and the pile of dust M'rain recognized from her flight from K'kor.

She pulled out her two empty sacks and began to fill them with a gourd they had brought, first making certain the hole in the corner had been tied shut. P'puck did the same as soon as he saw what she was doing.

"I see that Glick wishes us to remain hungry for a while longer. I see no signs of food or water here." P'puck gave the cave a thorough inspection.

"Yes. I expect he will lead us to the cave with food and water when our sacks are full. We will need to wash all signs of this dust off our skin or it will make us ill like K'kor. I remember that there is a small cave close by with water to wash in."

M'rain saw P'puck shudder as he realized that his arms and parts of his body glowed with the toxic stuff. "Then let us hurry." He gave the task of filling the sacks an added burst of effort. When all four were full and tied closed with thongs he lifted one up and examined it. "What of the dust on the outside of these? It will get onto our skin as we carry them."

"Brush off what you can. We will do it again when we have washed. I expect most of it will come off. And whenever we see water we will wash ourselves again."

P'puck gave her a dubious nod. "I hope there are many places to wash."

That made M'rain laugh. "Well, as you see, I have not gone mad from my having it on me...have I?"

P'puck's face split into a relieved grin. "I will answer that once we have returned again. This whole journey may be madness."

"We can leave the gourds here. They will be needed when we return."

"You must begin the trail here. You will need to be able to find this cave again, to replenish the trail. Begin with the smallest sack and leave it where the trail breaks from this one — and do not waste the dust. It must be sufficient for the entire journey."

M'rain had wondered when Glick would appear. She suspected he was never far from them, even when he did not choose to show himself. *"I had already thought of that, Glick. Will there be food at the bathing cave?"*

"Of course"

"Good, then we are ready to follow you there."

"Leave a torch at the entrance."

Outside of the chamber the line of light veered to the right, away from the way they had come. Behind them they could see it had disappeared altogether and been replaced by the trail of glowing dust they left behind.

"I am glad that these sacks will get lighter as they are emptied." M'rain led the way. She could only carry one sack as she needed her hands free to make certain the trail was not broken or became too thick.

That had left P'puck with the other two, having left the smallest one back at the dust cave as directed by Glick. His only reaction was a huff of effort.

"This one will soon be empty and I will take another from you."

"No need. I can manage." The grunt that followed as P'puck hitched his burden up a little made M'rain turn back to look at him. "We can switch places."

"No. Keep walking. Surely the bathing cave is near."

No sooner had he said this than the thread turned into a small cave and they heard a trickle of flowing water.

"Yes, this is it. The pool is at the back." M'rain tied the hole in the sack closed and set it down, reaching back quickly to help P'puck relieve himself of his burdens. With a groan of relief he stretched his back and rolled his shoulders. "Show me this pool. I want to wash this stuff off me."

"Refill your water skins first, or the dust will get into your drinking water."

"And then may we eat?"

"Look there, on that rock."

M'rain had already spotted the pile of grey fungi on the rock beside the pool, as she had known where to look. She laughed when P'puck made a face.

"That is our food?"

Aloud, M'rain said, "We must imagine what we would like to eat. That is what those lumps will taste like."

P'puck looked doubtful but said nothing. He began to strip off his loin wrap but Glick stopped him. *"That must be washed as well, to get the dust off."*

"Oh, yes, I suppose you are correct."

"I never suppose."

Both M'rain and P'puck snorted but neither deigned a retort. With a shared look of mirth and understanding M'rain indicated the pool with a jerk of her head and stepped into the water. "It is only as deep as my neck - something I did not know when Glick told me to wash. The bottom was slippery and I lost my footing. He almost let me drown."

"I am still here."

At the indignant remark both M'rain and P'puck laughed loud.

"I can remove the magic taste from the food."

M'rain merely laughed but a look of consternation came over P'puck's face. *"Oh, please do not do that, Glick. We were only teasing."*

"Hmph."

M'rain had already climbed out again and stood bent over wringing water from her hair. The sight made P'puck hitch his breath.

When he did not immediately follow her out of the pool M'rain noticed his stare. She stood up, tossed her hair carelessly behind her and headed for the food rock. "Are you coming or do you intend to stay in the water all day?" She realized she had begun to feel at ease with P'puck and was now reminded of his greater interest in her. She could not decide if it pleased her or not. One thing did impress her. He never complained.

M'rain handed P'puck a piece of fungi. "Think of what you would like to eat. That is what it will taste like."

"I know that is what you told me...but it looks so..."

M'rain made a show of popping a bit in her mouth. "Mmmmm, roast running bird."

P'puck eyed the piece in his hand. "I have never tasted your running bird. Do you suppose it will work for me, even though I do not know what it tastes like?"

M'rain shrugged. "I do not know. But there is only one way to find out."

"All right then." P'puck took a nibble and grimaced. "Ugh."

M'rain giggled. "Now we know. I am glad you were the one to try it."

P'puck sent her a glare that dissolved into one of his grins. "So now I imagine a food I know and like?" He gave the piece in his hand a disgusted look, squeezed his eyes shut for a moment, popped it into his mouth and chewed. His eyes flew open and a look of delight erased his earlier doubt. "Honey p'pone cakes."

When M'rain sent him a knowing grin his expression changed to one of mischief. "I wonder if you will taste my honey p'pone if I kiss you."

Before M'rain could react he wrapped an arm around her and placed his mouth firmly on hers. Her first reaction was to struggle and get angry, but his grip remained firm and she found she no longer wanted to pull away. Then she collected herself and gave him a shove. Before she could berate him he asked, "Well? Did you taste honey?"

The question erased the indignant comment she wanted to make from her mind. *What? Honey?* He had taken her completely unaware and kept her off balance. She took a moment to bring her thoughts back into some recognizable order and faced him as calmly as she could muster. She opened her mouth to speak, saw the play of emotions on his face and promptly forgot what she was about to say – again. Instead, her mind still in turmoil, she spun away from him, grabbed her share of their equipment and strapped it on. Then she strode out of the cave leaving P'puck to follow as best he could. Only after they had resumed leaving the dust trail, following a new thread of light, did she remember that she had only eaten one bite of the fungi.

P'puck, apparently, had noticed, because when her stomach growled audibly he reached out with a handful. In a subdued tone he said, "Here. I thought you might need this."

M'rain took the offering without looking at him or saying anything. She needed time to sort out what to say – and how she felt. This was not what she had bargained for. Yet, she had a feeling it was exactly what Glick counted on.

XXXX

THEY TRUDGED IN silence, their footsteps muffled by the dust of many lifetimes. The only breaks came when Glick would interject a, *"Leave a torch here"* to signal the intervals between torches.

The amusement in his tone did nothing to ease M'rain's confusion. It only added anger to it and made her wonder if Glick had been responsible for P'puck's impulsive gesture.

When the second sack of dust was about to run out P'puck broke the silence. "Let me lead to empty the next sack."

M'rain said nothing, but stopped when her sack no longer poured out more dust. She shook it flat, folded it and tucked it into her pack. Unable to avoid it any longer she turned to face P'puck. "Did Glick make you do that?"

He gave her a lopsided grin, part sheepish, part pleased with himself. "No."

"Then why?"

"I wanted you to know how I felt...feel."

M'rain raised her hands open wide, as if about to ask a question, then lowered them again. The words would not come.

Emboldened, P'puck asked again, "Well, did you taste honey?" The sideways look he gave her was both hopeful and teasing.

She could not allow herself to encourage him so all she said was, "No. And do not do that again."

His face fell slightly but he seemed to sense the lack of certainty in her voice because his smile did not disappear altogether.

M'rain sensed that the apology she wanted, the one that would help her recover her position of authority, would not be forthcoming.

Glick chose that moment to intervene. *"If you two lovers will stop squabbling for a moment you will see that your dust is half gone. You have reached the halfway point. That cave on your right is where you will spend the night. You will find food, water for your skins, and enough to wash the dust off as well."*

M'rain heard only one word. *"Lovers!"*

"No need to shout."

"How dare you."

"What? I did nothing."

"You made him do that."

"No. He is quite capable of playing suitor without my help."

P'puck grinned but said nothing.

M'rain sensed that the odds had turned against her. The only response she felt open to her was fury. *"Stop that. You are encouraging him."*

Glick ignored her tone. *"You did taste honey."*

M'rain turned on P'puck, knowing that to challenge Glick would only make things worse. "Do not touch me without my permission again. Understand?"

P'puck seemed to sense that things could take a bad turn and backed down. "As you wish. You know my feelings now. I do not regret it but I will not do it again."

Glick added, *"I cannot make anyone do what they do not wish to. His actions toward you are his alone..."* Then, addressing P'puck, he said, *"I suggest words might work better for a while."*

That brought the smile back. *"I bow to your wisdom."*

M'rain did not wait. She stormed into the cave and dropped her burden beside the pool. She had had the upper hand so far on their journey. Now she felt she had lost control and had no idea how to regain it. She was supposed to be the leader. How could she lead if he did not look up to her? The balance had shifted and it made her uneasy.

As P'puck followed her into the cave Glick sent an amused, *"Good night."* It was all she could do not to stomp her feet.

She heard P'puck set down his packs and stretch himself.

"M'rain..."

"The food is over there." With a jerk of her head she indicated the far side of the cave. "You will sleep on that side."

P'puck did not move, remaining standing behind her so that she could not stand up without bumping into him unless she stepped forward and turned to face him.

"M'rain..."

"I do not wish to talk about it."

With a tired sigh P'puck plucked his fur from his pack and took it to the far side of the cave. Then, after filling his waterskin, he peeled off his waist-cloth and sank into the icy pool. "Yow, that is c'cold."

M'rain forced back a smile. Defiant, knowing it would arouse him and that he could do nothing about it, she took off her wrap and followed him in, stopping half-way as the icy water proved too cold for a single attempt. With arms wrapped tightly around her she eased the rest of the way into the water, feeling P'puck's eyes raking her skin.

The cold took away any thoughts of lingering in the pool. P'puck left first, and rinsed his cloth in the water to rid it of the dust. Then, just as M'rain began to climb out he reached for hers and rinsed it out as well. He handed it to her as she emerged. She took it without meeting his eyes and wrapped it on before wringing out her hair.

"M'rain..."

"No."

"We will need to talk at some time."

M'rain shook her head and reached for the fungi on the stone.

P'puck gave his head a rueful shake. "I think I will add stubbornness to the things that I like about you."

His soft tone and the strangeness of his comment softened some of the tension M'rain felt, but she kept it to herself, not ready to think about what it meant nor agreeing to talk.

They ate in silence and retired to their respective furs.

XXXXI

P'PUCK SLEPT LITTLE that night, his rest interspersed with
deep sighs and much tossing and turning. He could hear the
same from M'rain's side of the cave. Aside from the unresolved
conflict, the penetrating cold of the cave floor did nothing to
dry out their wraps.

P'puck could not help but think they would both be much more
comfortable if they shared body warmth. But, alas, that was not to be, at
least not this night. Several times throughout the night he glanced in
M'rain's direction, a few times even wondering if he ought to approach
her about it. In the end he held back, afraid such a move would only
alienate her further.

He half expected Glick to show up but that did not happen. He
could have used his advice.

It seemed time did not pass in the normal way within the caves. He
remembered M'rain explaining how long each of the rescue journeys
had taken and suspected they had already travelled much longer than a
normal day before coming to this cave. Judging by the intervals between
leaving torches behind and counting how many they had left he guessed
they had travelled well beyond a day, perhaps close to two. The dust was
half gone, which confirmed they had reached their half-way point.

It also meant that he had only just over a day to mend his
relationship with M'rain, or, he hoped, to move it forward. He went
over the kiss several times in his mind, both savouring the memory of

his own pleasure from it and trying to make sense of M'rain's reactions. He knew he had an impulsive streak. It had caused him no end of trouble growing up. Now he questioned whether the kiss had been a good idea, or whether he had been too rash.

In the end he rejected that notion because he was sure that M'rain had, at least at first, responded in kind. That thought kept him in a state of semi-arousal for the entire night. A part of him wished he were more experienced where women were concerned. That might have helped him understand her better. Again and again he went over the incident, minutely examining every nuance of M'rain's reactions as he remembered them: the surprise, the response of her body and mouth, as if she wanted more, and lastly the angry shove. The more he thought about it the more confused he became. Yet, in spite of it all, he had no regrets. He would not apologize. On the other hand he would not touch her again without her consent either. He had given his word and would keep it, difficult as that might be.

That left only talk. And M'rain had made it clear she had no desire to talk.

He heard another long sigh from M'rain's side of the cave and looked over to see her rising off her fur. When she began to roll it up he knew she had given up on sleep. He got up and did the same. When he brought it over to set beside their other supplies he spotted a fresh pile of fungi on the food rock.

M'rain still refused to meet his eyes so they ate and packed up in silence. P'puck tried a couple of times, with no luck, to open conversation. He knew better than to attempt anything physical. When M'rain headed for the entrance to the cave and glanced back to see if he followed, P'puck made a bold decision. He sat down. The look of surprise on M'rain's face was exactly what he wanted.

"M'rain, we need to talk."

"There is nothing to say. We must be leaving."

"No, not until we talk."

"Are you refusing to follow me?"

P'puck did is best to keep his voice neutral. He really did not want this to take a wrong turn. "No, but it is no good with this silence between us. We need to talk first." Then a thought struck him. "M'rain, are you thinking I will no longer follow your lead...that I will try to become the leader?"

M'rain did not answer but the change in her expression told P'puck he might be on the right track.

"I have promised to follow your lead on this trek. That will not change."

M'rain took two steps toward him but remained standing. "And then. What do you expect when this journey is complete?"

"M'rain, please sit down so we can talk...please."

She still hesitated, then slowly lowered her pack and came to sit facing him. Was that fear he saw in her eyes. Did she not know he would never hurt her? Or perhaps it was not hurt she feared. Perhaps it was being controlled, being made to fit into his people's ideas of what a woman ought to be. He had not thought this through before so now he took some time before speaking.

M'rain did not move or speak. Nor did her expression change. Her body remained rigid as she waited.

P'puck chose his words with great care. "M'rain, I have no experience with women. If I had, perhaps I would have known better what to do to let you know how I feel." That brought no change in M'rain's expression nor did her body lose its rigidity. Time to change his direction, then.

He would never know why, or indeed if, Glick had anything to do with it, but the conversation he had had with Glick the first time they met came back to him. "M'rain, I know you are not like other women...that you will never be like other women. Nor do I want you to be." He managed a smile. "That would be boring."

Did he imagine it or had M'rain relaxed ever so slightly?

"More than boring. I know you would not be happy if you were made to be that way and I truly want you to be happy...and I hope that I can help you be happy." That made the furrow between M'rain's eyebrows deepen but she still said nothing. He knew he must tread carefully.

"I, too, am not like other men. I do not long for the life that others of my people are content with." He sent her one of his irrepressible grins as he remembered some of his childhood mishaps. "I cannot count how many times I was in trouble for asking too many questions, for challenging the elders – even for entering the cave past the trees. You know that I was the one who left food for you, do you not...that time when you fell asleep.."

"Yes, I know."

Encouraged, P'puck pressed on. "I have always wanted adventure. I wanted to explore. But that was not possible, so I had only my dreams." He leaned toward M'rain. "Then you came. I knew...er...took it as a sign. There really was more...more than the life I knew."

He took a deep breath, searching for the right words. "When I saw you sleep there, all dirty and looking so small, I wanted to protect you. But at the same time I already sensed that would not work with you. Already, I understood that you were not like the women of my people. I did not know what to do. So I returned to my duties. But I could not forget you. And I knew that I would see you again, that we would be linked somehow."

He could tell that M'rain was listening intently, now. The anger had drained from her body, which, while still tense, had lost the air of fear.

"You returned, as I knew you must. And in the pool, when all the dirt washed away" His breath caught and he felt something akin to pain as he remembered. "...so beautiful. Your hair shone blue, like the feathers of the cawbird in sunlight...and your skin..." He reached out to stroke M'rain's hand then remembered his vow and pulled it back again. He looked at his empty hand and opened it toward M'rain in a gesture of helpless regret.

Was that recognition he saw in her eyes? Did she understand? "M'rain, from that moment my life was pledged to yours. I have thought of no one else. Only longed for the next time you returned and hoping that you would like me, too."

Was that a tear forming in M'rain's eye?

"P'puck, I do like you. But I can never mate. I can never live as others. You must give up this idea."

"I cannot. I could as soon give up breathing."

Her only response was a sad shake of her head. When she rose again and began to prepare to leave he asked, "Are you still angry?"

"No, only sad. We cannot be more than friends. You must make peace with that."

P'puck sensed that that had to be enough, for now.

XXXXII

T HE REST OF the trek remained uneventful. They followed the thread of light, left behind the new trail of blue dust, deposited torches at regular intervals and spoke, ate, and rested only as necessary.

P'puck expected no more. He still believed that they would be life mates one day, and did his best to convince himself he could be patient.

When a glow of light appeared ahead on the trail and M'rain picked up the pace he knew they had reached the last of the caves.

He held back a little when M'rain broke into a sprint to the entrance of the great outer cave then halted abruptly in the opening.

When he caught up with her he saw great tears rolling down her face. Yet she uttered not a sound, her gaze fixed on the horizon as if in a trance. Something told him not to speak. He simply came and stood beside her, waiting until she was ready.

The wait gave him the opportunity to observe a world no description and no amount of imagination could have helped him picture. M'rain had spoken of it in the circle back in his village, but that did not prepare him in the least for what he now beheld. Ahead, beyond a short distance where bare rock showed through swirls of sand, stretched endless rolling dunes and flat vistas of sand. The sun blazed hot in the sky making the sand shimmer, blurring the outlines of the sand mounds. Some areas looked like pools of water, but he remembered M'rain explaining that these were tricks of the eyes and that the water did not exist. Here and there he thought he spotted plants of some kind, though, to his eyes they looked scorched and stunted. Nowhere could he see any signs of life. No birds, no fourfooters, not even sixlegs.

M'rain spoke first, her voice low and full of emotion. "It is even more beautiful than I remembered."

The landscape bewildered P'puck and its barrenness awed him. The only thing he could think of in response was, "It is your home."

M'rain looked up at him, her expression a mix of sadness and longing. "No, but I know the way, now."

"Shall we go, then? You must be eager to see your people again."

"No, not yet. See how low the sun sits in the west? If we go now darkness will fall before we reach my village. Darkness brings out the night beasts and poisonous crawlers and stinging hoppers. It is dangerous to travel after dark. We must wait until the morning."

M'rain shook her waterskin. "We need to return to the last pool to make certain our skins are full. We will need all the water we can carry. There will be none along the way."

Her remark made P'puck think she would turn back. Instead she sat down, cross-legged, just within the edge of the shade, and drank in the view in front of them.

P'puck sat down beside her, waiting and watching as she did. He sensed that something had changed in himself and wondered if this was a sign of maturity. His feeling of urgency, the impulse to act without thinking, had stilled, at least for the time being. He found he was content to sit beside M'rain, trying to see what she saw in this barren land. It did have a stark beauty, he decided. He wondered, too, about the dangers M'rain referred to. But he held his tongue and tried to picture her world as M'rain saw it.

A low murmur drew him out of his reverie.

"This is where it all began...where I changed."

P'puck struggled to find the best way to ask what he wanted to know. "What do you mean, changed? How have you changed? I do not think you are speaking of Glick's magic."

"No, not the magic. That set me on my journey but the change was mine alone." She paused. "And now I belong to no people. Not mine and not yours."

Her voice was so low that P'puck had to strain to make out her words, though he heard the pain in them. He thought about her answer and wondered how he could help her see that she need not be alone, that he would be there with her. No solutions came as the sun sank further and the air began to cool. When the sky turned crimson, and the sun became half a ball on the horizon, he voiced his thought aloud. "Perhaps that is why Glick put us together. So neither of us need be alone."

She did not let on she heard him but P'puck knew she had not missed it. He would wait for her to respond in her own time. He had not really expected her to at this moment. But since she did not disagree he sensed that she knew there was truth in it. It was enough for now.

XXXIII

THE NEXT MORNING they set out as soon as the sun rose high enough to send the predators burrowing away from the heat, or so M'rain said. He saw nothing moving.

He watched her closely and listened to everything she told him, doing his best to remember it all. This world was alien to him and he had a lot to learn.

"Now I have an idea of how strange you must have felt when you first came to our village."

"Yes, it was a lonely feeling. The worst was not knowing how I was expected to behave. But I looked for things that were the same and soon began to see that your people act a lot like mine." She had not looked at him but her tone was more relaxed and he thought he had detected a ghost of a smile at his observation.

He watched her keep her eyes roving over their surroundings, much as the hunters from his village did when searching for game. At least she had not asked him to hunt. He wondered what she would think of him when she learned he had such poor aim with a spear.

"Here." M'rain bent over and began to dig with the stick she had picked up at the mouth of the cave before leaving. "This is a root we cook in the pot. Help me dig it out."

He began to tug at more of the root as it was revealed below the sand but she soon stopped him.

"That is enough. If we take it all there will be none the next time we gather. We must respect the land and the things that grow in it or it will not provide us with the food we need."

"Oh, like the things we gather in the forest."

"Yes, like that. I know your people grow things but we cannot do that and must rely on what we can gather or hunt."

The day proceeded in much that fashion. M'rain showed him how to know which fruits could be picked from the prickle plant and how to break them off without getting the spines in his skin. "These are sweet. This is the right time to harvest them."

At one point P'puck spotted something moving in the sand. When he made to go after it M'rain put out her hand to stop him. "That snake is venomous. And we cannot eat its meat so we do not pursue it."

When M'rain spotted a small mound of sand that looked oddly out of place she poked the stick – the very one she had dropped when she had been captured, into the dark side of the mound. A small animal darted out, which M'rain killed with a clean blow from the heavy end of the stick. P'puck marveled at her skill.

"Meat for the pot tonight." She held the animal up by the tail with a proud grin.

P'puck gave the thing a dubious look. "Are all your animals so small? There is not much meat on that. That would not feed even one in my village."

M'rain laughed. It was the first time P'puck had heard her do so and the sound delighted him.

"We must take our bounty where we find it. This land is demanding and we are grateful for any food we can find. But sometimes the hunters catch a running bird. The running bird is very big, taller than you. We feast when that happens. It is my favourite food. We dry some of its meat to keep for the lean season."

"I hope I get to see one of those birds. From the name I think they must be hard to catch."

"Yes, they have great, long legs and run very fast. The hunters must work together to prevent them from getting away. It takes a lot of skill. And the bird has a huge beak that can injure a hunter. So the one who goes in close for the kill must be careful not to be struck or bitten. Sometimes the bird strikes out in an effort to escape and injures one of the hunters in the circle. When that happens they come back empty handed."

By the time the sun reached high in the sky both P'puck and M'rain carried a bundle of fibrous roots, prickle fruits, and M'rain's lone animal.

"Do you see that dark line on the horizon?" M'rain pointed far ahead.

P'puck strained to see but the shimmer of heat from the sand made it difficult. "I think I see something but I am not certain."

"It will become clearer. Those are the small caves where we store some food and occasionally take shelter from the rains."

"Oh, does it rain here?"

"Yes, but only for a short season. When the rains come many plants grow and the land is covered in bright blooms. The animals do not hide as deep in the sand. The hunt is always good and we feast on the plants and fruits we gather. Then the land goes to sleep again, as you see it now."

P'puck strained again in the direction M'rain indicated. "I think I see something, now."

M'rain looked up and followed his gaze. "Yes, we will be there very soon." She stopped and P'puck watched the play of emotion on her face: joy, doubt, hope, and finally trepidation.

"Are you afraid to return? Do you fear they will not welcome you?"

She gave a slow nod, her eyes remaining fixed on the grey shadow on the horizon. "I am not the same as I was."

P'puck thought about that a moment before responding. "No, you are not as you were when you left. You have become stronger and wiser."

"I no longer belong here. Perhaps I never truly did. Perhaps that is why I always went too far when out gathering."

P'puck nodded agreement. "Neither of us belongs where we came from any more. Glick called us travellers. Perhaps we are not meant to remain in one place."

She turned to him and met his gaze, her eyes sad and her voice low. "Perhaps."

P'puck knew they had been spotted long before he saw anyone because the entire village waited in a ragged line facing their direction. "They must think it strange that only one left and two return." A thought struck him. "Will they fear us? Will they harm us?"

"They will think us strange, especially you, as they have never seen you before, but no, they will not harm us. Those are the children, the women, and the old men who can no longer hunt. The hunters will not return until the sun begins to sink."

Long before P'puck could distinguish one person from another a single figure broke from the group and began to run in their direction. P'puck made to stand in front of M'rain to protect her but she pushed him aside and ran to meet the approaching figure, arms outstretched. "N'iri."

"M'rain."

The two women jumped up and down, hugging and squealing each other's names. Their joy at the reunion made P'puck smile as he approached. He waited beside them until M'rain noticed him. "N'iri this is P'puck. A friend."

"N'iri looked him over warily, then reached out and took his hand in both of her own, bowing her head. "Welcome, friend."

"N'iri is my beloved sister."

P'puck sent M'rain a questioning look and at her slight nod of encouragement returned the gesture. When he saw M'rain smile and nod he knew he had done the correct thing. This must be how her people greeted each other. He recalled what M'rain had said about observing how his people acted so she would know what to do and vowed to pay close attention.

M'rain held up the results of her foraging. "We come with food for the pot."

P'puck held out his additions for N'iri as well.

"I thank you. And welcome you both to our fire."

The travellers followed N'iri into the village where the people still waited, watching them approach. No one seemed eager to return to their duties.

N'iri held up her bounty as she came within hearing. "Let us welcome the weary and their gifts."

An old woman accepted the offerings and gave the formal head bow. "Welcome to our fire. We will feast tonight."

When pandemonium broke out P'puck understood that the formalities had been completed and the elder woman had deemed the pair harmless. Soon children tugged at his hands to propel him toward the circle of round huts which ringed the central fire, all of them directing eager questions at him at once. M'rain fared no better and he reveled in her laughter as they pulled her along.

Soon small gourds filled with a fragrant brew were pressed into their hands. When P'puck sent M'rain an inquiring glance she said, "Tea," and took a sip.

P'puck found it more pungent than the teas he was accustomed to but drank it down. He feared that to refuse would be seen as an insult to his hosts. By the last sip he no longer minded the acrid taste. It sent warmth into his belly that made him forget its bitterness and enjoy its effect.

In the chaos he became separated from M'rain and when he spotted her she was in deep conversation with N'iri. He watched N'iri reach for a plump infant and hand the child to M'rain, whose face lit up with joy.

He did not have time to enjoy the sight, however, as the children tugged at him to show him the rest of the village.

XXXXIV

N'IRI MY HEART is sad that I was not here for the birth and naming ceremony of your daughter." M'rain held the pudgy child and jounced her to make her smile. "I did have a dream, at least I think that is what it was. It showed me the birth."

"We missed you and believed a stinger or snake had killed you. We mourned your death." N'iri looked confused then smiled. "But now you have returned to us."

"Who named your daughter when I did not return?"

"We had no time to search for a better name parent so the duty fell to Mama. It was difficult for her. She wept for your loss at the same time she felt joy at the naming. I hope it will not cause M'rani's mind to become confused as she grows."

M'rain's eyes opened wide. "You named her for me – Little M'rain?"

"Yes, M'rani, so we would not forget you."

Tears sprang to M'rain's eyes. "I thought you might be angry, would want to forget me when I was not there to help with the birth."

"No one blamed you."

"And now – now you see I am not dead?"

"Now M'rani will know her aunt." N'iri gave M'rain a quick squeeze before taking back the squirming infant and putting her to her breast.

"N'iri, I have still not undergone the rite of womanhood." That had troubled M'rain, as she knew her people would not view her as an adult until the rite had been completed.

N'iri's hand flew to her mouth. "You must. Else you will never be able to take a mate, never be able to birth a child."

M'rain gave her a sad nod. "I do not know if I will ever wish to take a mate. But I do want to take the rite. I need the others to know I am an adult, a woman, not a child."

"We must consult with the elders."

The fire burned late, even to the dawn. Only the infants and children slept that night, mostly on mothers' or older siblings' laps.

M'rain felt that without the proof of P'puck sitting beside her they would not have believed the story the pair told.

The biggest barrier to acceptance of their tale was Glick. They believed in magic but had not seen any for time upon time. They had come to believe that magic only existed in the far desert, that it brought the rains that made the desert bloom and then went to sleep again. This was different - a real lizard, one who talked and told people what to do. Only the oldest sage, the one who kept the lore of the people and told the stories, did not shake his head in wonder.

Has he seen the magic? He nodded when we mentioned the snake that guards this village.

The air of doubt changed when M'rain brought out the honey, adding a small amount to the tea the villagers drank in copious amounts. The tea contained something that helped keep them awake.

M'rain held most of the honey back explaining that it would make the morning's boiled p'ona sweet and wonderful. When M'rain slipped the gourd back into its travel sack and tied it shut even the faces of the adults fell. Only the eldest expressed no desire for more of the sweet stuff. *Perhaps they are too old to enjoy something so unfamiliar.*

When P'puck cut up the crisp-fruits and passed them around, however, M'rain noticed that even the old ones looked like they enjoyed it. Perhaps the taste was more like the fruits they knew.

With the first hint of dawn the questions slowed and finally stopped. The women rose to begin the preparation of the morning meal. M'rain fell into the familiar rhythm with them. When the p'ona was almost ready she added a generous dollop of honey. The delighted grin from the women who got to taste it told her all she needed to know.

"Here," she said, handing the remaining sweet confection to the oldest crone, "There is enough for several more meals. I trust you will know how to make it last."

The old woman gave her the formal head bow of thanks and walked away to store the honey in her hut.

M'rain sought P'puck out after the meal to make certain he did not leave with the men to hunt. He did not have their training and skill. Not only would he hinder the hunt but M'rain suspected his lack of skill in their methods would cause him embarrassment.

"It is best if you remain in the village. I remember there was much to learn when I came to yours."

Already P'puck had several children around him. M'rain addressed one of the older ones. "B'ran, I leave P'puck in your care. Please help him learn how we do things here. Show him how we get clean, how we make our baskets. If one of the women needs help let her know P'puck wants to learn and will not feel insulted."

The lad gave her a proud nod and took P'puck by the hand. "Come, we will see the cleaning place first."

"Oh." M'rain stopped the pair. "P'puck, I intend to request the rite of womanhood. I need to do this this if the others are to respect my words. We have not yet spoken of the return and the future of the caves. Please do not until I am accepted as a woman."

"I will say nothing until you are ready." With that P'puck turned back to the boy waiting to lead him away.

XXXXV

THE ELDERS READILY agreed that M'rain must undergo the rite of womanhood. When they learned that P'puck had passed his rite of manhood they seemed relieved. M'rain wondered if they were uncomfortable with the idea that a strange person would become one of them instead of one of his own people if they performed the rite with him. Or perhaps they did not want to negotiate with a "child".

M'rain spent the next day in one of the small caves with three of the elder women. The women massaged her with oil from the fat of the running bird, made fragrant with petals from blossoms gathered in the rainy season. While they did so they chanted in low, rhythmic tones, ritual words explaining what it means to become a woman, to be a mate, to give birth, and even to die. They laid hands on her female parts, asking for her womb to become fruitful, for milk to flow from her breasts, and asking for a man to mate with her who would treat her with respect.

She ate nothing, and was allowed only a special tea reserved for the rite. It made her mildly dizzy. After a time the chanting began to sound like it emanated from the walls and floor of the cave. The women became shadow-like, almost as if they were no longer solid. They seemed to sway as they chanted. They repeated the anointing several times, chanting all the while until the voices became a drone she could no longer distinguish. She found it more and more difficult to focus.

Her body was no longer her own but merged into all the others. They were one. They were woman.

She saw, as though from afar, her body being laid on a mat of woven running bird feathers. She watched the eldest woman spread her legs and hold a writhing snake, the symbol of fertility, in front of her womb. It wove its head back and forth until it slowly uncoiled and entered her. When the elder pulled on its tail and drew it back out its head was covered in blood. The elder woman let it go and M'rain thought she saw it slither away toward the entrance of the cave. After more chanting in a more jubilant rhythm the two women left her alone on the blanket of feathers where she fell asleep.

When M'rain once more became aware of where she was the sun had begun to sink, leaving long shadows in the cave. She sat up slowly, trying to remember what had happened. Her head ached but she detected no other pain.

The memory of the snake came back to her and she scanned the cave for it. Near the entrance she spotted a coiled stick with a head carved to resemble a snake. She crawled over to examine it and discovered blood on the end that represented the head. *Did it come alive? Did it enter me and open my womb so it can quicken?* She went back to the feather bed she had lain on and discovered a small spot of blood in its centre. A glance at her thighs showed some there as well. But she felt no pain and the bleeding had stopped.

When she looked around again she discovered her wrap neatly folded beside the entrance of the cave. She wound it on and stuck her head out of the cave. The aromas from the cookpot told her it was almost time for the evening meal. The ritual was over. She was now a woman.

Like so many before her, she rose out of the cave and made her way back to the circle and the village fire. Each person she passed gave her the head bow of greeting and placed their right hand on their abdomen. "Welcome to the circle of women. May your womb bear many fruit." She returned each greeting with the formal head bow of her own. "I thank you for your welcome."

When she had received the formal greeting from everyone around the fire and shared the formal response with each woman there she sought out P'puck.

Before speaking he gave her the ritual greeting from his village, a bow and a gesture that made to touch her breasts and womb without actually making contact. "So you are a woman, now? Aside from the others listening to you as an adult has anything else changed?"

"No. I have a headache from the tea they made me drink and I am hungry. That is all."

"Good. I feared you would act differently."

The relief on P'puck's face made M'rain laugh. Then, serious again, she told him, "This night is meant to be a celebration. There will be feasting and a brew similar to the happy drink your people make. I fear we will not sleep again this night."

P'puck rolled his eyes in feigned dismay followed by a laugh. She answered with one of her own before resuming her serious mien. "But this means we may still not approach the elders about our plans. I will request to meet with them after the morning meal tomorrow. I think you and I must speak alone before then to plan what we will say. They will not want to hear from me because I am a woman – but they must."

"I will be ready when you wish it. You will know best how to speak to your elders and I will do as you ask." He gave her another long look. "There is something different about you. I cannot put it into words but something has changed."

"Did you feel different after your manhood hunt? Did it change you?"

"Nooo, not truly...and yet...The biggest change was that I left behind my younger friends and hunted with the men. I was treated as one of them, not someone still in need of training."

"I suspect it is much the same for me. I am still only M'rain."

He continued to study her as if looking for something elusive. "Yes, still M'rain but..."

A question had niggled at P'puck since they arrived so he decided to ask M'rain about it now, while they could speak alone. "M'rain, when we arrived we were greeted as visitors. You never mentioned outsiders or others not from your village. Are there others?"

"Oh. Yes, there is one other village about a day's walk from here. When our numbers became too many the food became scarcer so a group agreed to break away and set up another village outside our range for hunting and gathering. We meet together once every year right after the rainy season, when food is plentiful and the sun does not burn so hot. Many matings happen during those gatherings."

"I think I understand. So, when food becomes scarce some of you move away and hunt a new range? That is different from us. We have only the one village but food has never been a problem so there is no need for us to leave."

"I thought that was so when I heard your story-teller recite the tale of your people. He did not mention any others, except the ones who entered the caves. When you listen to our storyteller he will include the time of the dividing."

"So that is why your village is so small. Not everyone is here."

"Yes." M'rain changed the subject. "I have some time now. Let us sit behind my sister's hut where there is shade and talk of what we will say to the elders."

XXXXVI

A S THEY HAD agreed, M'rain took the lead in the meeting. At first the elders balked at this. Women here did not ask for meetings. If they had something to discuss they would ask a mate or parent to approach the elders with their concern.

This was different in P'puck's village. There women could ask to speak on their own. M'rain knew this and had explained to P'puck that this was why it was so important that she be the speaker. She wanted to establish that her role was not like that of other women.

"I need to show them that I do not need a man to speak for me. I need them to see that I am different, that I am a leader in spite of my sex." She half expected P'puck would side with the men. When he readily agreed with her she was surprised, pleasantly so.

"I will only speak if I have something to add, or if they need clarification...or if you ask me to."

"Even if questions are directed at you, let me speak first, unless the question is about you or your people."

"Yes, that makes sense. You are the leader and if I answer they will doubt it. I will defer to you in everything."

"Good. I know this is not normal, even among your people, so I thank you."

It looked like P'puck was about to quip something back, as he sent her a mischievous grin, but then he seemed to think the better of it and held his tongue. Instead he grew serious again. "I can see how important

239

this is, M'rain."

When M'rain requested to be allowed to speak the elders resisted. P'puck waited a moment or two then stepped in, saying, "M'rain has been chosen by the One Who Gives. I have heard Glick speak of it and I know this to be true. I follow her. She is all she claims to be. I ask you to reconsider."

M'rain wondered if they would reject him as well, as he was not of this people, but they agreed, although with a show of some reluctance and suspicion. Perhaps it was curiosity that drove the decision. *Perhaps it is a test to see if he really does follow me.*

While M'rain explained their purpose, the proposal of ongoing trade possibilities, and the future of the role of travellers, the elders sat in stony silence, refusing to meet her eyes. Now and then one would glance at P'puck, who remained silent.

A long pause ensued when she finished her presentation. Then, when P'puck still did not speak they began their questions. Almost every one was directed at P'puck, especially in the beginning. Each time, P'puck would turn to look at M'rain with an expectant expression, waiting for her to answer.

Eventually one elder, R'ebb, asked P'puck in a sarcastic tone, "So do all the men of your people follow women? Where is your manhood?"

M'rain almost gasped at the insult. P'puck was a guest. Guests were always treated with respect and hospitality. But when she looked at P'puck he seemed unperturbed and simply smiled before answering.

"Among my people men do lead. Our elders are all men. But our women may speak in the councils. They are given much respect and their opinions are valued. When important decisions must be made they add their wisdom and their voices to the consultation. It has caused no lack of manhood among the men."

P'puck paused a moment but before the elder could challenge him further he added, "I have agreed to follow M'rain, not only because Glick has told me I must, but because she has accomplished what no other person in our long story has done. She has traversed the caves alone without getting lost. She brought our lost people back to us. She has shown that she can be a leader, that she is strong, intelligent, and fearless. I follow her because she has the knowledge required for this mission. M'rain has the greater experience of the caves. It makes sense to me that I should follow and she should lead on this journey."

M'rain could have hugged him at that moment. She had to restrain herself from commenting, waiting instead, for the elders to take in what P'puck had told them.

When R'ebb looked stuck for words, T'ren, who M'rain knew to be less rigid, turned to M'rain and asked, "What is it you need from us?"

Victory! M'rain had to reign in her relief and joy. "We ask nothing at this time other than enough supplies for the return journey. P'puck's people sent gifts. Do you wish to send something in return?"

The elders looked at each other. When they seemed at a loss M'rain added, "As I explained, we intend to establish trade, to exchange between our peoples those things we do not have, to share those things we have more of than we need."

"We do not have more of anything than we need." R'ebb retorted, once more attempting to take the lead. "Each dry season we come close to starvation. We have nothing to share."

"I understand. However, the goods sent from P'puck's village to this one will replace what you send to them. Both peoples will benefit. You will have more, not less. P'puck's people have plenty and are generous."

T'ren's head bobbed in a thoughtful nod. "We have other things besides food."

"Yes." M'rain had given this a good deal of thought already but wanted the idea to seem to come from the elders. "The seed ornaments we make are beautiful, as are the running bird feathers. I think that the feathers, especially, will make good gifts. P'puck's people do not have anything like that. All their birds are much smaller."

Now P'puck did choose to speak up. "I agree. And our people have many things made of wood, such as large gourds. I have seen that trees are scarce here. Perhaps items made from wood will be welcome."

M'rain nodded, grateful he had chosen this point in their

negotiations to add to their bargaining. It would demonstrate that, while she led, he was not constrained to silence, much like the reverse among her people.

Now B'lar, the third elder, joined in. "The feathers are prized for their beauty and for what can be made with them. We have plenty. I suggest we begin with those, perhaps even a few items we make from them, to show how we use them." He directed his comment directly to R'ebb and T'ren. "And they are light-weight to carry."

T'ren nodded immediately. R'ebb sent the pair a scorching glare that told M'rain he felt betrayed.

M'rain thought she recognized the moment when R'ebb decided further protest would not change anything. Some of the rigidity left his body, though he kept his mouth set in a disapproving line. He said nothing more.

M'rain turned to P'puck. "Do you think your people will be happy with a gift of running bird feathers? You know them better than I." She deliberately deferred to P'puck to show the elders that they acted together and that P'puck also had influence.

"Oh, yes, I think they will like them very much. And I have seen the ornaments made of small seeds and feathers that M'rain spoke of. They are beautiful. If you have any to spare I can think of several women who will want to wear them."

R'ebb finally deigned to speak. "That is acceptable. What will you bring in return?"

Good. Negotiations are turning in the direction I hoped. The decision to trade has been made. Aloud, M'rain said, "P'puck, you will know better than I what your people will wish to send. What do you suggest?

Instead of listing items P'puck turned to the elders and asked, "What will your people desire more - food items, useful tools, or items that simply have beauty?"

He is a born negotiator. M'rain nodded her encouragement at P'puck. "That is an excellent question."

B'lar was first to answer. "We are early in our experience with your people, P'puck. Perhaps it is too soon to decide what we would like most. We welcome any suggestions."

A period of lively discussion ensued. In the end they all agreed that P'puck and M'rain would return with gifts of running bird feathers and seed jewelry. They would speak with the elders in P'puck's village. Then they would bring back a variety of items and see what M'rain's people liked most. To add a token of goodwill the elders agreed to add a sample of dried running bird meat to the gifts the pair would take.

When M'rain and P'puck could once more speak alone M'rain said, "P'puck, I think you were born to this. You are a skilled negotiator. I thank you."

"I did not overstep, then?"

"No, you showed them how we work together. Yes, I lead, but you do more than follow. It was well done."

P'puck beamed before the smile grew into one of his infectious grins.

Laughing, M'rain said, "Do not let your chest swell too much. It might burst."

P'puck blushed making M'rain laugh even more.

That night, as she lay trying to get some sleep, M'rain went over the events of the day and smiled. That night she dreamed of dancing with P'puck while all the members of both peoples clapped and beat the ground in rhythm as they watched. It was a happy dream.

XXXXVII

HEY STAYED TWO more days in the desert with M'rain's people. Some of that time was spent collecting the supplies they needed and packing the gifts they would carry back.

M'rain spent some time with her mother, N'iri, and her little niece. With the time remaining M'rain took P'puck to the small caves and showed him how they stored food against the lean season. She explained more of her peoples' customs and how those fit into their daily routines. She taught him as much as she had time for, showing him a few of the skills the children learned at the knees of their parents.

"Now I understand why you had such trouble weaving the willow basket." P'puck laughed as he tried to imitate how one of the children had shown him to carve out one of the small drinking gourds. He gave up with a yelp and a laugh when the sharp stone blade slipped and cut the palm of his hand. "I think some things are learned more easily when we are young."

M'rain took his hand to examine the wound. "Only a shallow cut. Let me put some heal-fluff on it. That will prevent festering."

"There is no need. It will heal on its own."

"No, we have so little water here that we cannot wash it as your people do. The heal-fluff is a wise precaution."

P'puck took it as a good omen that she did not let go of his two fingers as she led him to the hut where the healer-woman kept her stores. "Wait here." She let go of him outside the door and went inside, coming out with a wad of strange-looking dried stuff, like, but not like, the seed fluff of the blow-away plant that grew around his village. Breaking off a small wad she pressed this onto the cut. "Hold that there until we reach our packs. I want to add the rest of this to my bundle. It may prove useful."

When they reached the packs she stuffed the fluff into hers. "You can take that off, now. See if it has stopped bleeding. If not press it a bit longer."

P'puck did as she bade him and held his palm out for her to see. "The bleeding has stopped."

"Good, then you may throw that bit onto the central fire. We do not leave it on the ground because the blood attracts unwelcome pests. Stinger ants can give a painful bite."

"Yes, that is why our women always wash our food pots carefully before sleeping at home – except the drinking gourds after a late night of celebration. Sometimes the women find sixlegs inside them in the morning."

"And why we scour our food bowls with sand outside the village to remove any fat or food bits that cling."

"So many things are the same, yet different."

"Yes. It helps me understand that we are one people."

"And always have been."

M'rain raised her head from checking her pack to smile at him. "And always will be. And we, the travellers and those who come after us, will keep it so. We are the first." Her voice was low and held a tone of awe. "P'puck, do you see how important this is to both our peoples?"

"I do."

The simple words and the proud look that accompanied it warmed M'rain. She liked this young man more and more. They shared something no one else could understand. For the first time since her capture M'rain began to believe she was not alone, that she had a true friend who understood. She fussed with her pack more than necessary as she allowed that realization to settle. What did it mean? With no ready answer she gave herself a tiny shake and rose to strap on her burden.

"Are you ready?"

"Yes, let us go home."

M'rain was about to retort that it was not her home but the eagerness on P'puck's face stopped her. She would have to think more about what home really meant and how her new understanding of P'puck might change the way they related to each other. Certainly they already had a greater ease between them. She was glad, now, for his company. And she felt less need to be in control of their mission. This part of their journey looked much more promising than the first leg had been.

She noticed P'puck scanning the cave floor.

"Look, there is our blue dust trail." His head rose as he peered into the darkness ahead and gave a low whistle. "I still have the magic sight."

"Good, we will not need the torches then and can leave them for others."

P'puck strode with confidence into the darkness, not waiting for her to lead the way. M'rain found that she did not mind.

Their return journey seemed to take much longer. M'rain suspected Glick had something to do with that, or perhaps the first one had been shortened by him and this pass was more what travellers could expect.

"I think so, too," said P'puck when she mentioned it. "I think this will be more normal. It feels right to me, this pace."

"Here is the cave we stayed in that last night. It seems much farther away than I remember."

"I agree. And I am hungry. Shall we stop here to eat?"

When they had set their packs down P'puck looked around. "It appears Glick meant it when he said he would provide no more food. We will need to be satisfied with travel fare." He made a sad face. "No honey p'pone cakes." Then he grinned, eliciting a return smile from M'rain.

"I am afraid you are correct." M'rain grew thoughtful. "I wonder if Glick is still watching us. You remember what he said...about ending and rest."

"I remember...I hope he did not mean to leave so soon."

247

"I was so angry, before, and wanted to be rid of him...and now..."

They ate in silence, neither wanting to speak of Glick's demise. Finally, P'puck, in a much more optimistic tone announced, "He cannot be gone yet. We still need to set the light trail from the cave of dust back to the village."

Feeling much lighter M'rain nodded. "You are correct. We will still need to lay that trail."

They filled the time trudging to the cave in which they would spend the night with light banter. M'rain enjoyed P'puck's humour and found herself not noticing how heavy her pack felt or how tired her legs became. Not until they reached the sleeping cave and she set down her pack again did she feel the aching of exhaustion.

"Oh, I am glad to set this down." She rolled her shoulders and stretched her back in all directions grinning at P'puck as he mirrored her. "This is almost a dance."

"Indeed."

They laughed in unison.

◇◇◇

When they had eaten and spread their furs on the floor to sleep P'puck gave M'rain a long look, hesitating before he spoke. "You remember how cold this cave is? How neither of us slept the last time and we could not get warm?"

"I remember."

"I suggest we share body warmth and furs..."

M'rain looked away and for an endless moment P'puck feared he had overstepped again.

When she turned back and when she met his eyes once more they were full of doubt but not angry. "I trust you so, yes, we will share warmth."

She looked like she wanted to say more but lowered her gaze again and kept silent.

P'puck knew better than to press her for what she had wanted to say. This was a small victory and he had no wish to lose the ground he felt he was gaining. Instead he retrieved his fur and laid it over hers. His hand stole to the small pouch he kept tied around his waist to reassure himself that what he carried in it remained safe. *One day. One day soon I will present this to her.* He gave the small sac a squeeze and let it go.

When the two lay down between the two furs they remained rigid, flat on their backs, side by side.

"This is no better than sleeping apart." P'puck turned on his side facing M'rain. "If we are to be warm this night we must wrap around each other." He could feel M'rain stiffen. "M'rain if you turn your back to me I will fold myself against it and wrap an arm around you. You will be warmest but I do not mind a cold back."

To P'puck's relief M'rain slowly turned her back to him, though she said not a word. He spooned in behind her, wrapped the fur around them both, and tucked his arm underneath and over hers, taking care not to clutch anything other than the edge of the furs. "Is this all right?"

A whispered, "Yes," was her only answer.

P'puck did not know when he fell asleep. It had taken some time as he remained careful about how he touched M'rain. The trust she had shown was fragile, he knew, and he had no desire to test it.

To his great surprise, and delight, when he woke he found that M'rain had also fallen asleep. Somehow, his hand had become entwined with hers and now lay tucked under her chin, as if she had tugged it there thinking it was the fur.

He hardly dared to breathe lest she waken. Would the day ever come when she would do this waking, when she would receive comfort from his touch? For now he reveled in the scent of her and did his best not to sneeze as her hair tickled his nose.

When he twitched his face involuntarily to get the hair away M'rain moved and gave a deep sigh. She began to turn in his direction, then jerked away and sat up.

The spell had broken.

P'puck made a hasty decision to approach her with humour. "So, sleepy bones. I thought you would never wake. Although I am grateful that you do not snore." He rolled over on his back, folded his hands behind his head and gave her one of his best grins.

M'rain had, by this time, already risen to standing. It seemed his tactic worked because she gave him a hesitant glance, then placed her hands on her hips and quipped, "I am already up, as you can see. It is you must get your lazy bones upright and get to work." With that she gave his fur, the one on top, an exaggerated tug so that it came free. "Up, or I will throw cold water on you as well."

P'puck rolled onto his side and onto his feet in one fluid motion, taking M'rain's fur with him as he did so. He handed it to her and reached to take his back from her. "What, no morning meal before work?"

M'rain had already begun to roll her fur. As she tied it to her pack she sent him a sideways look. "We can eat as we walk. It is only travel food." A rueful smile followed her comment as she stood up. "I do miss Glick's magic food."

"As do I. I do hope he speaks to us again. I have some questions for him, ones I did not think of until after we met your people, questions about the duties of travellers and where the next ones will be found, how they must be trained. There is so much we still need to learn."

"I think Glick will come to us only if *he* thinks we need it."

"Hmmm," P'puck answered around a mouthful of dried meat as they exited the chamber, "I fear you are correct."

XXXXVIII

P'PUCK WAS HAPPY to follow behind M'rain for the first leg of the day's trek. He enjoyed watching the sway of her hips with each step, her slender legs, and her hair. It hung loose unlike the traditional braid of his people, and flowed side to side in the opposite direction to her hips, like water in a meandering brook. It hung almost to her waist in a shining fall and gleamed even with his dim sight. He imagined how it would feel as he ran his fingers through it and drew in a deep breath remembering the scent of it as they lay together. The rhythm of her steps echoed his memory of the drums during the mating ceremonies at home, the rhythm of hearts beating faster and faster. The thoughts awakened his arousal. Would she ever accept him?

When he heard M'rain call his name it pulled him out of his reverie with a start.

"P'puck, did you hear me? I asked if you thought we had walked a long time without coming to our next resting cave?"

"I am sorry. I was...thinking."

"Thinking? About what?"

P'puck hoped that their dim magic sight did not allow her to notice his blush and he shifted his burden to hide his arousal. Instead of answering her question he said, "I am getting hungry. Yes, it does seem much longer than last time."

"Now I am certain Glick has something to do with this. The journey to my people was much too short."

251

They both exclaimed at the same time, as they spotted a new thread of light leading away from their blue dust trail.

"Oh, what is this?" P'puck strode to where the new trail began. "I do not remember leaving half a sack of dust behind, do you?"

"No. This must be Glick's doing again."

"Well, I suppose we are meant to create a new trail with it. I wonder where it will lead?"

The trail proved a short one. The pair soon found themselves in an unfamiliar cave. This one had a large hole in the roof which let in some light. A trickle of water ran out of a crevice at the far end and created a shallow pool there. Around the pool, where the ground was touched by sunlight, grew a variety of mosses and lichens. One patch of fungus, off to the side and appearing out of place, looked tantalizingly familiar.

M'rain had set down her pack and now went to examine it. "I wonder if this is the magic food Glick leaves."

"Do not eat it. Most of those things are poisonous. We are not familiar with this one."

"It will not be here next time. You may eat it."

"Glick!"

"Hmph. Honey p'pone cakes, indeed. It is well honey is not more plentiful. You would grow fat."

Laughing, P'puck plopped down cross-legged in front of the lizard. *"Why, Glick, we are happy to see you, too."*

"Hmph."

M'rain called over her shoulder as she picked up a handful of the fungi. *"Thank you Glick. And I am happy to see you, too...I think."* With her hands full she came to sit beside P'puck and handed him a share.

P'puck popped a piece into his mouth, closed his eyes, allowed himself a moment of honeyed bliss, chewed, and swallowed. Chewing on the second piece he said, *"Glick, I will surely miss these gifts when you leave us."*

"Do not rush me. I am not gone yet."

"Good, because we have more questions for you regarding our mission and the role of future travellers." P'puck popped another bite into his mouth.

"But first," M'rain said, *"are you changing time? And how did this sack of dust come here, and this new path?"*

"Still so impatient, M'rain?"

"Well?"

"Very well. Yes, I made the journey out shorter – or to seem shorter. This is the normal pace. And it is well I left food here for you. You did not bring enough and would be hungry before you reach the other end."

P'puck had heard the impatience and annoyance in M'rain's voice. He did not share that mood and chided her gently. *"I am grateful for Glick's presence. Look at the food he has brought us. Have you forgotten that we feared we would not speak with him again?"* He hoped his smile would soften his words. When she made a wry face at him he took it as a good omen.

"M'rain does not like to be told what to do."

"I had noticed, Glick."

"Good. You will need to remember it."

M'rain's only response was to glare at them both, followed by a shake of her head that could not hide the mirth behind it.

"Ask your questions." Glick had become, once more, the taciturn guardian.

The pair learned much more about their roles as travellers, and as teachers of the ones who would follow in their footsteps.

"Two people, sometimes both men, other times both women, but usually one of each, will be marked as travellers. The elders, and indeed, many of the people, will see, as these children grow, that they are different, that they possess the special qualities needed for this task. Once they reach their age of adulthood and undergo the rites they will begin to accompany the current traveller pair and learn the skills needed to become travellers. They will learn how to make sure there are always torches available and how to replenish the dust trails so they do not fade. In this way there will always be two to take the place of the previous pair when they become too old to travel."

P'puck could not stop himself. He had to ask, though he knew better than to make it personal. *"You say it will usually be a man and a woman. Does this mean they will be mates?"*

M'rain stiffened at the question.

"Often. Not always."

"But what happens if they have children?" P'puck pressed on. *"Or do they not bear children if they become travellers?"*

"They do. The children travel with them for the early years. When they are ready they are left behind with others the travellers trust in the villages, to be trained in the ways of the people."

M'rain looked upset but did not ask more on the question about mating or children. *"Will there always be one from each of our peoples?"*

"No. You, as the first travellers, will train a pair from each of your peoples. Sometimes they will decide to work as one from each. Others, they will travel with someone from their own people. But they will travel in pairs, always four travellers. They will decide how to pair up."

After a pause Glick continued. *"Over time your peoples will mingle. Some will mate with someone from the other side. In time the only difference will be where they choose to live. Do not forget you were one people long ago and so must be again."* Glick gave them one of his sideways, one eyed looks. *"Do you not wish an answer to your question about the dust?"* Clearly he had told them all he planned to about traveling.

P'puck nodded. *"Yes."* He wanted Glick to stay.

"You left it here."

"But we do not remember that."

"No. You did not need to."

"And now?"

"Take the rest with you. You will need it one more time before you reach the blue cave and gather more for the remainder of the journey home."

"When?"

But Glick had gone.

M'rain turned her back to P'puck and picked up her pack. *"We must go. You take the dust."*

Her tense tone made P'puck wince. Had he gone too far with his questions?

XL

P'PUCK'S QUESTIONS HAD prickled M'rain. They had to be asked, she knew, because future travellers would need to know. But they brought up the problem of her relationship with P'puck, something she did not want to dwell on.

Before she had been captured she had assumed her life would follow the same course as all the women of her people. She had dreamed of more but had not thought it possible. All members of her people expected to mate and bring forth children. There were no exceptions. Now that had all been turned upside down.

P'puck had made it plain enough that he dreamed of having her as his mate. Even the prospect of children had not dimmed his eagerness when Glick had revealed how that would be handled.

Among her people, and, as she had observed, also among P'puck's people, all children were cared for by all the adults as soon as they walked. Even before weaning, which happened roughly at age two, any women would comfort a toddler, or reprimand or snatch a child from danger. Mothers could go about their duties secure in the knowledge that their children had eyes on them at all times.

On the other hand the bond between mother and child usually remained strong, especially for girls. Boys, when they came of age to be trained in the hunt, often strengthened their alliance to their fathers. But even then they relied on their mothers for advice on things unrelated to the hunt, such as how to please a woman or pursue a possible mate.

Children spent nights in their parents' hut, and were breast-fed by their mother, with exceptions if the mother was ill. M'rain's bond with her own mother had remained strong. Even on her return to the village, when others had shown reluctance to trust her, her mother had welcomed her with no reservations.

The new knowledge that travellers who became mothers would need to leave their young children as they plied their trade did not sit well with her. Independent though she was, she still felt strongly about the role of mother. That complicated an already thorny issue. Would she agree to mate at all? P'puck seemed the obvious, indeed the only, choice. How did she feel about that, about him, about mating in general, about the inevitable children that would result – and now, about the realization that she would not be with her off-spring for most of their growing years? Could she even contemplate that?

So, while she felt no anger toward P'puck for asking the necessary questions, the entire conversation left her unsettled.

Her thoughts wandered back to the night before, how they had shared warmth, how respectfully he had behaved. She had not believed she would fall asleep, but she had. Waking to feel his hand in hers, tucked under her chin, as she habitually did with the furs, had unnerved her. Tonight they would be in the same situation. She needed to come to some kind of understanding, not about P'puck – she knew where he stood – but about herself and how she felt about P'puck. She was sure of one thing. They could not go on long under their current tacit agreement. Either they would be a couple by default, betrayed by their bodies, or their friendship would founder due to frustration and indecision.

I do like him. He is pleasant to travel with. He has a good sense of humour and his optimistic personality will balance my, too serious, one. But am I ready to mate? Will he continue to treat me as an equal? Or will he fall into the traditional role of leader. I could not bear that. I cannot go back to how I was, not even a little. And if we have children, do I want to trek with them through these dismal, dark caves? How will that affect them? And how will I be able to leave them behind when it is time?

Fortunately, or perhaps not, P'puck did not intrude into her thoughts. When, once again, they saw a thread of light veer off and end at an unfamiliar cave he followed her in and both set down their packs.

This time M'rain saw no waiting fungi.

P'puck noticed it too. "I think we will need to rely on travel fare this night."

"So it appears." Making sure she did not make eye contact she bent down to untie her fur. "I suppose we will need to share warmth again." She stole a glance at him and winced at the look of relief on his face. *This cannot continue.*

P'puck had laid the trail of dust on the way in, leaving their last sack empty. He rolled it into his pack. "I see a pool at the back. We will be able to wash – or at least I will, to get this dust off." As he headed for the pool he added, over his shoulder. "That is another thing we must teach those who follow. That they must not leave the dust on their skin. That it will make them sick."

He waded carefully into the pool and when he reached its centre he called to M'rain. "The water does not come above my chest. Will you join me?"

M'rain almost declined but when she looked at her arms and feet and saw how dirty she had become she changed her mind. But she took off her wrap so it would remain dry. It would not give much warmth but if she had to wear it wet she would be even colder.

As she stepped gingerly into the chill water she could feel P'puck's eyes on her. *He says I am beautiful. Am I? What does that mean among his people?*

When she finally stood next to him and reached into the water to splash her shoulders clean she heard him take in a deep breath.

In a husky voice he whispered, "M'rain?"

She dared not look at him. "Yes."

"I want to kiss you." His fingers found hers and he slowly entwined them with his. M'rain never knew why she did not jerk her hand away but when she did not he became emboldened and pulled her toward him, still only holding her fingers. His other hand found her waist and turned her to face him.

"You promised." Her protest sounded weak.

"I know." He did not let go. Neither did he pull her closer. "Shall I stop?"

M'rain could not answer.

His head bent toward her and nuzzled her hair. There remained only the smallest space between their bodies. When she did not protest he drew gently at her waist until their bodies met. The hand that held her fingers let go and found its way into her hair, the thumb resting under her chin, gently tipping it up. His lips on hers were soft, tender - warm in spite of the cold water.

The kiss was long and languid. M'rain found that she did not want to withdraw. The warmth of his skin where their bodies met was so much more pleasant than the icy water.

It was P'puck who eventually drew away. "You are cold. Come out of the water." Once more he took her hand and led her out. "Here is your wrap."

Neither of them spoke as they pulled out their travel food and chewed the tough dried meat and fruit. When they had finished P'puck pulled out his fur and sat down on it. "M'rain, it is time we talked."

"Yes, it is." But she did not meet his eyes.

M'RAIN, AMONG MY people, with what has already passed between us we would be pledged to each other. How is it with your people?"

M'rain studied the ground as they sat facing each other, now with her fur wrapped around her shoulders. "It is the same. After the rites of womanhood and manhood have passed matches are soon made. It is expected. Our village does not have as many people as yours. Choices are few."

Puck nodded. "Even among my people matings happen soon after the rites. Often those who have been close playmates as children simply choose to stay together. They announce their intention, share the feast of celebration, and move to an unoccupied hut or a new one is built for them."

"It is the same among my people." M'rain stole glances at P'puck as he spoke but still could not meet his eyes. As he went on she played with the tufts at the edge of the fur in her lap.

P'puck leaned closer to her, more intense, now. "But our situation is different. We are different. You have expressed that you do not belong in either village, with either people." When he saw her small nod he decided to tell her the things about himself that she could not know. It would not be easy.

"Among my people I have always been a little different. When other boys could not wait to be taken on the hunt, to learn the skills of the hunt, I preferred to look after the penned animals, to tend the gardens and to explore on my own." He hesitated, uncertain if he should go on. But she deserved to know. "M'rain, it took me much longer than most boys to learn the skills of the hunt. I could not undergo the rite of manhood without making the ritual kill. I was a year older than most before that happened. When I succeeded it was as much a stroke of luck as it was skill – and I have never made a kill since without help. Even then, the others made it easier for me by holding the boar at bay. My aim is untrue. Perhaps there is something wrong with my eyes."

M'rain listened, her head now raised and her eyes intent. She offered no comment and he saw no judgement in her gaze.

"My urge to explore took me beyond the forbidden boundaries, past the safe parts of the forest. Once, when I was about eight years old, I went into the great cave. I wandered too far. It was late afternoon and the light left the cave too quickly. It was the time of year when sunset comes early. I could not see my way back. At first I wanted to keep looking for the way home. But something made me stop and think about what would happen, that I would become more lost and possibly die. I do not know what it was that made me think about that."

He sent M'rain a small smile and shrugged. "Perhaps, even then, Glick had something to do with it." He shrugged again. "In any case, I told myself that the light would return in the morning. And when it came I would know what direction to take to get home. And I promised never to explore the cave again."

He gave a rueful chuckle. "It was the only time I told my mother and the elders a lie. In the morning I did see the light and found my way back. When asked where I had been I told them I fell asleep in the woods. My mother shouted at me that I must be more careful, called me a disobedient and willful boy, and beat me with a switch." He smiled at the memory, a faraway expression in his eyes. "My backside was sore for two days. I understand, now, that she must have been very afraid that I would never return. But I knew if I told them where I had really gone it would be worse. I knew it would frighten them too much and make me appear even more different. And I feared the other children would find me strange and would no longer want to be friends."

M'rain nodded. "That is interesting. When I was taught how to gather and learned how to stay safe in the desert I always wanted to go beyond where I knew I ought to, too. The women often scolded me for coming back so late. That was how I was captured in the cave. I had wandered too far."

"So did you always feel different, even without knowing why?"

"No, but I got into more trouble than the other girls. Once I suggested to my mother that I ought to learn to hunt with the boys. She got very angry, and looked frightened. She told me never to speak of it again. So I tried harder to be like the other girls but I did not really like it."

"M'rain, did the others treat you differently?"

"No. As I grew older some would ask why I wandered so far - did I not want to mate and have children, did I not know the danger? They could not understand. But they did not press me about it often. Perhaps that is why my mother had me learn the birthing craft. Perhaps she thought that would be enough challenge to make me forget about wandering and hunting."

"That is a special skill."

"Yes, and I was good at it. It would have made me respected once my training finished and I had undergone the rite of womanhood. It was almost finished when I was captured."

"But even so, you wandered too far."

"Yes. I did not do it willfully. I would simply find myself far from home."

P'puck laughed at that. "So sometimes you dream when you wander, just as I do when I work in the gardens." He could see she had begun to relax. It gave him the courage to return to what was pressing him.

"So we have both always been somewhat different. We have both wanted to go too far from home. Do you not think this means something - that we were always meant to meet, to travel together?" He leaned closer again, intent on watching her reaction.

Her face became troubled and she seemed not to know what to say. Finally she gave a reluctant nod. "Yes, after what has happened to us both I do think we were chosen for this life of travel."

"M'rain...do you like me...as a man?"

"I...Yes, P'puck. You must know, now, that I do like you." She looked up at him, and quickly lowered her gaze again. "But I am also confused. There is much to think about, much that we do not know."

"M'rain, I have told you how much I want you, how much I like you. You must know that I would have asked you to be my mate before now, but I knew you were not ready to think about that. ...M'rain..."

"I am still not ready, P'puck. There are important questions I must have answers to."

"Ask." He could hear the wild pounding of his heart.

"Do you remember what Glick said about travellers' children?"

"He said they would have children if they mated and that the children could travel with them."

"Yes. Would you want to travel these caves with babes?"

"As long as we are with them I see no difficulty."

"What about the darkness, the danger?"

"They do not frighten me. I sense no danger unless we veer from the trails. If we see Glick again I will ask about the monster. I suspect he told us there was one only to frighten us into listening to him. Or that he made it and controls it. M'rain, the journey lasts only three days each way. I do not think taking young children will be impossible."

"You do not sense a darkness beyond the loss of light?"

"No....perhaps your earlier experiences here have created a greater feeling of danger than exists...or perhaps Glick has removed it."

It took a long time before M'rain spoke again. "I think only Glick will know who is right." She seemed to make up her mind and changed the subject. "There is another question about children. Do you remember Glick said we would leave them with the others in the village when they grew older? I cannot see travelling with children through these caves once they are walking and talking. If we disobeyed and wandered away as children what do you think will happen when they do? It is far too dangerous. They will become lost. That is why Glick said they must be left in the village." Tears sprang to her eyes and her voice cracked. "I do not think I could leave my children and travel without them."

"Oh," was the only response P'puck could muster for that. He had not thought about that possibility at all. *Is it because I am a man? Because men leave to hunt but women are always with the children?*

"I hope Glick returns. These are things he must be asked." P'puck's hopeful mood had turned melancholy. "I think it is time to sleep." He got up and laid his fur out.

M'rain added hers to it and lay down without a word, turning her back to him so he could spoon in behind her. When he draped his arm around her waist she made no protest. She took his hand and tucked it under her chin along with the fur. Under his embrace he could feel her weep with silent shudders. He pulled her more firmly against him to comfort her. There were no words. *Glick where are you?*

LII

'PUCK SLEEPS AND cannot hear me."

"Glick?" M'rain woke with a start. It took her a moment to remember where she was. When she felt P'puck's arm draped over her she froze. Then she recalled what Glick had just said – that he slept.

When she began to carefully extricate herself Glick ordered, *"Stay as you are."* His tone became suggestive as he added, *"It is where you wish to be – and if you move away he will wake up."*

"What do you want?"

"It is not what I want, but what you want."

"I suppose you are going to tell me what that is." Having been so rudely awakened from a deep sleep, M'rain was in no mood for idle banter, especially not while wrapped in P'puck's embrace and unable to move for fear of waking him. Once again Glick had the upper hand and, once again, it made her angry.

As if answering her thoughts Glick told her, *"It is almost morning. You have slept enough."*

"Why have you come, and why can P'puck not be part of this conversation?"

"Because it is not P'puck who seeks answers and needs guidance."

"What answers do I need that you have not already given us?"

"The ones that will allow you to accept him. You cannot deny that you want him."

"I do not know what I want."

"No? I disagree. You know what you want but are afraid to take it."

"Stop speaking in riddles."

"Very well, then, answer me this. You like him, yes?"

"Yes, I suppose I do." She was paying more attention, now, curious as to where this would lead.

"You told him as much."

"…yes."

"You desire him."

When M'rain began with an angry retort Glick broke in, *"Do not deny what we both know."*

Faced with that bold statement M'rain realized what she had been denying to herself. But that did nothing to ease her melancholy. When P'puck stirred in his sleep and pulled her closer she admitted that it felt good, that she felt safe and cherished in his arms. *"Yes, I desire him. What good does that do when giving in to that will result in children who will need to travel these dark caves, or who I will be forced to leave behind. I cannot go back to the life I was raised to, nor can I bring children into this horrid place full of darkness and danger."*

"There is little danger if you stay on the trail you have created."

"What of the monster?"

"What monster?" Glick's tone had become playful.

"So P'puck was correct. There never was a monster."

"There was once. You did not imagine it. But it is no more. The need for it has passed. It was created to keep the people out of the caves. Now the need is to travel through the caves. They are empty."

"But what of the fear I feel? P'puck does not feel it. Am I a coward?"

At this Glick actually laughed, a silent, strange, but unmistakable laugh. M'rain had never heard him do that before – chuckle sarcastically, yes, but not a true laugh. She saw no humour in her question and it roused her ire again.

"I see nothing funny in my question."

"It is funny because it is so ridiculous. No M'rain, you are no coward. There were times when I doubted you were the one chosen for this task. But you have erased all doubt. I know no woman braver than you have shown yourself to be."

"Then why do I feel fear?"

"I created the sense of danger in the caves for all who entered. It was necessary to keep people out, to keep them from entering, becoming lost and dying. That was also the reason for the monster. P'puck does not feel it because he entered after it was removed."

"Then why do I still feel it?"

"Memory. It will fade now you know there is no more need."

Though reluctant to believe Glick, M'rain decided she had nothing to gain by pressing the issue further so she changed the subject. *"Am I destined to mate with P'puck, then?"*

"That will always be your choice to make. I told him I do not interfere in such matters. Now I say the same to you."

M'rain had mixed feelings about this. On the one hand she was pleased that Glick would not interfere in that part of her life, but also annoyed that she would now have to make the decision herself, that she had not been relieved of that responsibility. *"So I am right back where we started."*

"Are you?"

"Riddles again?"

"Hmmm."

"Very well, answer me this. If I mate with P'puck will we have children right away? Will he be a good mate for me? Will he want to become my leader or will he continue as we are? Will I need to leave our children to travel? How old will they be when that happens?" The tightness in her chest and the sting behind her eyelids reminded her of the tears of the previous evening. She blinked them back and instinctively pulled P'puck's arm more tightly around her.

"So you accept him, then?"

"I do not know. Answer the questions."

"It will be several years before children arrive. You will need to negotiate how you and P'puck make decisions. But he loves you and will work at making you happy. Yes, you will need to leave your children when they can no longer accompany you safely. But each journey will last no more than ten days. Your children will understand and will welcome you home each time. You will not lose their affection to others."

267

"How many?"

"Oh, have you decided to accept P'puck, then?"

M'rain still did not want to give Glick the satisfaction of an answer. Indeed, she still was not certain, herself.

Glick did not wait for a response. *"P'puck wakes. I have left fungi on the rock by the pool. It is my last gift to you."*

Before M'rain could answer Glick had gone.

P'puck rolled away and stretched as M'rain sat up.

"Is it morning?"

"It is impossible to tell in this darkness, but we are awake so it seems a good thing to call it." M'rain rose and headed for the pool to look for the fungi. "Glick was here."

"What? Why did I not wake?"

"He did not want you to." She grabbed the fungi off the stone and came back to where P'puck still sat on the furs. "Here, he brought us food. His last gift, he said."

P'puck's hand stopped mid-air, before stuffing his mouth. "What did he mean 'last gift'? Will we never see him again?"

"I do not know. Perhaps he only means that he will not leave food again. We now know how long the journey is and how much food we need to take with us." She ate quickly, rose and began to pack. "Come, we will be home before this day is done. Our next stop will be the cave of dust. We will need to get more to lay the last part of the trail."

She did not look back as she hoisted her pack and strode from the cave, leaving P'puck to scramble after her. He dared not ask what she and Glick had discussed, not when she had made it so clear she was in no mood to talk. Instead his hand searched for the reassurance of the small pouch at his waist.

LII

P 'PUCK LOOKED AT his hands, covered in blue dust. "Do you think we ought to go back to the cave with the pool? It is not far."

M'rain set the half-filled sack of dust down. She had held it open so P'puck could fill it without getting a lot on himself. Only his hands were covered. "I could pour some of the water from our waterskin over your hands. We will not need more before we reach the village."

"But we have not eaten our midday meal, yet."

"That is so. I do not like the thought of eating if any of the dust remains on our hands." She lifted her own. "Mine have a little on them too. Yes, let us go back and eat by the pool. I do not like this cave."

"We can leave the rest of our packs here. I will bring the food."

The cave with the pool was only a short distance away. Soon they had both washed off all traces of blue dust and sat across from each other to eat.

"Are you eager to be home, P'puck?" M'rain had noticed his silence, unusual for P'puck, and the serious look on his face.

"No."

Surprised, M'rain asked, "Why?"

"Because I have not finished what I set out to do on this journey." His hand travelled again to the pouch at his waist.

M'rain noticed it this time and felt a shiver of apprehension. But

269

P'puck took his hand away again and searched her face.

"M'rain, are there any more questions that plague you about our duties as travellers?"

The knot in M'rain's stomach tightened. "No…"

"Besides knowing that we would have to leave our children when we travel is there anything else that keeps you from me?"

M'rain lifted her hands to hold P'puck back then lowered them again. *So, this is the time of decision. I want more time.* But she had no more time. More time would not ease her misgivings, her dilemma. Glick's comment echoed in her mind. *You want him.* Yes she did want him. But what of the consequences? What of their children?

She studied P'puck, his tense body, the look of profound earnestness, the worry, the hope. She watched his tension increase as she thought about his question. Finally she whispered, "No. I have no more questions."

Without taking his eyes from her face P'puck reached down inside the pouch and drew out something that remained hidden in his palm. "M'rain, among my people we have a custom. When a man asks a woman to be his mate he offers her an anklet made of seeds and nuts strung on a leather thong. The bigger ones, the nuts, have symbols carved into them by the suitor. They are chosen with great care, to show what he thinks of his chosen one, what she represents to him that sets her apart." His voice had become low and solemn. "I began making this after our first time in the bathing pool." He opened his hand to reveal the anklet. Then he drew her attention to one nut. "See, this one is your hair. See how it flows and seems to move?" He drew out a second one. "And this one has two sides, one light, the other dark. They represent your journey, light for home and dark for the caves."

M'rain admired the exceptional skill that had gone into the carving. She had seen other beaded thongs on the ankles of some of the women in the village but had not known what they represented. The carvings on these nuts, as small as her thumbnail, were much more intricate than any she had seen. They took her breath away.

P'puck held up a third bead. "This one represents the two of us.

See how the circles are entwined but not joined? See how they are of the same size, one not bigger or more important than the other? I carved that one after Glick told me you would never be like other women, that you would never follow and obey. I do not wish to change you. I do not desire that you must obey me."

All of the carved beads were separated by several gleaming seeds so small M'rain could not understand how holes could have been made in them for the thong.

P'puck looked up at her, his eyes questioning, then held out the fourth and last carved bead, larger and of a different kind of nut.

"This one shows us as travellers. See the trail ahead of us, the packs on our backs?"

He held the treasure out to M'rain, his hand open. "M'rain, it is the wish of my heart that we be mates. If you accept this gift you have my oath that I will not break the promises these beads represent."

He does not expect me to change, to obey him. That settled the final question that had plagued M'rain. A lump in her throat prevented her from speaking. But speech was unnecessary. With a trembling hand she reached out and slowly lifted the beads from P'puck's palm, watching his face as she did so. The joy she saw there lifted the darkness out of the cave and made it feel as if the sun filled it with warmth and light. Finally she could speak past the lump. "I accept."

She stuck her foot out ahead of her and sent P'puck a questioning look. At his nod she tied the thong around her ankle and held it out for P'puck to see. "P'puck, I have never seen anything so beautiful. The carving is perfect. You have such skill."

P'puck beamed as he reached out to adjust the anklet so the beads could be seen clearly and stroked her foot with his thumb. When he raised his head to meet her eyes he looked shy. "M'rain, it is the custom among my people that when two are pledged they announce it to everyone around the fire at the evening meal. Then, after the feast, when it is time to sleep, the couple goes to the hut assigned them. They are mates. I have a hut already, as you know, since both my parents died of a fever when I was almost a man, their hut became mine. That will be our hut now." He looked down at the ground. "But until then, our bodies must remain apart." He met her eyes again, this time an eager, soft smile on his lips. "It has been hard to wait, but it will not be long, now."

This time the silence held only promise. M'rain examined her beads more closely, turning each one carefully to see every detail. When she finally looked up again she found him watching her with a proud, tender smile, eyes soft and liquid. She returned it without hesitation. After another moment she rose. "Come, it is time to go home."

"Our home."

"Yes, our home." She belonged once again.

EPILOGUE

THE STORY TELLER looked at each of the waiting faces around the fire. The people never tired of this ritual story. It was their story, the story of their people, the story of the world.

In the time before time we were one people, one village. Now we are many villages but we are still one people. Then, as now, we lived in peace. Game and food were plentiful. Only one thing was forbidden us by the One Who Provides – the Great Caves. All who entered were doomed to become lost. None returned. The spirit of the caves did not release them home.

A time came when some rebelled against the One Who Provides. They believed they could travel the caves without getting lost. For a long time they wandered, hungry and afraid. Many died. But the One Who Provides took pity. Some were led out of the caves and into a new land, a land of sun, and sands, and heat. They were told to remain in this new land. These few made a home there. Life was harsh. Food was scarce, water scarcer. But they lived, had children and their numbers grew. When the land could not provide enough some went farther away and formed another village. They, too, survived. Each year these two villages met after the rains to feast and choose new mates. They remained one people.

They remembered the story of the first people, of the One Who Provides, and the mercy shown those who had disobeyed. Once more the caves were forbidden. But they lived far from the caves. The cave did not call to them. They did not go into the caves when they hunted or gathered. Some began to believe the caves did not exist as no one had seen them for time upon time.

It happened in those days that a woman, M'rain by name, wandered too far over the sands in search of food. She came upon a great cavern and knew it to be the cave of the stories. It being late, and the sun being hot, burning high in the sky, she sought shelter in the shade of the cave's mouth. There she fell captive to the clutches of a demon. This demon also held others in thrall, enslaved and starving.

M'rain had not come to the caves by accident. Oh, no. The One Who Provides had destined that she come there. He decided the demon must be defeated and his captives returned to their home on the other side of the caves — returned to a people she knew of only in the stories. It is told that, to aid her, the One Who Provides sent a messenger, a guardian in the form of a lizard, who had dwelt for time upon time in the caves. Glick was the name he told M'rain. He had magic, and gave her some of his magic. He gave her sight in the caves. He gave her paths of light to follow. He slew the monster that hunted the caves. He protected her.

At his command M'rain defeated the demon and led the lost ones back to their home on the other side of the Great Caves.

But the One Who Provides had not finished. He decreed that the two peoples who had become lost to one another must once again become one, as they had been in the time before time. Once again he chose M'rain. But the lizard, Glick, knew that M'rain could not do this alone. And so He chose a companion for her, to be her mate, the man named P'puck. Together the pair became known as The First Travellers. They and their children, and their children's children have travelled and have taught more travellers.

Ever since that time there have been pairs who walk the trails between the villages and trade goods, one with the other. These pairs are still named Travellers. They are the living links between all our villages on both sides of the caves.

But none since the first travellers have ever seen the lizard or felt the magic. It is said Glick left because he was no longer needed. The travellers have no need of magic to traverse the caves. The caves no longer hold danger for those trained in how to travel them.

Now and then one is born who speaks of the magic, who says he feels it, and is touched by it. But others call them mad, or that they dream only. No one knows if the magic still lives.

We are many villages now. We grow in numbers, we have plenty to eat. We learn new skills that help us grow more food. We have new tools that make the hunt safer. We have discovered the black rocks that burn longer than wood and created trails so we can mine them.

And so we remember M'rain. Because of M'rain we are again one people. And so it will remain from the beginning unto the end.

The fire had burned down to embers and in the deepening darkness the storyteller's face was obscured into eerie planes and angles. He jabbed his hand into the dying light and shook his rattle, startling his audience out of its trance.

The rattle had the shape of a lizard. Did it writhe as if alive or was it a trick of the disappearing light?

◇◇◇

Thank You

THANK YOU FOR taking the time to read this book. I hope you have enjoyed it. That is the goal of every author. As a self-published author I do not have a publishing company promoting my work to find new readers. If you have enjoyed my work there is one thing you can do that will help get the word out to others who may also do so. That is to leave an honest review on the sites where it is sold. Even if it is only a sentence or two this is the best gift you can give an author. Authors always appreciate reviews. Readers also like them as they help connect them with new books they might be interested in.

ABOUT THE AUTHOR

Yvonne Hertzberger is a native of the Netherlands who immigrated to Canada in 1950. She is married with two grown children, both married, and one grandchild. She resides quietly in Stratford, Ontario with her spouse, Mark, in a 130 year old, tiny, brick cottage, where she plans to live out her retirement. She calls herself a jill-of-all-trades. Her many past paid jobs included banking, day care, residential care for challenged children, hairdressing (her favourite), retail, and customer service. She enjoys gardening, singing, the theatre, decorating and socializing with friends and family.

Hertzberger is an alumna of The University of Waterloo, first with a B.A. in psychology, then and Hon. B.A. Sociology and stopped ½ a thesis short of an M.A. in Sociology. She has always been an avid student of human behaviour. This is what gives her the insights she uses to develop the characters in her writing.

Hertzberger came to writing late in life, hence the label 'late bloomer'. Her first Fantasy novel "Back From Chaos: Book One of Earth's Pendulum" was published in 2009. The second volume in the trilogy "Through Kestrel's Eyes" arrived in 2011 and the third and final volume, The Dreamt Child is now available.

◇◇◇

Links to Media

Smashwords:
http://bit.ly/1oZuVWq

Twitter:
https://twitter.com/YHERTZBE

Facebook Author page:
http://on.fb.me/1oZv4cH

Amazon author page:
http://amzn.to/1nLWC3T

Amazon. UK:
http://amzn.to/1nXAo3l

Goodreads:
http://bit.ly/1n6wc0T

Website/blog:
http://newfantasyauthor.com

◇◇◇

Also By Yvonne Hertzberger

Back from Chaos:
Earth's Pendulum Book One

Battle and bloodshed have upset the Balance, crippling the goddess Earth's power to prevent further chaos. Unless it is restored more disasters will ensue: famines, plagues, more unrest and war.

Four chosen: Lord Gaelen of Bargia, Klast, his loyal spy and assassin, Lady Marja of Catania, and her maid Brensa. Each is unaware of the roles they must play in restoring that Balance.

Most important of these is Klast. It is he who must rescue the kidnapped maid, he who must unmask and bring to justice the traitor who threatens all their lives. It is also he who must deal with the scars from his tormented and abused past before he can accept the final part he must play in Earth's recovery. But he is a most reluctant and unlikely hero and time is short.

◇◇◇

Through Kestrel's Eyes:
Earth's Pendulum Book Two

Through Kestrel's Eyes begins seventeen years later. The peace that followed the end of the Red Plague is shattered when the lords of Gharn and Leith are toppled by traitors, throwing the land into chaos.

Liannis, the goddess Earth's seer, her apprenticeship interrupted by the death of her mentor, must help restore the Balance. Until it is, Earth's power is weakened, preventing Earth from sustaining the rains needed for good harvests. Drought and famine result.

Liannis battles self-doubt, the lure of forbidden romance, and deep loss as she faces tests that take her to the brink of her endurance.

But Earth sends a kestrel that allows Liannis to see with her eyes and a white horse to carry her, both with the ability to mind-speak.

Time is short. The people with starve if Earth cannot heal and the Balance cannot be restored.

◇◇◇

The Dreamt Child:
Earth's Pendulum Book Three

Liannis, the goddess Earth's seer, can no longer deny the meaning of her recurring dream. She must join (marry) with Merrist, her devoted hired man, and bear a child – one with great gifts. Earth has decreed it. But the people resist the changes, bringing danger to the pair and strife to the lands. Both Liannis and Merrist must face tests, sometimes without each other, to fulfill their destiny and bring The Dreamt Child forth into safety. They must succeed if they are to initiate the new era of peace and balance so desperately needed.